W9-CFM-093

Booklist (April 1, 2012 (Vol. 108, No. 15))

Grades 8-11. Seventeen-year-old Jamie only joined the cultish Right & the Real Church of Christ because her boyfriend was a begrudging member, but then Jamie's own father became a devoted convert. When Jamie refuses to sign the loyalty pledge demanded by the Teacher, she is disowned. Unwilling to be sent away to live with her deadbeat mother, Jamie takes up residence in a sleazebag, pay-by-the-week hotel, scraping for money and praying she'll still get into the New York City acting institute of her dreams. Those expecting juicy details about cult life will be disappointed—little of the novel focuses on the church, though the glimpses we get of a naked Teacher being massaged by his various wives are indeed decadent. Instead, this is a story about homelessness and, of course, romance: that cute boy at the coffee shop sure seems nicer than her current boyfriend, eh? The best character by far is the hulking LaVon, the brusque ex-felon who keeps the room next to Jamie and becomes her staunchest defender. A not-too-intense look at some very intense situations.

G. P. PUTNAM'S SONS • A division of Penguin Young Readers Group.
Published by The Penguin Group.
Penguin Group (USA) Inc., 375 Hudson Street, New York, NY 10014, U.S.A.
Penguin Group (Canada), 90 Eglinton Avenue East, Suite 700, Toronto, Ontario M4P 2Y3, Canada
(a division of Pearson Penguin Canada Inc.).
Penguin Books Ltd, 80 Strand, London WC2R 0RL, England.
Penguin Ireland, 25 St. Stephen's Green, Dublin 2, Ireland (a division of Penguin Books Ltd.).
Penguin Group (Australia), 250 Camberwell Road, Camberwell, Victoria 3124, Australia
(a division of Pearson Australia Group Pty Ltd).
Penguin Books India Pvt Ltd, 11 Community Centre, Panchsheel Park, New Delhi—110 017, India.
Penguin Group (NZ), 67 Apollo Drive, Rosedale, Auckland 0632, New Zealand
(a division of Pearson New Zealand Ltd).
Penguin Books (South Africa) (Pty) Ltd, 24 Sturdee Avenue, Rosebank, Johannesburg 2196, South Africa.
Penguin Books Ltd, Registered Offices: 80 Strand, London WC2R 0RL, England.

Design by Marikka Tamura.
Text set in Adobe Caslon.
Library of Congress Cataloging-in-Publication Data is available upon request.
Anthony, Joëlle. The Right & the Real / Joëlle Anthony. p. cm.
Summary: Homeless after her father kicks her out for refusing to join a cult, seventeen-year-old
Jamie must find a way to survive on her own.
[1. Cults—Fiction. 2. Self-reliance—Fiction. 3. Homeless persons—Fiction. 4. Fathers and daughters—
Fiction.] I. Title. II. Title: Right and the Real.
PZ7.A6283Ri 2012 [Fic]—dc23 2011013312
ISBN 978-0-399-25525-0
1 3 5 7 9 10 8 6 4 2

This book is dedicated to

Linda Anthony—
for encouraging both my love of the theatre
and my passion for writing.

The Brouhahas,
for walking every step of the way with me on this story.

And Victor Anthony—
for everything.

THE TIGHT COLLAR OF THE BRIDESMAID DRESS didn't help my bad mood. I stood in the dark supply closet, my body tense and the odor of bleach stinging my nose. Josh's familiar footsteps sounded in the hallway, and then there was a flash of light as he slipped inside and shut the door behind him.

"Jamie?" he whispered.

"I'm here." I reached out and pulled him to me, taking some comfort in the softness of his kisses and the taste of warm, minty Chapstick, but after a few minutes I couldn't do it anymore. I pressed my face into the front of his dress shirt.

"You okay?" He rubbed the back of my neck. I shook my head against his chest. Usually, kissing Josh sent tingles through my whole body, but tonight I barely registered he was there. "You'll have to come out pretty soon," he said. "The ceremony starts in ten minutes."

His mouth found mine again, and I mumbled through the kisses, "I can't let him marry Mira."

Josh squeezed me tighter, but instead of reassuring me, it made me angry, and I pulled away. "It's all your fault," I told him. "I never should've come to this stupid church."

1

He leaned his body into mine and I gave in and let him hold me. He was so warm and comfortable. Maybe we could stay in the closet forever. Maybe if no one could find us, they'd put the wedding on hold. Maybe . . . oh, who was I kidding? And why was I taking solace in Josh when it really *was* because of him my dad was getting married tonight?

"It's your fault," I said again, but my voice was muffled against his chest.

"I know . . . I know. . . ."

A light tapping noise made us both jump, and the closet door opened a crack. "Josh, I know you're in there," Derrick said. "Mom and Dad are looking for you."

"Is anyone around?" Josh whispered to his brother.

"Nope. You're good," he said, "but hurry up. They're gonna start soon."

Josh tried to pull himself away, but I clung to him. "I can't do this."

He stroked my back. "Come on, Jamie," he said. "It won't be that bad."

"How can you say that? It's going to be horrible." I wanted to hit him, but I sagged against him instead. He opened the door and led me into the hallway. Derrick was gone, but the Teacher stood there, looking benevolently at us both.

In a normal church, the Teacher would be the same as the pastor or minister, but here the congregation was supposed to consider him Jesus. Seriously. Jesus. I know . . . insane. That should've been my first warning the people here were crazy. Actually, when Josh asked me to a church dance for our first date, and all the teenagers were dressed in clothes they'd obviously ordered from Amish.com, I should've known there was something odd about his church, but did I care? No. And why not? Because someone besides the drama boys had finally noticed I was alive. And not just anyone, but Josh Peterson, the hottest guy in the twelfth grade.

For the first three years of high school, I'd spent all my time in the theater department. My best friend, Krista, and I had made our own funky clothes, colored our hair with streaks of blue, worn black lipstick, and put holes in our fishnets on purpose. But over the summer between junior and senior year, I'd landed the part of Peter Pan at a professional theater downtown, and I'd had to cut off all my crazy hair. And once it was gone, I'd seen something I hadn't noticed before.

I was pretty.

My naturally light blond hair framed a face with perfect skin, sparkling blue eyes, deep dimples, and straight teeth. For the first time, I saw *all* my potential as an actress. Not only could I sing, dance, and act, but I had a fantastic and very marketable all-American look, perfect for commercials. And as it turned out, also perfect for landing the star football player as a boyfriend.

The fact that the church was super conservative actually made it kind of fun at first. Since Josh's parents hardly ever let him go out on real dates, I'd joined Bible Study and Youth Group, and after meetings, we'd made out in every dark corner of the church. We'd spent so much time locked away in closets that, when we were apart, it was how Josh's body *felt* against mine I remembered, not so much how he looked. The thickness of his neck under my small hands and the feel of his rock-hard shoulder muscles when I caressed them—these were burned into my memory. And his smooth skin against my face, except for the spots he missed shaving, which were prickly and left red patches on my skin. . . . Sometimes, I actually had to think hard to remember his eyes were hazel, because I hardly ever spent any time gazing into them.

Meeting in secret was fun. And it wasn't like we *had* to do it; it just sort of made the whole thing more thrilling. Except for times like now, when someone caught us. Then it was kind of embarrassing.

"Ahhh . . . young love," the Teacher said. "I hope you were showing Jamie proper respect."

"Yes, sir," Josh said. "We were just talking." He blushed from his neck all the way up to the roots of his blond flattop. I needed to give him a few acting lessons.

"Good," the Teacher said. "You two better run along. It's almost time for the wedding."

That sobered me up quickly, and again I felt stupid for being so clueless about the church and its members. The Teacher looked like he was trying to pass himself off as one of those drawings you see on cheap Christmas cards featuring Jesus—wispy brown hair, a long white robe, and leather sandals.

He'd gone into his office, and Josh and I were still standing there when, like bees leaving the hive, twenty-two bridesmaids in dresses just like mine swarmed out into the hallway from one of the meeting rooms. Sarah, the ceremony coordinator and queen bee, drove us all toward the lobby. "You go take your seat, young man," she buzzed at Josh. "Places, bridesmaids. Places." She reminded me of a stage manager in the theater, but this was no play—this was a real wedding. In fact, it was twenty-three real weddings, and one of the couples was my dad and his fiancée, Mira.

Sarah lined us up in the lobby, and one after another, we walked down the center aisle. More than five hundred members sat on fold-ing chairs under blazing fluorescent lights, staring at us. One of the freakiest things about this place was the way everyone looked alike. Women in pastel yellows and lavenders, men in dark suits, kids dressed like miniature versions of their parents, right down to purses and ties. Throughout the auditorium (I couldn't call it a church—partly because it'd once been a grocery store), big TVs showed the service to the people sitting in the back, and video footage of us in our hideous flowered dresses splashed across them. I'd watched plenty of recordings of me on stage in plays or singing, and I usually liked see-ing myself on a big screen, but not like this.

I wanted to run away, but some tiny part of me hoped Dad would look into my eyes at the very last minute and see what he was doing to me . . . to us. If I didn't go to his wedding, he didn't stand a chance of ever getting out from under Mira's thumb, or the control of the church, so I kept walking, my hope dying a little more with each step, the cheap white flats pinching my toes.

I took my place in the front with the other bridesmaids. You'd think someone besides me would clue in that a group wedding was not only impersonal, but a little disturbing too. I swallowed hard to keep back a sudden sob. All the ceremony and rituals at this church freaked me out, not to mention my new stepmother-to-be and her fanaticism. Mira acted very sweet and innocent, but I'd seen the crazy glint in her eye more than once when she talked about the Teacher and how he was going to save us all from hell and damnation.

And the whole reason we were here was my fault. I wanted to blame Josh for getting me involved in the first place, but I was the one who let Dad come along with me to a Sunday service. Stupid, stupid me. For years he had dragged me to every house of worship imaginable: Catholic, Baptist, Jewish, Mormon, Lutheran, Unitarian, Jehovah's Witness, and one where they did yoga and meditation, but called it Spiritual Redefining. He never attended more than two or three services, though. This was the first time something had stuck.

Before my grandpa died last year, he explained the whole church fascination was because my dad was searching. *He's unhappy,* he'd said, *because he couldn't help your mother.*

My parents had met in rehab and, against the advice of everyone at Alcoholics Anonymous, especially their sponsors, they'd dated anyway. According to my dad, who has almost nineteen years clean and sober, they'd been good for each other. At least until I was about three and Mom started missing the party life.

The wedding march blared, loud and long, momentarily snapping me out of my misery. As I watched the twenty-three brides, all in identical white dresses, my stomach churned. Tonight was what they called a Ceremony Night. Besides the group wedding, new members and anyone over thirteen who hadn't done it already would take the Pledge of Loyalty. I'd read it, and it was nothing more than an archaic vow where members agreed to be ruled by the Teacher and disciples. At the Right & the Real Church of Christ, they called what amounted to elders "disciples." All of them wore white robes with sandals and had beards like the Teacher.

The brides had lined up by height, and elegant, petite Mira led the way. She'd pulled her dark hair back in a severe bun, and meticulous makeup hid the lines in her face, making her look younger than forty-four. I couldn't believe my dad wanted to marry someone five years older than him. I thought men liked *younger* women.

All the bridesmaids had to stand off to one side in two straight rows, but there were chairs for the brides. Through their veils I could see different emotions cross their faces. Joy, fear, sadness, anger. I clearly wasn't the only one who thought this group wedding was disturbing.

The Teacher walked to the podium. "Welcome, everyone, on this joyous night of faith and celebration," he said into the microphone. His words echoed off the concrete walls. "While each time we worship is special, tonight we are blessed with the entire Red Sea Choir."

A rustling sound filled the auditorium as, behind him, two hundred people stood and opened their music, their scarlet robes a wash of color across the TV screens. There were so many members at the Right & the Real Church—over fifteen hundred, I think—that they had to take turns going to services on Saturdays and Sundays. Tonight was invitation only. The Teacher turned to face the choir and gestured in the air, waving his arms. "Raise up your song to God so He may hear you in Heaven and bestow His blessings upon us."

The keyboard player sent a crashing chord through the church, and the voices of the choir joined in. A little chill ran through my body just like when I'm doing a musical and there's a big chorus number and all the different vocal parts sound so good together. Halfway through the song, my anxiety level had risen to the point where my hands shook as if I'd had a double mocha, but I wanted them to sing forever because I knew as soon as they stopped, it would be time for the Pledge. Once Dad took that, it was all over. I'd never get him out of here single.

Eventually, it ended with a *hallelujah* and an *amen*, and the Teacher took his place at the microphone again. "Thank you, my brothers and sisters," he said. "And now we must join together and welcome the newest members to our flock. Please come forward, pledges."

The whole first row stood. They were all guys about my age or younger, except my dad and two other men. All the girls who were pledging were also bridesmaids. Josh had taken the oath a while ago, but I knew he thought it was crap and did it only because his dad made him. If he'd believed it, I definitely wouldn't have been dating him.

"The Right & the Real Church is happy to envelop you into our fold," the Teacher said. "There are many things to remember if you wish to be a child of God, but the disciples and I are here to help you, to guide you, and yes, to be Christ here on Earth in order that we may keep you on the right path."

My mom was never much into religion except for a brief moment when I was in second grade. I lived with her before Dad got custody, and one day she'd "found God." That had lasted only until she'd found Hank, but the preacher there had sounded a lot like the Teacher—loud and certain.

"There are many people and organizations who claim to know the true path to God," he continued, "but here we have been blessed because I myself am Christ." He gestured at the men sitting together near the front. "The disciples you trust with your lives are the true servants of Jesus. No other church on Earth is as blessed as we are because, as Christ resurrected, I will lead you all to salvation."

"Amen," said the congregation.

I was pretty sure most religions would call that sacrilegious bullshit. I definitely did. But my dad couldn't see this, and I knew the reason was Mira, the first woman besides me to pay attention to him in a decade. That, and he had an addictive personality. His therapist would say this was another addiction. Except he'd fired Dr. Kennedy a couple of months ago, saying he didn't need him anymore because he had the church.

"Fellow pledges," the Teacher said. "Please repeat after me: Our lives can be lived only if we give them over to the idea of Headship." Around me, the pledges repeated his words. "God is the head of Christ," he continued. "Christ is the head of Man."

This was it. With every word spoken, the gap between me and my father, the only adult in my entire life I could count on, widened. Dizziness almost overcame me, and I thought for sure I'd faint from the stress of it all. Would that stop him? Probably not. I took deep, slow breaths to calm myself, like before I go on stage, but I still felt way more nauseated than I ever did when I performed.

"Man is the head of Woman," the Teacher said.

"Man is the head of Woman," they repeated.

I stared hard at Dad, willing him to look at me, but it was already too late. He couldn't see me anymore.

"I have here on this podium a scroll with your names on it," said the Teacher. "The choir will sing 'Here I Am, Lord' as you take your turn signing and receive a blessing from me."

Each of the pledges stepped forward to sign the paper. My dad was at the end of the line, and the closer he got to the podium, the more rage and panic welled up inside me. I considered trying to drag him outside, where the cold January air might somehow miraculously clear his head, but before I could act, he signed his free will away with a flourish of the pen. He smiled brightly at Mira, a glazed look in his green eyes, his balding head shiny from the hot lights. And then he took his place beside her, ready for the wedding.

THE TEACHER TURNED TO THE BRIDESMAIDS WHO
had pledged. "And now you may sign," he said to them. The girls
stepped forward, their eyes revealing that same blank submissiveness
so many of the women had here. The first girl signed her name and
then she lifted up her face to the Teacher, and he laid his hands on
either side of her head. I seriously thought he was going to kiss her
on the lips, but instead, he murmured something and laid a wet one
on her forehead. Still, totally gross. I swear I heard the juicy smack. I
was still standing there, reeling in disgust, when the Teacher snapped
me out of it by saying my name.

"Jamie?" He motioned me to the podium.

"What?"

"Please sign."

"Oh, no. . . ."

He looked at my father, and so did I. Dad nodded at me.

"Ummm . . . no," I said. "I'm not signing the Pledge. I'm just a
bridesmaid." And after those kisses he gave the others, I wasn't going
near him.

The Teacher smiled, but anger flared in his eyes. "You're a member of our flock and over the age of thirteen. It's time you committed to us."

"I can't." It came out weak and unconvincing, even to me.

"Jamie," Dad said, "sign the Pledge so we can begin our new family under God's guidance."

I stood where I was, feet planted, growing roots through the ugly gold carpet right down into the concrete below. They couldn't make me sign. In three months, I'd be a legal adult.

"I'm sorry," I said, "but I don't believe. I mean, I believe in God, but not the Pledge."

A murmur ran through the crowd. I knew the microphone had picked up what I'd said and amplified it. Josh was the only person in the whole room who wouldn't hold it against me. I didn't want to think about what his parents would say.

"Your father is the master of his daughter," the Teacher said to me. "And he has spoken. Step forward and sign the Pledge or prepare to be recognized no more as a daughter of this true believer."

This was unreal. *Prepare to be recognized no more?* It sounded like a line from a straight-to-video release. If nothing else, that one phrase should've broken the spell and made my dad laugh at the absurdity of it. I couldn't be the only one who could see through this charade.

When I didn't move, the Teacher turned again to my father. The members shifted in their seats, trying to see what would happen. Everyone wanted to know who would give in first.

"Your daughter needs your guidance," the Teacher said to Dad.

"Jamie, look at me." Dad met my eyes, and anger filled his voice. "You cannot expect Mira to come and live with a sinner."

His words stabbed as deeply into my heart as if he'd used a real knife. I was his only child, and he'd rescued me from a drug-addicted mother. He *knew* how much I needed him.

Dad crossed over to me and whispered fiercely in my ear, his breath hot against my skin. "Jamie Lexington-Cross, do not ruin this for me."

"But . . . I can't. . . ."

"Sign the Pledge," he said, moving closer to the microphone as if he wanted everyone to hear. "If you don't sign, I will be forced to choose between you and Mira."

"You wouldn't choose *her,*" I said, the words barely audible.

The Teacher looked out over the congregation and said directly into the mic, "It is only fair to tell you, Jamie, a husband in the Right & the Real Church always chooses God first, and then his wife. Rebellious children before you have been excommunicated so they do not poison the flock."

The Teacher could hardly kick me out, since I wasn't part of his demented church. Still . . . I knew from the past few weeks that Dad would do whatever the church told him to do. He'd already quit his job as an ad salesman at the newspaper because the Teacher made him believe his new path lay in serving God. Now he spent his days in their office creating reading material that was, as far as I was concerned, sheer propaganda for the ministry.

I couldn't risk losing my father. I took two steps toward the podium, telling myself it wouldn't be that big of a deal if I signed. I'd pretend it was another role in a play. I could *act* like a believer if I had to. Josh had done it, and he hadn't changed.

The Teacher held out the gold pen to me with what looked like a real smile, but I didn't believe it. I took it, my hand shaking. My father nodded curtly at me. I pressed the pen to the paper, and I'd already written *Jamie* when Dad's words skittered through my mind again. *If you don't sign, I will be forced to choose between you and Mira.* Of course

Dad wanted me to sign—it would make everything easier for him. He knew he'd choose me. He always had. If I refused, though . . . well, he'd have to forget Mira, and I'd get him back.

I drew a line through my name and dropped the pen. "I can't do it, Dad," I said.

When he didn't step forward immediately and tell me it was okay, I didn't know what to do except leave and hope he'd follow. All the way down the aisle, my slippery plastic shoes clacked against the linoleum floor. *Choose me, choose me, choose me.*

I heard murmurings from the congregation and tried to block them out. *Did she sign? Where's she going? What happened?* The heat from the lights beat down, making me sweat. I wanted to get out of there fast, and it took everything I had to simply walk, but I wouldn't give the Teacher the satisfaction of running me out of his stupid church.

In the parking lot, the cold wind hit me like a slap to the face. I stood outside, freezing in my thin cotton dress, knowing Dad would come. Goose bumps rose on my arms as I waited, and I hugged myself to stay warm. And then I heard the choir start to sing again.

It doesn't mean anything. He'll still choose you in the end. He's not strong enough to walk out in front of all those people, I reassured myself. Even if he married Mira tonight, it would be okay. By the time they got back from the beach on Monday, he'd have realized he'd made a huge mistake. We'd be fine. We had to be.

I snuck back inside and got my purse and coat from the meeting room. Dad and Mira weren't taking a real honeymoon right now because they planned to go on a three-week church retreat in the summer. Tonight and tomorrow night, they were staying at a bed and breakfast and I was sleeping over at Krista's house. She had my SUV, and I'd ridden to the church with Dad and Mira. I texted her to come get me.

Shivering outside the R&R, I tried to tell myself I was just cold, but it felt more like that deep-inside-you shakiness from fear rather than from the weather. Part of me still hoped Dad would come after me, but I was also a little afraid that if he did, he might bring disciples with him to drag me back inside, so I stood in the shadows. The doors stayed firmly closed, though, and a little piece of my heart cracked. I held my breath to keep from giving in to racking sobs, but I couldn't stop tears from running silently down my face.

The overcast night should've made my surroundings dark and foreboding to match my mood, but instead, the church parking lot glowed like the Main Street Electrical Parade at Disneyland. Dozens of security lights flooded the church grounds, bouncing off windshields and mud puddles.

The concrete building stood on what had once been a strawberry field between Portland and the city of Gresham. Off to the right of the parking lot, two guards protected the entrance to the trailer park and the driveway leading to the Teacher's mansion. A six-foot fence with three rows of barbed wire encircled the residential compound.

Josh's dad was one of the disciples, and his family lived in a double-wide trailer about three-quarters of the way down the little gravel road. Once, when his parents had gone away on a mission trip, he'd convinced the guards I'd come over for Bible study. Instead, we'd watched movies and eaten frozen pizza with Derrick.

I thought about walking out to the street to meet Krista, but I stayed put in case Josh managed to make some excuse to his parents and came to check on me. And then, like I'd conjured him up, I felt his hand on my arm. I whirled around to face him. "Oh, I'm so glad—"

"Jamie. You shouldn't have done that in there," he said. "You should've just signed. It doesn't have to mean anything."

"But I thought if I refused, Dad would choose me."

"They'll never let him choose you," Josh said. "The Teacher has plans for your dad's inheritance."

I didn't know for sure how much my grandpa had left Dad when he died last year, but I found it hard to believe it was more than five or six hundred thousand dollars total. And Grandpa had set it up in a trust that would only pay Dad a small allowance each month for the rest of his life, because sometimes he wasn't the most responsible guy in the world, and Grandpa knew it.

"It's not a lot of money, Josh."

From the first day Dad had gone to the church, he'd flaunted his wealth, putting a hundred-dollar bill in the collection plate. I knew he'd done it so they'd notice him—and, boy, did they ever.

"My parents told me the Teacher got your dad to sign a monthly pledge to the church," Josh said.

"Are you serious?" I asked. "Why didn't you tell me before?"

He shifted his weight and wouldn't meet my eye. "I didn't want you to worry."

"We're talking about my life here, Josh. You should've told me."

"I know. . . ."

Krista's headlights swung across the entrance to the church, lighting up Josh's face, making him look ghostly. His hand shot out, and he yanked me to him, kissing me so hard he bruised my lips against his teeth. Then he shoved me away.

"Jamie," he said, "forgive me."

"For what?" I asked. But he'd already slipped back inside the church.

15

I ALMOST RAN AFTER JOSH, BUT KRISTA BEEPED the horn. "Get in," she shouted over the music. "I just got it warm in here."

Once inside, I held my frozen hands up to the heater. Grandpa had left the Beast to me last year when he'd died, but I drove only when I had to. I know teens are supposed to be all excited about having their own car, but I wasn't at all. The Beast was so huge, it reminded me of the time I rode on a giant tractor on a school field trip to a farm. When I drove, I was afraid I'd crush some pedestrian or flatten a cyclist as I lumbered along. New York City rocked because I could walk or take the subway everywhere, and I could hardly wait until Krista and I moved there next year for school.

Krista loved everything about my SUV, though, from its all-leather interior to the custom floor mats and fantastic sound system. When I asked Dad if she could drive it, he said he didn't mind as long as she didn't get a ticket. She'd been hauling us around ever since. The Beast was almost more hers than mine.

"Wow," I said, checking out Krista's clothes. Sometimes it was hard to believe I used to dress just as crazy as she did.

"You like?" she asked.

We'd stopped at a light, and she turned so I could get a better look at her getup. She'd obviously been sewing, because she'd pulled her long hot-pink hair into a high ponytail to keep it out of her way.

"For you," I said, "it's way cool. For me, not so much anymore."

She laughed. She'd taken my new "generic look," as she called it, in stride. Her wardrobe changed pretty fast because she could sew so well. She was always ripping out seams and putting things back together into new outfits. Tonight she had on what looked like a paper bag made of metallic purple material, long-underwear bottoms, combat boots, and lace fingerless gloves.

"I call it Boy George meets Prince," she said, stomping on the gas when the light changed.

Before Krista's obsession with eighties glam fashion, she'd been totally into the seventies, and I'd pretty much gone along with whatever she wanted to do. But way back in freshman year, we'd both dressed in vintage nineteen-forties. I kind of missed the seamed stockings and elegant fitted dresses, but as a future designer, she had to keep mixing up her look.

"The only problem," she said, "is I can't get it off without help because the sleeves are straight-pinned on. I'll end up stabbing myself."

I laughed in spite of the sinking feeling in my gut. I planned to tell Krista everything when we got to her house, but I didn't like to distract her when she was driving. Especially if she had straight pins sticking out of her clothes.

What a crazy night. I wondered what Josh meant, *forgive me*. . . .

"How come you're done so early?" Krista said. She bobbed her head in time to a rap song. "Boring reception?"

"Something like that," I said.

"Should we get ice cream?" she asked.

I looked down at my bridesmaid dress. "We're not exactly dressed to go out," I said.

She laughed. "Maybe you're not, but I look good." She was right, of course. She could pull anything off. Most people thought she was really cool, not weird at all. "Drive-through coffee?" she suggested instead.

"Can we just go back to your house?"

She turned the stereo down. "Are you okay?"

"Not really. But I want to change into my pajamas and get warm. Then I'll tell you, okay?"

"Deal."

Krista's bedroom looked like a working design studio. She had a sewing machine in one corner, a drafting table by the window, and an ironing board attached to the wall. In her closet, her clothes were hung by color and her shoes sat lined up neatly on racks.

The twin beds sported hot-pink and purple comforters with a ton of throw pillows she had made herself with bargain fabrics. She also had two matching beanbags with a fuzzy rug and a TV in one corner. Instead of books, her shelves were stuffed with beauty magazines. Krista practically ran the costume shop at the theater, but what she really wanted to do after high school was study fashion at Beaumont Design in New York.

After changing into pajamas and covering my lap with a plush blanket because I couldn't seem to shake the chills, we sat down to talk about my evening. I held Krista's hand and painted her fingernails a sparkly silver. Focusing on my task gave me distance from everything as we hashed over the details again and again. Krista's one of those eternally optimistic people, and usually she can talk me out of my low moods, so I was counting on her tonight.

"The idea the Teacher thinks he's Christ resurrected is so unbelievably creepy," she said.

"I know. The whole place is just freaky."

"That's what you get for dating a boy outside the theater department," she said lightly.

I knew she was only half kidding, though. She'd never thought much of Josh because he thought she was weird. After I finished her nails, I sat on her bed trying not to think while she sent texts to her fashionista friends in New York. I picked at the last piece of pizza, but couldn't force myself to eat any of it. The time on my cell changed from 11:16 to 11:17. Every time I slept over at Krista's, my dad called to check in. Tonight my phone sat ominously silent. When it changed to eighteen after, I kind of lost it. I wrinkled up my face, squinting my eyes, in this weird way I do when I'm trying not to cry, but it didn't help.

Krista abandoned her texting. "It'll be okay," she said, wrapping her arms around me while trying to keep her still-tacky fingernails clear of contact. "You'll see. By the time they get back from the beach, he'll be all relaxed and happy, and everything will be fine."

"But he didn't call," I said. "It's like he's totally abandoned me for Mira."

"I don't want to gross you out or anything," Krista said, "but it *is* his wedding night. He's probably kind of busy."

"Oh, yuck. Yuck! Don't say that!" I couldn't help it, I laughed. And then I shoved her off the bed. "Gross! Why did you have to remind me?" I demanded.

19

She grabbed her laptop. "Come on," she said, "let's look for apartments on Craigslist. That'll cheer you up."

We wouldn't need a place in New York for another eight months, but checking out the listings was one of our favorite pastimes. It made our future real somehow.

"Yeah, okay," I said. "Start with the luxury ones. They're more fun."

We spent the next day vegging in front of reruns of *America's Next Top Model*. Krista critiqued the clothes from head to toe, and I mostly zoned out. I think I might have dozed a bit. I wanted to call Josh, but he's not allowed to use his phone on Sundays. He can't watch TV or IM on the computer, either. It was an R&R rule, and his parents held him to it.

"What do you think he meant by 'forgive me'?" I asked Krista during a commercial.

"The same thing I thought the last fifty-seven times you asked me," she said. She grabbed a bag of chips out of my lap. "He thought he upset you by saying the church wanted to keep your dad in their clutches."

I sighed. "Yeah . . . you're probably right."

"I'm always right," she said, grinning at me. She hit the volume on the remote, and we both sang along with the latest Gap commercial. She covered the melody, and as usual, I did some awesome harmony.

By the time we finished the homework we'd ignored all day, it was almost midnight. I'd left Dad three messages, all light and cheerful, telling him I'd see him after school on Monday, but he never called back. I wasn't too worried about it anymore, though. Krista had convinced me it would all blow over.

• • •

We made our usual stop at the bathroom by the theater wing, and while Krista checked out her makeup, Liz glided gracefully into the vicinity like the dancer she is.

"Sucks to be you," she said, wrapping her arms around me and giving me a squeeze. Her chestnut hair was in its usual sleek ballerina bun, but a wisp had strayed, and it tickled the side of my face.

"Don't I know it," I said.

Liz propped her foot up on the windowsill to stretch. She reminded me of that ballerina in *The Red Shoes*. It was like she couldn't stop dancing for even a second. She is my second-closest BFF, and after Krista had threatened to drive over to Josh's house to ask him what he meant by "forgive me," I'd called Liz to get her two cents.

I'd told her only the minor details of Saturday night, so when she said, "Did Josh really push you?" I knew someone had filled her in with a bit more info. I glared at Krista, who was reapplying liquid eyeliner so thick I thought maybe her eyelids would get glued together. What she needed were her lips sealed. Sometimes I hate that my best friends are into theater. Everything has to be a soap opera with them.

"He didn't *push* me," I said, even though he had. It sounded really bad like that, like abuse. "God, Krista. Inflate the drama much?"

"Oh, please," she said. "Since when do you keep secrets from your best girls?"

I sighed and headed for the locker I shared with Krista. "It's not that I'm keeping secrets," I said when they caught up with me in the hallway. "It just makes him look so bad, and he didn't mean it. I don't want the whole school to hear about it."

"I'm not just anyone," Liz reminded me. "Besides, who would I tell?"

"Yeah, I know . . . ," I said. I put my arms around the two of them as we walked. "I'm just feeling blue."

I looked for Josh on the way to each of my classes, but I didn't see him in his usual spot by the gym, and when I called him at lunch, I got his voice mail. In spite of the cloud of dread that had followed me around all day because I'd have to talk to my dad after school, a certain amount of excitement pulsed through me too. Today was the first company meeting for *West Side Story*. The dancing and singing numbers are super complicated, so our drama teacher, Mr. Lazby, decided to try something new this year. He'd held auditions for the spring musical right after winter break and formed a company of actors instead of giving us our parts right away.

We'd spend February learning the big dance numbers and the songs as a company, and then in mid-March, we'd find out who we got to play. After that, all the usual intensive rehearsals would start, culminating in May with eight evening performances and four school matinees.

It was going to be tough to win the role of Maria because I'm short, blond, and pale. And Liz, who definitely had her eye on Maria too, was tall, dark, and could easily pass for Puerto Rican. Plus, Maria has a ballet number with Tony, and I knew that was going to be my weak point. But I intended to do everything in my power during these rehearsals to persuade Mr. Lazby to give me the role.

After the last bell, I rushed to my locker, grabbed my stuff, and headed for the theater. The lights were on in the lobby, and the main doors stood open. From inside, I could hear the hum of voices, and I got that little rush I always get when I enter a theater.

The cast milled about for a while, talking noisily, until Emily, the stage manager, came in and let out an earsplitting whistle. "Sit in the orchestra pit," she yelled.

I found Liz and Krista, and we plopped down on the floor together. Around us, everyone laughed and shoved each other, making a lopsided circle. Just as Mr. Lazby strode across the stage above us, Liz's little sister, Megan, wedged herself in next to me.

"Megan, don't you have your own friends?" Liz asked.

"I'm the only freshman who made the cast," she reminded us. Her face glowed with pride. Freshmen almost never got cast in the musical, but like Liz, Megan had danced her whole life, and she'd kicked ass during the auditions.

"Shhh," I said. "Mr. Lazby's waiting."

He towered over us from the apron of the stage. Imagine John Travolta with a belly, a beard, and a bad attitude about the acting biz, and you had Mr. Lazby. Still, he was a fantastic director, and even though he was known to throw a tantrum without warning, everyone loved him. His sheer bulk seemed to cast a shadow over all of us, and almost instantly it got so quiet, you could hear the proverbial pin drop.

"Welcome," he said, his voice somehow low and still carrying all the way to the back row. "Emily, please call the roll."

Things went quickly for a minute or two, but then Emily called out, "Marissa Stephens?" and someone answered, "She had a dentist appointment."

"What?" Mr. Lazby roared. "Well, if Ms. Stephens doesn't want to be in *West Side Story* enough to come to the first meeting, then just scratch her off the cast list, Emily."

Around the room, a few girls who were on backstage committees and didn't have roles perked up, thinking maybe they'd get Marissa's spot, but we veterans knew Mr. Lazby was just blowing off steam. If you looked up drama queen on Wikipedia, you'd see his name for the definition.

For the first time all day, the worry I'd been carrying around in the pit of my stomach dissolved. With all my friends around and people laughing and the excitement of the show, I totally forgot about my dad and the R&R. Emily handed out rehearsal schedules, Mr. Lazby talked a bit about the history of the musical, and then we played a few improvisation games to get us on our feet and release some energy.

After rehearsal, I dropped off my friends and headed for home. Twice I had to wipe my sweaty palms on my jeans because they slipped on the steering wheel, and I didn't think my nervousness had much to do with the traffic. That chill from Saturday night crept through me too.

It took me three tries to get the stupid Beast parked, and in the end, the front tire was wedged tightly against the curb, with the back stuck out into traffic a little. I gave up. There was a big stack of cardboard boxes on the porch, and my pulse flickered with excitement. Maybe Dad had ordered me the new bedroom suite from Ikea like he'd been promising. But then I saw they all had U-HAUL printed on the sides of them and decided they must be more of Mira's things.

I was just about to stick my key in the front door when I saw the light blue envelope taped to the top of one of the boxes. It had my full name, Jamie Lexington-Cross, scrawled across it in my father's handwriting. Puzzled, I yanked it off, slicing my finger on the edge of the envelope as I opened it. A single slip of blue paper fluttered to the ground, and when I picked it up, the words swam in front of my eyes.

January 24th

Jamie,

You made a sinner's choice, and now God has made mine for me. You are banned from our home. Don't come back until you're willing to take the Pledge.

In Christ's name, Richard Cross

I TORE AT THE PACKING TAPE ON THE FIRST BOX. Inside I found all my shoes. In another, all my summer clothes. Jeans and warm sweaters were stuffed in a third one. Then I saw the labels. *Books & CDs. Mementos. Theater Stuff. Contents of Desk.* I didn't believe for a minute he really meant to kick me out. He's just trying to scare me into signing, I told myself.

Some people might be able to disown their own children, but not my dad. We were a team. We'd stuck by each other through it all. Even when I was in eighth grade and he let those recovering addicts move in with us and one of them stole my piggybank, I'd forgiven him.

And it wasn't like I could go to my only other living relative. Dad knew how to get ahold of Mom, but I didn't know, and I didn't want to. She'd moved to Hollywood when I was in sixth grade with some guy whose name I chose to forget as soon as I saw the back of him. Supposedly she had a job as a personal assistant for some two-bit movie producer. More likely, she was the person who scored his drugs.

Dad would never do this to me. It had to be Mira's idea. At first, I'd thought she was nice. Her big, doe eyes seemed kind, and her voice was soft. For their first date, she'd insisted on including me and had cooked dinner for us at our house. She'd set the table with beeswax candles, the real silver we'd inherited from my grandmother, and cloth napkins.

I had actually been happy for Dad because he'd stopped planting himself in front of the TV every night. Or relying on me for entertainment. For years, I'd read aloud to Dad from plays, which was fun for both of us, and I think helped me to become a better actress. But it was also exhausting after a long day of school and rehearsal. With Mira, he had a distraction, and I'd been grateful.

Gradually, I'd seen a change in her, though. Slowly, but methodically, she started taking over our lives. First it was ironing my dad's shirts. Then doing the grocery shopping. Those things weren't so bad, but then I noticed some of our favorite knickknacks, like the Mickey Mouse clock we'd bought at Disneyland and the Winnie-the-Pooh lamp we'd gotten on a trip to England, had disappeared.

In their places were religious statues. And one of them had a little plastic figure on the cross, but I swear it had the Teacher's beaky nose and didn't look anything like how you might expect Jesus to. I tried to reassure myself it was a coincidence, but honestly, it kind of freaked me out.

On Sundays Dad gave Mira a ride to church "because a lady doesn't drive herself when she has a man in her life." And she expected him to go to Wednesday Night Fellowship and to chaperone the Friday Mixers too, wearing the new, dark suit she'd bought him. When I complained he spent too much time with her, he said, "You're growing up, James. It feels good to have someone to take care of again."

"I thought your therapist warned you about giving up your life for someone else," I reminded him.

He ruffled my hair, a new habit since I'd had it cut short, and added, "Don't worry. It's not like when I was with your mom. I'm not trying to fix Mira. She's perfect the way she is."

I wasn't dumb enough to believe she was really perfect, but it was such a relief to see a smile on his face, I'd ignored my gut feelings, and now I was homeless. As I stood there, sucking my cut finger, I got the uncomfortable feeling I was being watched. The front curtains were drawn, but maybe Mira was peeking through, trying to see how I reacted. I cringed at the thought of her hands touching my stuff. But Dad had clearly written the note himself. Maybe he really had packed it all.

I grabbed the box on top and lugged it down the driveway. Fueled by anger, I dragged the rest of the boxes to the Beast and loaded them into the back in record time. Once I was behind the wheel again, though, the hurt of Dad's betrayal rushed through me. I knew how susceptible he was to persuasion, and I knew he'd been brainwashed, but it still just about killed me to think he could kick me out.

I needed to talk this over with someone, and if there was anyone who could give me some advice about the Right & the Real, it would be Josh. I hit number four on my speed dial, but it went straight to voice mail.

This is Josh—leave a message.

"Ummm . . . hi. It's me," I said. "Missed you at school today. Hope you're not sick or anything. Could you give me a call? Okay . . . well . . . bye."

There was only one place to go, Krista's. But halfway there, I fell apart. My whole body trembled in my seat, and for the first time, I understood what it meant to cry so hard you felt like you might throw up. I gulped for air, my hands holding tight to the steering wheel, while I looked desperately for a place to pull over.

Even though I could barely drive, there was this tiny voice inside telling me, "You can use this experience in your acting." That happens a lot to me, and sometimes it makes me wonder if I'm actually a really shallow person, but I don't think so, because tonight, the pain felt very real.

Once I'd gotten onto the shoulder of the road, I made myself do some deep breathing, and after a few minutes, I looked around and got my bearings. I wasn't too far from a side street that dead-ended into a little park where the drama kids would sometimes go late at night to mess around and drink, and so I drove there.

It was only five o'clock, but almost dark already. I sat there, leaning my head against the steering wheel, and the tears came again. They poured down my face, dripping onto my jeans, leaving dark blue splotches. By the time I'd cried out every drop, the streetlights had come on, giving the park an unnatural glow. The merry-go-round sat deserted, calling to me.

A minute later, I grabbed the icy bar and ran around and around and around, my shoes sending up a spray of sodden dirt and gravel. When my legs felt all rubbery and cold air stung my lungs, I leapt up onto the rough platform and threw myself down on my back. Above me, the night sky alternated with the streetlamp, making a blur, and I held on, gripping the cold metal to keep from being flung off.

The merry-go-round creaked and groaned, eventually slowing down and then stopping. I lay there, waiting for my insides to catch up with my body and the dizziness to subside. A cloud shifted, and a tiny bit of moon poked out. The cold air had cleared my head; now I knew what to do.

I'd go to the Right & the Real for Wednesday Night Fellowship, and I'd sign the Pledge. And then my dad would let me back in the house. I knew he was just trying to scare me into thinking he was serious about kicking me out, and I decided I'd make him sweat it out a little. It wouldn't hurt him to worry about me for a few days.

At the Coffee Espress-O, I washed my face in the bathroom sink and then I ordered a bagel and a double mocha and sat by the electric fireplace for a while. Before I left, I bought Krista a vanilla latte because it was her favorite and drove over to her house.

"Do you think your mom and George would mind if I stayed a few more days with you?" I asked when she answered the door. "The lovebirds want to be alone." I forced a smile.

"Sure," she said, taking the drink I offered her. "Mom had to go to Seattle for her job, but George won't mind. Come on in."

I could've told Krista what happened, but after all the crying, I didn't really have the energy to talk about it. Besides, I only needed a place to crash for two nights. By Wednesday, I'd be back at home, so she would never need to know my dad had kicked me out.

"What are all those boxes for?" Krista asked me, when we climbed into the Beast the next morning.

I kept my voice light. "Just stuff Mira wants me to give to the Salvation Army."

"I can barely see." She adjusted the rearview mirror. "Maybe we should dump them off on the way to school."

"I doubt they're open," I said. "I'll do it later."

She shrugged. "Okay."

• • •

In the locker room after PE, I mentally counted my money while I tried to make my hair look like Ms. Fitzpatrick hadn't run us ragged in ballet. It was beginning ballet, and I only took it because it was better than volleyball or field hockey, plus it kept me in shape for my real dance classes, which I took on Saturdays at the Bright Lights Studio.

PE ballet was pretty easy, but I always worked up a sweat anyway. Short hair was tough for me. When it was long, I'd worn it in a bun like Liz, and it always looked pretty okay afterward, but now it was a damp bird's nest. I gave up on it, applied fresh lip gloss, and touched up my eye shadow.

I had plenty of cash for lunch and gas because Grandpa had always given me money for birthdays and Christmas, which I'd tucked away. And I'd saved almost all the money I'd earned last summer for acting in *Peter Pan* too. I'd be fine, even if it took Dad a little while to cool off after I signed the Pledge. Krista had to go to her father's for the weekend, but I could stay with her until Friday if I needed to.

I stuffed my dance clothes into my bag and fluffed my hair one last time. I still looked pale under my makeup, and dark circles ringed my eyes, but boys don't notice that stuff. At least, I hoped Josh wouldn't. I still hadn't seen him today, but he never missed lunch.

In the cafeteria, I found Krista and Liz poking at their hot lunches—a gray lump floating in brown gravy. I decided to opt for the salad bar. "Why are you guys eating that?" I asked when I got back to the table.

"She dared me," Liz said. "I don't know why she bought it."

"Death wish." Krista stabbed the meat loaf with her fork. "Calculus test next period."

I speared a limp lettuce leaf. "So did you guess right?" I asked Liz.

Krista had outdone herself this morning when we were getting dressed, and we'd made a bet Liz wouldn't be able to figure out her inspiration. Today she wore slinky tights, a short skirt, and about four layers of torn-up T-shirts in neon colors. She also had a ton of metal and rubber bracelets weighing down her arms, and she'd pulled all her hair back on one side and teased out the other.

"At first I thought a young Madonna," Liz said. "Because of the neon. But then I remembered that chick with the shaved head on one side."

"Cyndi Lauper," Krista reminded her. "It was kind of both of them anyway."

Liz rumpled Krista's hair. "Our friend is whacked," she told me. "Totally."

"Hey! Don't touch the 'do!"

"At least she doesn't listen to the music," I said.

Krista wrinkled her nose like she'd smelled something even worse than the food. "As if. Give me some credit."

I scanned the cafeteria, looking for the football players. "Have you guys seen Josh?" I asked.

They exchanged frowns.

"What's wrong?"

"Rumor is you two broke up," Krista said. "But we know that's not true because you would've told us."

I swallowed back my surprise. "News to me."

"We figured," Liz said. She pulled the chopstick out of her bun, shook her hair loose, and retwisted it up into a knot, which she does about fifty times a day. "Megan told me she heard it from Ashleigh Robertson, who heard it from her brother. Never trust little sisters."

I forced myself to smile and tried not to think about how Josh hadn't returned any of my calls or texts. "We didn't break up," I said firmly. "I'll go find him."

I hadn't even stood up yet when Josh and Derrick strolled into the cafeteria. Josh looked great in jeans and an old University of Oregon football jersey. My heart literally raced at the sight of him. He was so gorgeous. Sometimes I could hardly stand it. I know every girl's supposed to fall for his type—friendly, tall, blond, straight teeth, and all that—but usually I was attracted to his total opposite. The skinny, dark-haired, moody, and dramatic types. Or loud, funny, and kind of awkward. And yet, every time I laid eyes on Josh, I turned to jelly, just like stereotypical girls in books.

What was kind of weird, though, was Derrick had the exact same big build, blond flattop, and blue eyes, but he wasn't attractive at all. I think it was the sour look he always had. He didn't like school very much. They headed over to the pop machine, shoving each other out of the way to get to it first. Then they fed dollar bills into it while they laughed and joked around.

I snuck up behind Josh and put my arms around his waist. As soon as I did it, his whole body stiffened and he pulled my hands apart. Derrick stood there watching us, his arms crossed like those guys on that *Iron Chef* TV show . . . the one where they try to look all hardass, but all you can think is, *Really? A tough chef? How stupid.*

"Uh, Jamie," Josh said, "let's talk over here."

He took me by the elbow and led me to the corner where you dump off your tray. Derrick followed so close I could practically feel him breathing on me.

Josh shifted his weight back and forth and wouldn't look me in the eye. Finally, he said, "We have to break up."

"What? Just like that?" I couldn't believe it.

"I don't have any choice."

"If it's because of Saturday nigh—"

"I have to go," he said. And then he just walked off, leaving me standing there with the iron chef. I started to run after him, but Derrick grabbed my arm.

"Just leave him alone," he said. "He's not allowed to talk to you."

"Because of the Pledge?"

Derrick moved in closer; his hulky body hovered over me. "You're not supposed to talk about it at school."

All the kids from the R&R were homeschooled except Josh and Derrick, and the two of them tried to keep their involvement in it a secret. Derrick never talked about it because the Teacher had convinced him the other kids would try and shake his faith, but Josh kept his mouth shut because he was embarrassed to be part of the church. The only reason they got to go to public school at all was that they had athletic promise. Josh's dad was convinced his boys had a shot at the NFL if they could play high school and college football, and the Teacher had made an exception for them.

"Well, is that why he's upset?" I asked in a low voice. "Because I didn't sign?"

Derrick nodded like I was an idiot. "Duh. You can't expect someone like my brother to date a sinner."

"But I'm not," I protested. "I'm going to sign tomor—"

"Forget it," he said, walking off.

I tried to grab his arm, but all I managed was a handful of his jersey.

"Derrick, wait!"

"What?"

I leaned in confidentially. He smelled like gym socks and too much cologne. "I . . . I made a mistake." The next bit was going to kill me, but I pretended like it was a line from a play. "And I'm ready to do *it* tomorrow night," I said.

Derrick made a noise, something between a snort and a laugh.

"The *Pledge*," I whispered. "Tell Josh I'll be there. At Wednesday Night Fellowship."

"Too little, too late," Derrick said, and he jogged off after his brother.

I HAVE ADVANCED DRAMA LAST PERIOD, AND I spent it being consoled by Liz and Krista on pillows in the downstairs rehearsal room. They had their arms wrapped around me and were taking turns stroking my hair and telling me it would be okay.

Emotional meltdowns in the drama room were so common, no one bothered to ask us why I was crying. Besides, by then, everyone had heard anyway. Mr. Lazby was holed up in the costume shop as usual. We were supposed to use the class for homework so we wouldn't get behind because of rehearsals, but no one ever did.

"I've got to talk to Josh," I said.

"Honey, just forget him," Liz told me.

Then Krista said, "Speak of the Devil."

Josh stood in the doorway, scanning the room, his arms crossed. He couldn't really get inside because Juan and Patrick, two guys in our class, were using half the floor space for a sword fight. Well, one sword and one fencing foil, since that's all they could find in the prop room. Juan swung the sword at Patrick, yelling out some improvised Shakespeare, and Patrick dodged and lunged with his foil.

"I seek revenge for the fair maiden," Patrick shouted. "Your head is mine!"

Josh spotted me and tried to get around them, but they jumped and flailed their weapons so much, he had to back into the hallway. Juan danced out of the way of the foil. "Egad, man. Is that your best effort? I will cut your miserable life short with my sword before you—"

Patrick dived at Juan's legs and took him down with a tackle that left them wrestling on the floor. "You cheat, man, I say!" shouted Juan from underneath him. One of them cried out in pain, and they rolled apart.

"Watch my stuff," I told Liz and Krista.

"Do you want us to go with you?"

"I'm good," I said.

By the time I got into the hallway, Josh was already heading into the scene storage room like it was just one of the zillions of times he'd ditched his last class to come see me.

"Where are you going?" I asked.

"I've got a library pass for the whole period," he told me. "I thought we'd hang out like usual."

"Ummm . . . excuse me, but didn't we break up at lunch?"

He pulled me inside the scene shop and shut the door so Lexi and Matt, a couple of big-time gossips who were standing around the bulletin board in the hallway, wouldn't hear us. Instead of switching on the glaring overhead fluorescents, he turned on the little flashlight I'd given him for his key chain.

"I didn't break up with you. Didn't you get my text?" he asked.

"My phone's in the car," I said.

"Wait a minute! You really didn't get it?" The light played eerily across his features.

"What part of 'it's in my car' don't you understand?" I demanded. What was wrong with him? "And what do you mean you didn't break up with me at lunch?"

"Jamie! I'm so sorry." He tried to reach out and take me in his arms, but I pressed myself up against the wall so he couldn't. "I wasn't really breaking with you. That was all for show . . . for Derrick."

"Excuse me?" I said. "What the hell are you talking about?"

"I would never break up with you," Josh said. "Come here . . . come here. . . . I'm so sorry. I love you . . . really. . . . I would never dump you like that."

What was he saying? He'd pretended to break up with me? My body relaxed a little, and he slipped his arms around me, pulling me close. As I snuggled up next to him, his familiar warmth pulsed through me. I was still confused about what had happened in the caf, but Josh's body was so comforting. I felt a shudder go through me, and his arms tightened around me.

He whispered into my hair that he had to break up with me or his dad and the Teacher would pull him out of school and he'd lose his scholarship for the University of Oregon next year. He didn't want Derrick to have to lie for him, so he'd come up with the idea of a fake breakup.

"Jamie," he said, nuzzling my neck, making my skin tingle, "you looked so hurt in the cafeteria, all I could think was, *Wow, she really is a great actress*. I had no idea you hadn't gotten the text I sent. I'm so sorry."

I clung to him tighter, glad it had been a misunderstanding. I couldn't take my dad and Josh abandoning me in the same week. "It's okay." I stroked his hair. I was still maybe a little angry, or hurt, or whatever, but at least I had my boyfriend. "So what happens now?" I asked.

"We'll have to see each other in secret," he said.

My body tensed up. This wasn't exactly what I had in mind when I thought of being in a relationship. "I don't like it, Josh," I said. "It makes me feel . . . I don't know . . . like—"

He tilted my face up and kissed me long, soft, and sweet. Any apprehension I'd had about being in a secret relationship dissolved with that kiss. Besides, once I took the Pledge tomorrow night, we could get back together.

"It'll be fun," Josh said, his voice soft and husky. "Like when we sneak off into closets at the church. You like that."

I laughed a little. "Because it seems wicked."

"I like it when you use that word," he said, running his hands up and down my back.

Josh was as familiar with the storage room as any drama student, and he picked me up and carried me through the maze of old scenery flats. All the set furniture was piled haphazardly in the back, and over the years, students had arranged some of it into a little sitting area. When we got there, Josh laid me down on the couch. He pulled the chain on the single bulb over the prop storage shelves, so a faint light washed over us.

"I like to see how hot you look when I kiss you," he said. And then he lay down on top of me.

Sometime later, Josh's phone buzzed, and he dug in his pocket for it and turned off the alarm. He always set it for when class was over because we tended to lose track of time. Reluctantly, we separated ourselves. It felt like being pulled out of safe warm waters and plunged into icy ones. It wasn't until after Josh was gone that I remembered I'd never told him about being kicked out of the house.

For some reason, when Dad had packed my clothes, he'd kept my three church dresses. Maybe Mira wanted them. We were both the same height, five-foot-one, and wore the same dress size. Luckily, because Krista practically lives in the costume shop, she was able to score me something to wear on Wednesday night.

After a quick pasta dinner with Krista and her stepfather, George, we went upstairs so I could get ready. She zipped up the powder-blue dress for me.

"I look like Hodel in *Fiddler on the Roof*," I said.

She grabbed my hands and swung me around in an impromptu dance, singing, "Matchmaker, matchmaker, make me a match, find me a find, catch me a catch."

"Shut up." I covered her mouth, but she fought me off. We wrestled around on her fuzzy carpet, laughing and trying to outsing each other until we heard a seam rip. Then she had to stitch me up before I could leave for Fellowship.

I got to the church early, and the parking lot was only about a quarter full. Inside, when I passed through the lobby, I could hear people in the auditorium. I wondered if my dad was in there, and I almost stopped to check, but first I wanted to catch the Teacher alone if I could, so I went directly to his office.

"Enter," he called out when I knocked. Inside, I found him sitting in a swivel desk chair, pretty much naked. I backed out into the hallway. "No, no . . . ," he said. "Come in, Jamie. You're not interrupting."

He had a towel draped across his midsection and his feet in a basin of water. A woman, who I swear wasn't more than twenty and was wearing a dress almost exactly like mine, knelt beside him, gently scrubbing his feet with a loofah sponge. Another girl, who I think might've been even younger than me, stood behind him, and he rested his head against her small breasts while she rubbed some sort of oil into his bare shoulders.

It was no secret that the Teacher loved the opposite sex. He had three wives that I knew of, all members of the church, but only one of them lived in the mansion. The others had trailers in the compound. He had a whole bunch of kids too, some from each wife. No one had ever told me if they were consecutive wives or if the R&R really did condone polygamy, but I was starting to think it was the latter. Seeing the two girls caressing him made me feel sick to my stomach, but I tried to hide it by keeping my face as passive as possible.

"Maybe I should come back," I said.

"Don't be shy. This is just my preservice cleansing." He waved his arm, gesturing at me. "Come in, child. I was expecting you."

"You were?"

"For some reason," he said, smiling sadly, "the Devil was in you on Saturday night, but I had a vision this morning you would see the way and return for guidance."

"Well . . . yes."

"Wonderful." He waved at a metal chair. "Have a seat."

The last thing I wanted to do was sit down and watch those girls touching his bare skin. But if I was going to play the part of the repentant daughter, I had to pretend like it didn't matter. I pulled the chair away from the wall, but not too close to him. "I'd . . . I'd like to sign the Pledge."

"Of course you would. And we here at the Right & the Real are happy to welcome you into our flock."

The girl standing behind him picked up one of his arms and massaged his biceps.

"So . . . will I do it at the Fellowship meeting tonight?" I asked, looking at a red stain on the carpet so I wouldn't have to watch those girls. "Or maybe right now?"

"What's the rush?" he asked me in a cooing voice. "Let's talk first."

"Ummm . . . okay."

"There are some things you need to understand," he said. "Because you didn't sign at the ceremony, and because you humiliated your father, you will have to pay retribution to be welcomed back into the church. Bad deeds can't go unpunished."

"What do you mean?" I hoped it didn't involve washing his feet.

"You'll need to spend some time with Mira doing Bible study."

Oh, great. I pasted a smile on my face. "I think that's probably a good idea," I said.

"And, of course, you'll leave school right away . . . tomorrow. That should help tame any rebelliousness."

I shook my head. "I can't quit now."

"Young ladies here at the Right & the Real stop schooling at menstruation. Am I correct that you are a woman?"

The heat rose up my face.

"I have to graduate," I said. "I'm going to drama school next year, and I need my diploma."

I hadn't gotten the results of my audition back yet, but I knew I'd study acting somewhere, even if I didn't get into the Redgrave Actors Conservatory, which was my first choice.

"Jamie," he said, leaning slightly forward. The girl sitting on the floor stopped washing his feet, and I knew she was watching me under her lashes. "I've discussed this with your father. Either you sign and agree to leave school tomorrow, or you're banned from the church and his home forever."

"But I can't," I said. "Josh and Derrick go—"

"They're boys. They're not susceptible to the evils of the world."

"Neither am I," I argued.

He shrugged his bare shoulders. "Sign or don't sign, Jamie. God has given you an opportunity to make up for your wickedness and to honor your father, but this is your last chance."

I stood up so fast my chair tipped over. "I want to see my dad."

He folded his hands together into a little tent and smiled up at me. "I'm sorry. He's not allowed to see you until you've signed the Pledge."

"You can't keep me from him."

He leaned forward and pushed a button on the phone on his desk. "I already am," he said, still smiling.

This wasn't a religion, it was a cult. I'd known the people at the R&R were fanatical, but it hadn't really hit me until the Teacher said he could keep my dad from seeing me. He controlled people in a way no regular minister ever would.

"If you're not going to sign," he said, "it's time for you to leave."

"But—"

Two men in brown servant robes appeared in the doorway.

"Show our visitor to her car," the Teacher said. "She's no friend of God."

They reached out as if to take my arm, and I pushed past them and ran for the lobby. A small figure wearing a pale green dress that looked awfully familiar hurried down the hallway ahead of me.

Mira.

I sprinted after her. "Wait!" I said. When I reached the lobby, it was empty, but I heard the door to the women's bathroom thud shut.

I threw it open. "I know you're in here, Mira," I said.

"What do you want?" she asked from the end stall.

"Why did you do it?" I asked. "Why did you convince Dad to cut me off?"

"I didn't," she said. "It wasn't me. It was Jesus."

I'd always thought Mira was manipulative but sane. Now I wasn't so sure. "What do you mean?"

"Jesus told him to do it," she said.

I stared at the pink metal door dividing us. "What? Like in a dream?"

The door flew open and Mira faced me, her cheeks flushed, her eyes bright. "Not in a dream! The Teacher is Jesus Christ our Lord come again."

Oh. My. God. I'd heard the Teacher say that a million times, but I guess I never realized people actually took it literally.

"And he told my dad to disown me?" I asked in the kind of non-threatening voice one uses with a crazy person.

She nodded. "Yes, yes! He told us that you are evil and all you want is Richard's money. But now, the church will safeguard his inheritance for him, and you are banned. Praise God."

"And my dad believed him?"

"Of course," she said. "Jesus would never lie to us."

I was still taking this idea in when Mira darted around me and ran out through the bathroom door.

6

I HEADED TO KRISTA'S.

None of this had seemed real, but now I couldn't believe I'd been stupid enough to think Dad would go to the trouble to pack my stuff and kick me out just to make a point. As I climbed the stairs to Krista's room, part of me was surprised at how little emotion I felt. Sappy commercials can leave me a weepy mess, and those crazy stories, like the one where someone has a heart attack and then the doorbell rings and it's the pizza guy, only he's actually an out of work paramedic and he saves the day . . . I cry rivers over. And I'd sobbed buckets on Monday, but now, when my whole life was falling apart, all I felt was cold. A deep, bone-chilling iciness.

I'd told Krista I was signing the Pledge so Josh and I wouldn't have to date in secret. She hadn't liked that at all, but I'd decided I'd rather let him take the blame than tell her my dad had kicked me out. Now that I wasn't going to get to move back home, I'd have to tell her the truth. Stepping into her cheerful room should have snapped me out of it, but everything looked sort of surreal instead.

"Hiya, chickie," she said, glancing up from her sketch pad. "How'd it go?"

"Ummm . . . not that good." I perched on a twin bed.

"Why? What happened?"

"Well—"

Someone knocked twice and then opened the door a crack. George poked his head into the room. As usual, he needed a shave. Krista and I always joked that her stepdad was half gorilla.

"Okay, I'll turn down the music," she said.

"It's not the volume, although, now you mention it . . . Actually, I have a special-delivery letter for you, Miss Kris." George held up a thin envelope. "It was still in the mailbox when I got home. Probably nothing important," he said, "but the postmark *is* New York."

Krista laid down her drawing pad, her expression a mixture of terror and hope. She took the envelope from him like she was afraid it contained snakes. Slowly she tore it open and pulled out the letter.

"I got in," she said, almost too quietly for us to hear. "I got in to Beaumont Design in New York!"

George and I threw our arms around her. We laughed, and hugged, and congratulated her. Pride for Krista swelled up inside me, replacing all my worries. She'd worked so hard for this, and for the first time in days, the tears that leaked out of the corners of my eyes were happy ones.

"I have to call Mom!"

George gave her another hug. "Good job, kiddo," he said. He saluted us and backed out of the room. "As you were."

Krista dialed her mom, but got voice mail. "Call me back as soon as you can," she said.

She grabbed the huge file we'd put together full of brochures, maps, and the school's catalogue, and we pored over it, excited because it was finally happening—our dreams! Or at least Krista's. The thought did occur to me that our big plans would be ruined if I didn't get into drama school, but I pushed it away.

"You know what would be the ultimate New York experience?" she asked. "If we could find a brownstone to live in. I mean, ones that are apartments, not a whole house."

I tugged at the hem of the Day-Glo orange tunic she had on. "You're going to have to raise the prices on your website for your clothing line to afford that."

"Don't I know it," she said. "I probably can too. Now that I got into such a prestigious school. Besides, I meant a really tiny apartment."

"Like maybe someone's walk-in closet?"

"Exactly," she said.

I slumped deeper into the throw pillows and watched Krista shuffle through the papers. Her eyes had that same glittery, excited look we always shared when we planned our future together. How could I tell her about getting kicked out now? Without my dad's support, I'd never even get to New York. Krista would have to find someone else to room with, because at that moment, I didn't know where I was going to live next week, let alone next year. I couldn't bring her down like that when she was so happy. But I had to tell her something.

"Krista—"

Her phone blared the theme song from the TV show *Fashion Escapades*, and she grabbed it. "Hi, Mom. No, everything's good. It's fabulous news, actually. I got in to Beaumont Design!"

I heard her mom scream in excitement through the phone. Krista had chosen Beaumont because it was a tiny boutique school, and they only took in twenty new students each year. Most of their graduates got great internships with big-time designers. It was a huge accomplishment to be accepted straight out of high school too, and as she talked with her mom about the program, I had to fight a surge of jealousy.

If I told Krista what happened at the church, I could make her promise to keep quiet, but I wasn't sure it would work. Your best friend suddenly being homeless is exactly the kind of secret *Seventeen* magazine always gives you permission to tell an adult about. And Krista thinks that, in spite of their extremely *safe* fashion choices, the writers are goddesses, so she might spill.

Maybe getting an adult involved was a good idea, but not Krista's mom, Margie. She'd gone to high school with my mother, and no matter how many times my mom bummed money or a place to sleep off of her, she always believed her when she said she was getting clean. Margie had told me a bunch of times that Mom was doing great in LA, but what I wanted to know was, if that was true, why did she still cash the checks Dad sent her every month?

I also knew Margie didn't like my dad because of that time when I was in eighth grade and he let a bunch of homeless druggies move into our house. Eventually, Grandpa had found a shelter for my dad's friends and stayed with us for a month, getting my father into therapy, but Margie never forgot it. Dad had been a pretty good parent ever since, though. Until this church thing, anyway. Now Grandpa was gone, and if Krista's mom found out I was on my own, there'd be no one to stop her from forcing a mother-daughter reconciliation. She'd probably even buy the airplane ticket herself. Krista thought I should give Mom a chance too, which burned me.

I flipped through the travel brochures while Krista and her mom gabbed about maybe taking a scouting trip to Manhattan in June.

"Of course I told Jamie," Krista said. "She's staying over. Yes, again." She rolled her eyes at me. "Yes, I know . . . Mom. She doesn't want to talk to you. Okay. Fine." She held out her cell to me.

"Why?" I mouthed.

She shrugged.

I gave in and took it. "Hi, Margie."

"How are you, Jamie?" she asked, her voice all smooth and concerned.

"Uh . . . fine."

"Krista tells me you've been with us since Saturday. I thought you were only staying two nights."

I couldn't tell if she was prying or if she knew something. I wouldn't put it past her to have found out from a network of neighborhood friends that I'd been seen taking boxes off my porch and loading them into the Beast.

"Well, my dad and Mira . . . they wanted some time alone since they didn't get a real honeymoon. . . ."

Krista made kissy noises at me and then started moaning and saying "ohhh, Mira . . ." under her breath.

"Stop it!" I whispered at her, trying to kick her off the bed, but she moved out of reach, laughing.

Margie had been talking, but I'd sort of missed it. "I'd be happy to," she said.

"Ummm . . ." Crap. "Happy to . . . ?"

"To go over and talk to your dad and Mira. I'm sure it's hard for you all to adjust to a new person in the house, but I've been through this before. When George and I got married, there was a lot—"

"Oh, no," I said. "I mean, no thank you. Please . . . you don't need to go talk to my dad."

"Jamie?" Margie said in that slow I'm-a-mom-so-don't-even-try-to-bullshit-me voice she had. "Is anything wrong at home?"

49

"No. Of course not."

"Mira's not a drug addict or an alcoholic, is she?"

"Definitely not," I said, telling the truth for once. But my voice was totally squeaky.

"Has your dad been going to his therapist?"

Oh, God. This was so embarrassing. "Everything's fine, Margie. Really."

"Are you planning to go home on Friday night, or will you be there when I get back?"

"No. I mean, yes, I'm leaving when Krista goes to her dad's. I won't be here."

"You would tell me if something was wrong, wouldn't you?"

"Sure."

"Or George. He could help you too," she said.

"I know. Thanks, but I'm fine. Everything's fine."

"All right. If you say so."

I'd have to be really careful around both Krista and her mom because I did not want to end up in Los Angeles living with Mommy Dearest.

By the time we'd turned out the lights, the coldness in me had thawed and raw pain had replaced it. Part of me wanted to throw myself on Krista's bed and tell her everything, but I was her best friend, and she was so happy.

"Hey, Jamie," Krista said, her voice heavy with sleep.

"Yeah?"

"You never told me what happened at the church."

"Tomorrow," I said. "Tell you then."

"Okay. Night, chickie."

Her breathing slowed to a regular rhythm. For the first time since my encounter with the Teacher tonight, I thought about Josh. I'd seen him briefly at school and told him my plan to sign, but I hadn't gotten a chance to tell him about Dad kicking me out, because Derrick had come out of the locker room while we were talking, and we'd just walked away from each other.

We'd both been so sure that once I signed the Pledge, we would be able to date in public again, but now we'd have to keep the whole relationship a secret after all. And he'd asked me not to call or text him either. I'd have to find him as soon as possible. He was the one person who could help me, because he knew how the church worked. He would know what I should do.

chapter 7

I SAW JOSH FOUR TIMES BEFORE LUNCH, BUT whenever I tried to get close to him, he ducked into a bathroom or out a side door, which kind of pissed me off. I'd made sure Derrick wasn't around first, so I didn't know why he had to treat me like that. On my way to the caf, his lab partner, Marissa, found me in the hall and held out my favorite blue hoodie.

"Here. Josh Peterson said you left it in his locker." She gave me a sort of pity look, like she was sorry for me, which I didn't buy for one second because I knew she crushed on him. A lot of good it would do her.

"Thanks," I said, taking it.

I slipped it on, breathing in the scent of Josh's aftershave left over from where his letterman's coat had pressed against it in the locker. I thought maybe this was a sign he wanted to see me, and I headed for the south stairwell, where we used to meet at lunch, but he wasn't there.

After a while, I sank down onto the floor to wait, pressing my back against the cold cinder-block wall, my arms wound tightly around my knees. The faint smell of Josh on my hoodie conjured up pictures of us together, and I let my mind wander to when we first started dating back in September. By our third date, I'd worried something was wrong with me, like BO or bad breath, because Josh never, ever made a move. After yet another totally chaste date, Josh had dropped me off at Krista's with a quick shoulder squeeze good-bye, and I'd run into the house looking for her.

"Smell my breath," I said, blowing in her face.

She shoved me back. "God, Jamie. Personal space. Please?"

"It's bad, isn't it?"

"No, it's fine," she said, "but if someone's gonna get that close to me, I want dinner and a movie first."

"Ha-ha." I grabbed her and gave her a big smooch on the cheek. "I can't get any action, so you'll have to do."

She wiped my lip gloss off her face. "Maybe it's because you have a chaperone," she said.

Derrick did go with us everywhere. But you'd think Josh would kiss me at the front door at least. I mean, yeah, his little brother was in the car, but he probably wasn't spying on us. I highly doubted he wanted to see us making out any more than we wanted him to, but seeing people kiss wasn't that big of a deal. He must've seen tons of couples hooking up at school.

When Josh finally did get around to kissing me, it was worth the wait. The best part about it, the sweetest thing, was that he'd actually *asked* first. I'd been attending the Right & the Real regularly for a month or so, and I'd met Josh's parents and received their approval, so they let us go to homecoming together without taking Derrick as a chaperone. On the dance floor, Josh towered over me, and my arms barely reached around his neck. His strong hands wrapped around my waist, we swayed to a slow song.

"Jamie?" he'd said.

"Hmmm?" I answered, loving the warm tickle of his breath in my ear.

"I know I'm supposed to wait until I take you home, but . . ."

I lifted my head from his chest and looked up at him. "But?"

"Could I kiss you now?"

I couldn't help it, the laugh bubbled out of me. I knew I was his first real girlfriend, because his parents were so strict, he'd never really dated, and he probably was just shy, but once I started giggling, I couldn't stop, which made everything more embarrassing for him. I stood there, shaking with laughter in Josh's arms while the color crept up his neck. He let go of my waist.

"No . . . wait," I said, grabbing his hands. "I'm sorry, I didn't mean to laugh. It was so sweet. No one's ever asked to kiss me before."

"You've never been kissed?" he said.

Then it was my turn to blush. "Well . . . I mean . . . I just meant . . . no one's *asked*."

"Oh."

When I finally swallowed the last giggle, he took me back in his arms and kissed me. His lips were cool, and he tasted like minty Chapstick.

The cold of the tile floor seeped through my jeans, and I squeezed my arms around me tighter as if they were Josh's. It took me a minute to realize tears were running down my cheeks. I guess maybe because even though we were still together, everything was different too. I searched the pocket of the hoodie to see if by some miracle there might be a tissue. My fingers touched crisp paper instead, and my heart soared. I pulled it out expecting a note from Josh, but instead I found three twenty-dollar bills folded together.

I fingered them like I'd never seen money before. I didn't remember leaving cash in there. It was possible, but it wasn't like I had so much I could forget about sixty bucks. As I unfolded them, a tiny slip of paper fell out.

J— Heard about your dad kicking you out. Are you OK?
Staying at Krista's? Don't answer. We'll talk next week.
Derrick's watching me all the time. Love you. Josh

Next week? It was only Thursday. I had been counting on Josh to help me figure out where to go this weekend. This was just great. I fingered the cash. Maybe Motel 6 would rent me a room.

After school on Friday, while Krista packed her weekend bag, I crawled into the backseat of the Beast and pulled out a few of my boxes. I'd rearranged them so they weren't blocking the driver's view anymore, and when Krista asked why I hadn't dropped them off already, I just pleaded laziness.

With Krista going to her dad's, I'd asked Liz if I could stay with her, but her grandma was in town, so I was on my own. I checked to see if my sleeping bag was in one of the cartons in case I had to camp out in the car. My dad must've kept it, but I did find the whole set of Princess Pink linens he'd bought me for my sixteenth birthday. That was one good thing, at least. I'd stacked a bunch of boxes in the driveway while I searched and was loading them back in when I saw the one labeled *Theater Stuff.*

I ran my hand over the cardboard, caressing it. This had to be all my scripts, plus my theater memorabilia. It probably had all the books I'd bought on that trip to New York City with the drama group, photocopies of scripts for plays we'd done at school, and the photo album from performing arts camp in it too.

It had only been six days since the wedding, but it already felt like I'd been in limbo for weeks. I had such a longing for my old life, I vowed right then I wouldn't open this box until I was in New York at drama school. Or at least until I had my dad back and my life was on track again.

"Hey," Krista said, startling me so I hit my head on the doorjamb, "when are you going to get rid of these boxes? You can't be that lazy."

"Ummm . . ." I should tell her right now. She could help me figure out what to do. "I—"

A horn beeped twice as a blue minivan pulled into the driveway behind us.

"Mom!" Krista said.

Margie climbed out. "My meetings ended early." While they hugged, I quickly shoved the last of the boxes back inside and slammed the door.

"Hi, Margie," I said, walking toward her, smiling my brightest smile.

Later, I took Krista to the mall to meet her stepmother, Lisa. "Don't forget about your phone," Krista said to me before they drove away.

"I won't. I'm going there now."

For some reason, I wasn't getting any service. I made my way to the end of the mall to my cell provider. I paced around the tiny phone center, looking at headsets, cases, and hands-free adapters for almost an hour, waiting for my turn to talk to one of the two gum-chewing, multitasking salesgirls. Finally, I was up, but this big guy with a beer gut and a toddler wrapped around his leg tried to cut in front of me.

"Ummm . . . excuse me," I said. "I'm next."

"I just need to buy this battery," he told me.

"Yeah, well, I've been waiting for, like, an hour."

The girl took it from him. "I'll ring him up real fast."

My nerves were wound so tight, it took every ounce of self-control not to totally lose it, but I managed to hold it in. Fifteen minutes and two phone calls later, she finally said, "Okay. What can I do for you?"

I took a deep breath to keep from screaming, gave her my name, and told her the problem. "There's something wrong with my cell. It charges, but it's not getting any service."

While she looked up my account, she took a call on her own phone, and I had to fight back the urge to rip the earpiece out of her ear. I knew part of my problem was general anxiety, but honestly, she was pushing every button I had by taking a personal call. Her fourth one since I'd walked through the doors.

"No, I can't," she said into her headset. "I've got to close tonight and then I'm meeting Spencer." She typed a few more things into the computer. "What's your name again?" she asked me.

"Jamie Lexington-Cross," I spit out. "But the account's in my dad's name. Richard Cross."

"Hmmm. . . ." She chomped on her gum. "He never said that."

"What?" I asked.

She shook her head at me and mouthed the words, "I'm on the phone."

"Yeah, I got that," I muttered, and she gave me a wide-eyed look like, *What's your problem?*

"Okay . . . here it is," she said. "Your service has been canceled."

I seriously thought she was still talking to whoever she had on the phone.

"Your service was canceled," she said again, when I didn't respond.

"Me?" I asked.

She nodded. "Yeah, earlier today. Must've gone over your limit one too many times and pissed your dad off." She laughed. "Happens all the time. He'll get over it, but it will cost him fifty bucks to reinstate it. Good luck."

I couldn't believe I hadn't realized this the moment it stopped working. I'd been so focused on all my other problems, though, and I'd actually thought the phone was dying because it was ancient; I'd had it for over a year. But still, how stupid could I be? He'd kicked me out. Of course he'd cancel my phone. Before I could ask about maybe getting a new plan, she had turned her attention back to her call and walked off.

"Ummm, hello? Salesgirl with the phone attached to your ear?" I said extra loudly. Everyone in the store turned to look, and a few people snickered. "I'm not exactly done here? Could you hang up and give me some customer service?"

The girl stared at me, her eyes wide again. "Ummm . . . I gotta go," she said to her friend. She stepped back to the counter like I might slap her if she got too close. "How may I help you?" she asked formally.

"You could give me a little more information," I said. "What do you mean, my account's canceled? Like closed, or like he forgot to pay the bill?" I asked, even though I already knew.

"It appears your phone line was removed from the account by Mr.

Cross earlier today," she said stiffly. "Perhaps you would like to open a new one? I need to see a driver's license and credit card."

"I don't have a credit card," I said.

"We have some prepay options as well," she continued, as if she were reading out of an employee manual.

Suddenly it was too much. It was like my dad kept pecking away at me, making things worse and worse. Why couldn't he have let me have this one thing? He knew I couldn't afford a phone. I grabbed my purse off the counter and wove through the half dozen people who were crowded into the store, waiting.

"God, what a bitch," I heard someone say.

"It's called customer service," I yelled over my shoulder, but I kept going without looking back. I had to talk to my dad. And not just about the stupid phone, but about everything.

BY THE TIME I FOUGHT MY WAY THROUGH THE RAINY
Friday night rush hour traffic, my determination to face Dad had
weakened. I must've circled the neighborhood for half an hour trying to work up my nerve before I finally turned down our street and
parked across from the house, but I left the engine idling and the
windshield wipers whooshed back and forth, brushing away the rain.

The driveway was empty, but light leaked out of the living room
into the yard, and after a few minutes, I saw my dad's shadow pass
behind the drapes. I killed the engine and started to get out, but then
a second, smaller silhouette joined him and my body tensed. If only
there was some way to get him alone.

I sat there for a long time, but after a while I knew I'd never go up
to the door with Mira inside, so I drove around for an hour. When I
passed the bright lights of a Mobil station, I realized how stupid I'd
been. The Beast sucked down gasoline like Josh gulping Gatorade
after a game. I only had thirteen hundred seventy-two dollars in my
savings account, which wouldn't last very long. Even with Josh's sixty
bucks, I couldn't drive around randomly ever again. At least not until

I got a job, which was next on my list, right after finding a place to live.

Normally, I would've gone to Coffee Espress-O, but I was afraid I'd run into too many people I knew, so I drove over to a little café called the Coffee Klatch that my dad and I had discovered last summer on a dusky evening bike ride. It was in kind of a paradoxical area of town where the houses had all been redone, the lawns were trim, and kids played hopscotch on the sidewalks, but you could also hear the constant traffic on Sandy Boulevard just a few blocks away. The busy, wide street cut across Portland on an angle, and along this stretch, it was lined with dicey hotels, fast-food places, and taverns. The café was on the ground floor of an old brick building that sat right in the middle of a residential neighborhood.

I made my way to the counter, past businesspeople in ties, teens with backpacks, and college students dressed in black, who congregated on soft couches, eating, drinking, and flirting. There wasn't anyone working behind the counter, and I stood there, waiting. After about five minutes, I decided to go somewhere else, but then the swinging door to the back opened a couple of inches and a voice yelled out, "Trent! I thought you were watching for customers."

A guy who was sitting on one of the couches behind me yelled, "Sorry. I got it."

He ran across the room and leapfrogged the counter so he was facing me. He brushed floppy brown hair out of his eyes and smiled at me so intensely it was like I was the only person in the room. For some odd reason, instead of it being creepy, I got a rush from it. And then I blushed.

"What can I get you?" he asked.

"Ummm . . ."

I must've looked a little doubtful or confused, because he said, "It's okay. I work here. I mean, I'm not working now, but I can make you a drink." He nodded toward the swinging door. "Girl trouble, so I'm covering."

"Oh. Okay. I'll have a mocha." But then I remembered I needed to watch my money. "Actually, make that a regular coffee with room for cream."

I waited while he got it for me, and even though it took forever, I was so distracted by the fact I had nowhere to sleep, I didn't even notice he had made me a mocha until he asked if I wanted chocolate sprinkles.

"Ummm," I said, "I ordered a coffee."

"But you *wanted* a mocha." He squirted a huge mound of whipped cream on top, and it wobbled as he handed it to me. "Free upgrade for having to wait."

It honestly made me want to cry, which I knew was not the reaction he was hoping for. "Wow. Thanks."

"Anytime. Well, not actually anytime," he said, "because I can't give away free drinks for no reason, but you know, if you have to wait or you're unhappy with the service or—" I started laughing even though my insides ached. He smiled back. "Anyway . . ."

One of his bottom teeth was just the tiniest bit crooked, and I wondered what it might feel like to touch it with my tongue. Like if we were kissing. God! What was wrong with me? Clearly I was losing my mind. *Hello, Jamie! Remember Josh?* I couldn't believe I'd even thought that.

"Okay, well, thanks," I said, moving away to check out the crowded bulletin boards before he noticed I was blushing again.

"See you around," he said.

"Thanks again," I said, heading over to the bulletin board.

Yesterday, I'd read the ads in three newspapers looking for apartments, but found out everyone charged thirty-five dollars just for the credit check. Plus you had to be eighteen, with a job and a security deposit. I wouldn't be eighteen until April, and I barely had enough for one month, let alone two. I scanned a bunch of handwritten ads for rooms to rent and tried not to think about the fact that the cute coffee guy was wearing an NYU sweatshirt. Did he love New York too?

I shook off thoughts of him and used a pay phone by the bathroom to call on a couple of listings. The first turned out to be all the way across town and too expensive anyway. The woman who answered at the second number said I had to be at least twenty-one because if the police found minors drinking in their house again, they were "soooo busted." I promised I wouldn't drink, but she blew me off.

After that, I sat on one of the couches making a list of what I might be able to sell for cash. I never wore jewelry because of dance class, so I didn't have any of that. And my dad had kept the computer, which was a two-year-old desktop anyway, so it wouldn't have been worth anything. So far, all I had on my list was my autographed photo of Laurence Olivier, which Grandpa had given me for my fourteenth birthday. It was a rare picture and worth a lot, maybe as much as six or seven hundred dollars, but I'd never sell it. I'd rather starve first. I crumpled up the paper and tossed it in the recycle bin.

I ended up closing down the café, but the coffee guy didn't talk to me again. Although he did give me a little wave around eleven o'clock when he left. At midnight I found myself in the Beast, wondering where to go next. My eyelids drooped. A week of barely sleeping had finally caught up with me right when I had no bed to crash in. I tried to think of someplace safe to park and ended up at the Doughnut Shoppe because it was open all night.

Two police cars were parked across the street at the convenience store, which made me both nervous and reassured. Would they notice me? Maybe it didn't matter. I parked on the outer edge of the lot and then I shifted a few boxes to the front and stretched out on the backseat, using my pink comforter and pillow for bedding.

Even with my clothes on and tucked under the comforter, I shivered from cold. Sounds of cars pulling in and out, their doors banging, made me uneasy. I buried my head under the pillow, but that gave me a crick in my neck. Finally, I must've drifted off because a couple of guys yelling at each other about cream-filled doughnuts jarred me awake.

"Dude. I dibbed that one first," a voice shouted.

I peered through the window, staying down so they wouldn't see me. Two guys in Oregon State sweats wrestled and laughed over a box of doughnuts. I watched as they got into a little gray Honda and drove away.

I plugged in my iPod, found my well-worn copy of Laurence Olivier's biography in my dance bag where I kept it for those times I was early to class, and read by the light of the streetlamp. The next thing I knew, it was dawn and the book was pressed into my cheek, probably leaving a mark.

"Ow, ow, ow!" I said, rolling my head around, trying to loosen the stiff muscles in my neck. If my breath was half as bad as my mouth tasted, I felt sorry for anyone who got within ten feet of me.

I stepped into a puddle when I climbed out, soaking my right sneaker, and splashed across the lot toward the Doughnut Shoppe.

Inside, I washed my face in the bathroom and tousled my hair with a little water. I'd forgotten my toothbrush, so I used my finger, but it did absolutely nothing, and I still felt totally gross.

"What can I get you?" asked the girl behind the counter.

I ordered the dollar-ninety-nine special. Sitting on a stool at the counter, I tore off tiny pieces of a blueberry muffin and forced myself to eat them. It was fresh, the coffee inky, and the crossword puzzle someone had left behind impossible. It wasn't even eight o'clock yet, and my tap dance class didn't start until nine, but I finished my food and left anyway, tucking one of my precious dollars under the saucer for a tip.

When I stepped inside from the windy, rainy cold into the warm, almost humid foyer of Bright Lights Studio, the familiar odor of floor polish, wood, and sweat enveloped me like a hug. No matter how chaotic things were in my life, the hushed voices of parents, the monotonous tones of ballet teachers calling out positions, and the soft tinkling of the piano always relaxed me.

I walked past the toe class where Liz and Megan spent their Saturday mornings, and I peeked in. I picked them out of the row of ballerinas standing at the barre, listening to Madame Zubrinski. If they saw me, you'd never know it. They both had the still, concentrated look of all the rest of the dancers in the class, and their gaze never shifted from Madame's face.

Ballet at school was really simple stuff, and I enjoyed it, but when it had been time for me to go up on toe shoes here at Bright Lights, I'd decided to give it a miss. I wanted to be an actress, not a dancer with messed-up feet. Sometimes I envied my friends' grace and dedication, though. Hard work had gotten Liz early acceptance at Oberlin too, and I was still waiting to hear about drama school. Assuming I could even figure out a way to go if I got in.

I stopped by the office to make sure my classes were all paid up for the quarter because the last thing I wanted was for one of my dance instructors to take me aside and tell me I owed the school money. Luckily Dad had paid for me through the end of March. What I'd do then, I didn't know. Dancing on Saturday mornings was practically my religion.

After class, I had taken a shower in the changing room and was getting dressed when Megan and Liz rushed in and grabbed their stuff out of their lockers.

"We're late for the ballet matinee with my grandma," Liz explained, rushing out.

"Have fun," I said.

"We will," Megan called as she ran after Liz, who was probably halfway to the car already.

I spent all afternoon on one of the Coffee Klatch computers, surfing the web. By the evening, I had a whole pile of printouts on cults and religions that I wanted to mail to my dad. I'd gotten a bunch of different envelopes from the dollar store, and I tried to make it look like it was correspondence from people he knew or business letters, and not from me, so he'd open them. Once they were addressed, I walked to the corner mailbox and dropped them in.

I'd also found a company on the web who would send in a team to rescue people from cults, and I called from the pay phone at the café. What did I have to lose?

"Hello," I said, when a man answered the phone. "I'd like some information on your services." I explained about my dad.

"No offense, but you sound kind of young. How old are you?"

"Why?"

"Well . . ." He stopped talking, and a hacking, wet-sounding cough filled my ear. Yuk. "Sorry. Bronchitis. As I was saying, our services don't come cheap."

Figures. "How much?" I asked.

"Three thousand for the capture. Plus expenses. Six thousand a week for deprogramming. Usually takes one to six weeks."

"Oh."

"Still interested?" he asked.

"I guess not."

"Have a nice day."

"Yeah . . . thanks," I said, but he'd already hung up.

When I came outside, rain poured down in sheets, and by the time I was behind the wheel, my drenched body shook with damp cold. The Doughnut Shoppe had seemed safe enough, so I parked there again. It took me a while, but eventually I fell into a really light, dream-filled sleep. In it, I wandered around in a snowstorm without a jacket. When someone knocked on the window, I sat up fast, totally disoriented. I peered through the glass. Two uniformed police officers motioned at me to join them.

I pulled on my coat and climbed out. "Hi," I said.

The cops stood there like a pair of blue salt and pepper shakers— exactly the same size, shape, and posture. It wasn't until the one on the left spoke that I realized she was a woman.

"You living in this vehicle?" she asked. Her voice was deep and gravelly, not like a cigarette smoker, but like after you've had laryngitis and it's still sort of raspy and almost sexy. She was definitely Pepper.

The cold air shocked me awake fast. "Ummm . . . no."

"Runaway?" asked Salt, stepping forward. He peered into the SUV, shining his flashlight on my stuff. "What's with all the boxes?"

"Oh, those? That's just my stuff," I improvised. "I go to . . . to Southern Oregon U, and my dad's moving, so I had to drive home and pick up some of my things from the house to take back to the dorms."

The woman officer met my eye. "So why are you sleeping in the parking lot?"

Good question.

"Oh, yeah . . . well"—I tried to keep my voice as casual as possible—"I was supposed to stay at my boyfriend's house, but somehow we got our wires crossed, and I can't get ahold of him. I'm heading back to Ashland as soon as it gets light. I didn't want to drive through the mountain pass in the dark."

"Right," Pepper said. I couldn't tell if she believed me or not.

"I thought it was safer than driving five hours at night," I explained. "Sleeping here didn't seem like a big deal."

"A girl alone in a car is always a big deal," she said.

"Yeah . . . I guess."

The weather gods chose that moment to do me a huge favor, and a gust of icy wind ripped through the parking lot. The light drizzle turned into a driving rain, and I put my hands up to shield my face from the stinging drops. "It's only for a few hours," I yelled over the wind.

"Well," said Salt, grabbing hold of his hat to keep it from flying off, "make sure you're gone in the morning."

"I will."

"And lock your doors," added Pepper.

I dove into the Beast and huddled under my comforter, wide awake, for a long time. I couldn't afford to be questioned by the police again because they might ask for ID and discover I was only seventeen and my dad's house was less than three miles from here. They'd probably take me back to him, and if he said he didn't want me, they'd ship me off to my mom's in Los Angeles. Somehow I doubted they'd care that the last time I lived with her, not only had she been arrested for shoplifting beer, but they'd also found stolen lunch meat tucked under my Big Bird T-shirt. I had to find some-where besides my car to sleep.

ON SUNDAY MORNING, I PULLED THE BEAST INTO the grimy parking lot of the Regis Deluxe Motel. It was more like a strip of narrow spaces with faded white lines than an actual lot, and most of them were empty. McDonald's and Burger King wrappers fluttered around, accumulating in little piles by some dead-looking bushes near the front doors. VACANCY flashed in the window, but both the Cs were burnt out. Below it was the sign that had caught my attention.

CHEAP WEEKLY RATES
FRIDGE INCLUDED

I got out and made sure all my doors were locked and set the alarm. I didn't want the two guys in greasy jean jackets who were huddled together against the wind, smoking cigarettes, to get any ideas. I had to pass them, but they stared without comment.

Inside, stale smoke had permeated the peeling wallpaper, leaving it yellow-stained. And when I walked by a dead palm tree near the door, it reeked of urine. I prayed the rooms wouldn't be as gross as the lobby. A sign said to ring the bell, so I tapped it quickly and then wiped my hand on my jeans. A thick tree trunk of a man lumbered out from the back.

"What can I do for you?" he asked.

I glanced around, looking for the owner of the voice because it sounded exactly like Marilyn Monroe, but we were alone. It had to be him. He wore two gold hoops in his ears, and a silky pirate blouse, but he was no woman. The handlebar mustache was a dead giveaway.

"Ummm . . . ," I said, studying the MOTEL RULES AND REGULATIONS sign on the counter so I didn't stare at him. "I'd like to see a room."

"See one or rent one?" he cooed.

"Rent?" I said.

"I have a strict no-runaway policy, darlin'. You eighteen?"

"Yes," I lied. "But I don't have a credit card."

"I only accept cash up front. You got it?"

"I can get some from the ATM."

"Follow me." He sashayed down a threadbare carpeted hallway. His round, bald head balanced on his shoulders like a golf ball on a tee. "Name's Stub, by the way."

"Oh. Okay. Uh . . . Jamie."

One lightbulb lit up the middle of the hallway, and an exit sign glowed over a doorway at the far end. "We recently installed security bars on the ground-floor windows," he said, like it was a selling point. He led me into what amounted to an eight-by-ten-foot box. The walls were a dirty gray-white, and there was a metal-framed cot under the window with a filthy-looking, stained bedspread. There was also a dilapidated dresser, a table that leaned to one side, a rickety-looking chair, and a lamp.

Stub opened the bathroom door, and the odor of rotten eggs wafted into the room. "Smells a bit," he said, "but I cleaned it myself. That's about it. It's two-sixty-five a week, utilities are included, but if you bring a TV, it's an extra six bucks tacked on. So, you want it?"

I couldn't believe my choices had come down to this room or my car. The scary thing was the motel was giving me flashbacks to second grade and places my mother and I used to live in. She'd ramble on about the elusive *man that would change her life forever*, while we ate Cheerios with water for dinner. As far as I knew, the closest she'd come to finding her handsome prince was my dad, and she'd screwed that up royally.

I hadn't seen my mother since she and that slimeball ran off to Hollywood, but there was one thing I knew for sure. I was not her, and I would never become her. Even if I did have to live here for a while.

"I know it's not the luxury you were expecting," Stub said, "but will it do, sweetheart?"

"Ummm . . . can I think about it?" I asked.

"Sure. But these rooms go fast."

I didn't believe him, but I should have. "Okay." I tried to smile. "Thanks."

He pointed at a door under the flickering exit sign. "You can go out that way," he said.

I pushed through it out onto the pavement, gasping for fresh air.

After hogging the pay phone for four hours, calling every ad for a roommate on Craigslist and striking out, I was back to say I wanted the room, but Stub had rented it out already.

"You don't have anything?" I asked. At this point I'd have been willing to take a supply closet if the door locked and I had access to a bathroom.

"Well . . . ," he said. He smoothed the ends of his mustache with his fingertips and thumbs like a villain in an English pantomime. "A room on the third floor just opened up, but I haven't cleaned it yet."

"I'll take it," I said, afraid some other homeless person would come in and snap it up before I could.

I didn't think I'd ever fall asleep in the smelly, damp room, but I must've because a sharp rap like gunfire made me bolt upright in bed, confused about where I was.

"Yo! John, open up," said a man in the hallway.

Was he knocking on my door or the one across the hall?

"Dude, it's me." He lowered his voice a little. "I got your money, and I need a hit, man."

I stared through the darkness at the door and saw shadowy movement in the gap at the bottom where it didn't quite meet the dirty carpet. I wanted to tell him to go away, but my voice was caught in my throat, stuck there by fright.

"It's me, dude. I got something you want," the man said, louder this time.

When I didn't answer, he yelled for me to open up. "What the hell is wrong with you? Come on, Johnny. I need to see you. I got your money."

"Go away," I croaked, but he didn't hear me because he'd given up being patient and was now thumping hard with heavy fists. My heart raced. The door rattled under the blows. I'd checked the deadbolt at least six times before going to bed. I couldn't see if the chain was hooked because the streetlight that bled through the single dusty window was so dim, but I was sure I'd fastened it. What should I do? Maybe hide in the bathroom. But then I'd be trapped if he got inside.

"Man, I know you're in there! I said I got your money. I'm not lying. Open up."

I tried to answer, but by now I was so scared all that came out was a squeak. All the vocal projection tricks we'd learned in acting class had deserted me. I scooted into the corner of the bed, my back against the wall, and pulled the comforter up around me, hiding.

If he did get inside, he'd know right away I wasn't this John guy he was looking for, because pink comforters were not standard issue in this dive motel. The first thing I'd done when I moved in was strip the thin, grimy sheets off the bed, throw them into the far corner, and put on my own clean bedding. The pounding increased, his blows sounding like a kid banging on a drum without rhythm or reason, and even in the low light, I could see the door straining. I looked around for a weapon.

"Goddammit! Open up!" he shouted.

"Go away," I finally forced myself to say loud enough for him to hear me. "You've got the wrong room."

He stopped knocking. "What? What'd you say?"

"I said go away. You've got the wrong room."

"Man, don't tell your bitch to talk for you. Open the door. I need some shit."

He began to rattle the knob with one hand and batter with the other. With every thump, my heart pounded like it would burst open. Sweat dripped down inside my sweater. I was glad now I hadn't changed into pajamas.

Would my cell still call 911 even though it was disconnected? I grabbed my purse, but then remembered I'd been so angry, I'd thrown the phone into the backseat and left it there. Besides, I doubted the police cared about people who lived in rooms you had to rent by the week.

The man was kicking at the door now, and I swear I heard wood splinter. I got out of bed and put on my shoes, in case I had to make a run for it. Then I grabbed the lamp to bash against his head if I had to and stood by the door, ready. Why hadn't Stub come up to see what was going on? You'd think someone would've complained by now.

Other tenants had to have cell phones, didn't they? Maybe one of them would call the cops. Although the residents I'd seen in the lobby—the filthy woman with long brown hair and the rail-thin man passing her a plastic baggie of pot—didn't exactly look like the kind of people who would ever call the police voluntarily.

"If you don't open up, man," he threatened, "I'm gonna bust this door down and kick your ass."

I didn't have any doubt he could do it. I held the lamp in one hand, and my purse and keys in the other. I'd have to sleep in the Beast again if he got inside. Assuming I managed to escape. Then I heard a door bang and heavy footsteps on the creaky floor.

"What the fuck is goin' on?" yelled a deep, menacing voice. Clearly not Stub's.

"Dude, mind yourself," the guy outside my door said. "I need John, and his ho is in there sayin' he ain't here."

"The cops picked him up this afternoon. Now get the hell outta here and don't come back. I need my beauty rest."

"Are you shittin' me, man?"

"Do I have to tell you twice?" asked the growly voice.

"No, dude. Chill. I'm goin'. I'm goin'."

He gave the door one last kick and then I heard him moving away, swearing. The door down the hall slammed shut, and I put the lamp down, my hands shaking. What was I doing here? This was crazy. It was only my first night, and a man had already tried to break into my room. I'd end up dead, living in this sleazy motel.

The empty dresser was made of thin, cracked plywood and probably wouldn't stop anyone, but I tried to shove it in front of the door anyway. It wouldn't move, though, because it was nailed to the floor. Then I got a better idea. With shaking hands, I shifted all of the cardboard boxes, containing everything I owned, in front of the door, making a five-foot-high barricade. If the place burned down in the night, I'd go up with it, unable to get out, but at this point, I wasn't sure I cared anymore.

KRISTA HAD STAYED SUNDAY NIGHT AT HER DAD'S, and he was driving her to school, so she didn't need me to pick her up, but I still timed my arrival to match the late bell so I wouldn't have to explain to my friends why my hair was so gross. I'd been way too scared to take a shower.

In our locker, I'd found three of my favorite dark chocolate bars and a love note from Josh. I couldn't wait to see him at lunch, but it was only third period English, so I had to content myself with doodling his name on my notebook while Mr. Lazby grumbled about the standardized testing coming up.

I tried not to think about Krista's reaction to the candy bars. "What?" she'd said. "Chocolate is supposed to make up for him humiliating you in the caf?"

"You know it was an accident," I said.

"Yeah, well, this whole undercover relationship blows," she said. "You're better than that, chickie."

She just didn't understand because I hadn't told her everything. If she knew how much Josh was trying to balance—the church, his dad, our relationship, school—she'd be more sympathetic. But I couldn't explain everything to her or she'd freak out about the motel and get her mom to call my mother. I was going to have to live with her disapproval.

I wrote Josh's name on my English folder again, making the *o* into a heart, and continued to ignore Mr. Lazby's lecture. It was no secret how much he hated teaching his two English classes. He used to hold them in the drama room until the vice principal found out he was just assigning everyone time to read to themselves and disappearing into the costume shop like he did during drama class. After that, he had to teach English in a regular classroom so the department head could check in on him. I think the only thing that kept him from getting fired was he'd taught here for twenty-two years, and they knew he'd retire eventually. Plus all the drama kids loved him because the shows he produced were so good, it made them feel like they were almost professionals.

For about a millisecond, I considered telling Mr. Lazby what had happened with my dad, but then I dismissed it as stupid. He pretended not to notice us hooking up in dark corners, but he was still a teacher. Besides, if there was an issue in the theater, Mr. Lazby could handle it like a pro. But real life? He'd hand off my problems to the school counselor so fast I wouldn't know what happened. And she would definitely turn me over to social services, who would find my mom.

The bad night I'd had, coupled with Mr. Lazby's droning voice, must've put me to sleep because the next thing I knew, he was standing over my desk, nudging me with his big hand.

"Would you care to join us, Jamie?" he asked.

I snapped to attention. "Sorry. . . ." The class snickered.

"Late night?"

"Something like that."

Mr. Lazby had once been tall, dark, and handsome (I'd seen his acting headshot), and he still had broad shoulders and looked pretty okay for his age, but not great. His crushed Hollywood dreams had completely soured him on the acting profession, though. I wouldn't call him bitter, exactly, but he was definitely jaded, and mostly he tried to discourage us from studying theater in college. I was the exception, which is how I knew I actually had talent.

I managed to stay awake for the rest of class, but when the bell rang, Mr. Lazby called after me. "Walk with me, Jamie," he said.

As usual, it wasn't a question. I think all his years of giving orders directing high school students in plays had made it impossible for him to actually ask someone to do something.

"But I have—" I stopped talking because Mr. Lazby was already out the door.

When I caught up to him, he glanced down at me and said, "Oh, there you are."

I had to take three steps for every one of his strides, but he plowed through the hallway, and everyone gave him plenty of room, so at least I didn't get swallowed up by the crush. We'd reached the top of the stairs that led to the drama room before I could tell him I needed to get going and change for dance class.

"Mr. Lazby, I—"

He'd stopped walking to look through a file folder of typewritten pages.

"Can you believe they've got me teaching Applied Language Arts again?" His sigh echoed down the stairwell. "You wouldn't want to skip your next class and correct these atrocious essays for me, would you?"

I'd done that for him before, and believe me, I didn't want to read those papers any more than he did. The only good essays were the ones kids bought off the Internet.

"I have dance class," I said, "right now."

Mr. Lazby finally gave me his attention. "Dance? With Ms. Fitzpatrick? I don't know why you bother with that woman." And then he ran down the stairs so I had to follow him.

"Mr. Lazby," I said, "did you want me for something, or was it just to correct the essays?"

"Oh, right," he said. "Any word?"

"About what?"

"Your audition."

Finally he was making sense. "Oh. No. Nothing yet."

"Well, no news is good news," he said. He pulled an orange out of the top drawer and peeled it. The sharp citrus smell filled the room, and my mouth watered.

It had been less than a week since Krista got into Beaumont Design, and she'd asked me each and every day if I'd heard anything from drama school, but I was still waiting. Last fall, before the church had really gotten ahold of my dad, the two of us had flown to New York for the weekend so I could audition for the Redgrave Actors Conservatory and see some shows. I'd called my dad and left three messages asking him to drop my mail off at the school office, but so far he hadn't.

"I thought maybe you didn't make the cut," Mr. Lazby said, handing me a section of orange. "You've looked depressed lately."

I knew he really wanted me to succeed, despite being a frustrated actor himself. "The website says two to four months," I said, "so I should find out by next week at the latest."

"Great. Well, let me know." He popped the last piece of orange in his mouth. "Sure you don't want to take a crack at those papers?"

"Definitely not," I said. "But thanks for asking."

He laughed. "Can't blame a guy for trying."

On my way to lunch, it occurred to me maybe Dad had simply thrown out my mail. I was so busy imagining what I'd say to him if I found out he had that I didn't see Josh until I ran right into him.

"Sorry," he mumbled.

I grabbed his sweatshirt before he could get away. "Josh, wait. I need to talk to you."

"I can't, Jamie. Derrick's meeting me."

I pulled at his arm, leading him into the stairwell. In spite of the chocolate, I was kind of mad that Josh hadn't tried to find me before. I had so much to tell him, but he looked so yummy with his blond hair, and bright eyes, and wide shoulders that I got distracted and tried to kiss him instead of talking.

"Not here, J," he said, prying my arms off of his neck.

"What? Embarrassed by PDA now?" I asked, laughing. It felt good to laugh after the weekend I'd endured. "I miss you."

"I miss you too, but if Derrick sees us . . ."

I crossed my arms. "He never uses these stairs."

He nodded at the stream of kids going up and down around us. "Someone else might tell him."

"We're keeping this a secret from *everyone*?" I asked. Somehow I'd missed that part of the deal, and I didn't like it.

"We have to," he said. "Please?"

I sighed. "Whatever. But I have to talk to you. I have a lot going on, and I need your advice."

"Later," Josh said. "I'll find you." He ducked through the door, leaving me standing there feeling like an idiot for counting on him.

This whole secrecy thing was crazy, and it was pissing me off too. I had to get Josh alone, and there was only one place I knew for sure I could do that, but I'd have to check the wrestling schedule to find out which day would work.

Josh was still mostly avoiding me for Derrick's sake, but we did get a few stolen minutes behind the bleachers on Tuesday, and on Wednesday, we actually spoke for more than ten seconds. I tried to tell him how horrible the motel was, but once he'd heard I had found a room, that seemed to be all he cared about, and he'd distracted me with more kisses. He also slipped me another twenty bucks and a DVD of *Love Me Twice,* a romantic movie we'd seen together last fall, which was kind of useless to me since I didn't have a television. I wondered if I could return it for cash.

On Thursday, Derrick had a wrestling meet across town, so Josh and I made a date to meet in the weight room after school. During drama, I changed into my workout clothes, and when class was over, I headed for the gym. The weight room was long and low ceilinged, with mirrors covering one wall, and it smelled like feet. I made my way through the exercise equipment to the far end, where there was a pile of red mats, and I sat down to stretch next to them.

As I leaned forward, laying my chest against my legs and grabbing my toes, I felt a familiar warmth flowing through me. Some of the day's tension oozed out too. I remembered the first time I'd stretched like that in front of Josh, and a small laugh escaped in spite of the sucky week I'd had.

"How can you do that?" Josh had asked, amazed.

"Do what?" I said, lifting my head.

"Fold yourself in half like that!"

His legs were stuck out in front of him, but he had to bend his knees and point his toes up toward the ceiling to reach them.

"Lots of practice," I said. "Years and years."

"I've been stretching my whole life," he said, "but I'll never be able to do that. It must be because you're a girl."

"Ummm . . . there are plenty of male dancers who can do this too," I said.

He scowled at that, and I was sure he was going to make some homophobic comment, which would cause me to break up with him, but instead he said, "I think I'm so tight because I mostly lift weights. But it would be great for football to be more like you. Can you help me?"

"Sure. It'll be practically painless," I'd lied with a smile.

I sat up straight and reached for the ceiling, arching my back. My eye caught movement in the mirror, and I saw Josh watching me. He probably wanted to get cozy in a corner, but I needed to talk to him, so I said, "Want to work out?"

"Yeah, okay." He plopped down beside me onto the mat. "You doing all right?"

"I guess." I pressed my chest against my knees again, wrapping my hands around my feet. Now that we finally had time to talk, I wasn't sure how to start. I wanted to tell him everything: how I'd spent the last four nights in hell, how I missed my dad in spite of everything, and most of all, how scared I was. But we'd always talked about Josh's problems. When we weren't making out, I helped him with his English so he wouldn't flunk and listened to what a mean bastard his dad was. Had we ever even talked about me?

Josh gave up on touching his toes and crouched on the balls of his feet, bouncing. The real reason he wasn't limber was because he only stretched for about thirty seconds every day.

"Ummm . . . Josh . . . I've been thinking . . . this whole secret thing—"

His phone buzzed in the pocket of his sweatpants. "Yo," he said, answering it.

Derrick's voice on the other end was so loud I could hear him through the phone. "Wrestling meet was canceled, dude. Their gym ceiling caved in or something."

We heard one of the guys from the team yell, "They're a bunch of pussies!" And everyone else cheered.

"You're kidding," Josh said.

"Not even. Coach wants us to lift today since we're not wrestling."

Josh's eyes just about popped out of his head. "In the weight room?"

"Duh," Derrick said. "Where else?" He made his voice go all high and squeaky. "Boys, do you want to work out in the *theater*?"

We heard a lot of laughing. The drama department is always an easy target for the jocks.

Josh yanked me to my feet and started pushing me toward the only door.

"So you gonna meet me, dude?" Derrick asked.

"Already there, bro," Josh said.

"Cool. See you in thirty."

All the tension in Josh's body deflated from relief. "Thirty minutes? You're still on the bus?" he asked.

"No, dude. Thirty *seconds*. We're in the parking lot."

Josh snapped his phone shut. "We've got to get you out of here," he said.

"It's a little late for that," I pointed out. "There's only one exit."

"You have to hide."

"What? Josh, no!"

But he was already herding me back across the room. "Lie down there," he said, pushing me between a roll of sweaty rubber mats and the wall. "I'll cover you up with stuff from the lost and found."

"Jo—" I said as I got a face full of smelly sweatshirts and God knew what. I shoved them away and tried to sit up.

"Do you want me to get pulled out of school and lose my football scholarship for next year?" Josh whispered, forcing me back down.

"No, but—"

"Every night my dad asks Derrick if I'm seeing you."

"He'd cover for you," I said.

"He'd try, but he's a terrible liar."

The door at the other end of the room banged open, and the wrestlers' voices echoed around us, bouncing off the mirrors. "Fine," I hissed, lying back down. "But get rid of them fast."

Josh sat on the stack of mats, squeezing me against the wall until I could barely breathe. From above me, I heard him whisper, "We'll just have to wait. I'll make sure Derrick and I leave last, so you'll know you're clear."

This was crazy. Did Josh really think I would stay crushed up here like a partier at a rave for the next hour while a bunch of Neanderthals tried to outlift and outstink each other? This secret thing totally blew, and I was over it. Nothing was stopping me from just getting up and walking out right then. Nothing except the fact I couldn't move because Josh was holding the mats against me with his weight.

I lay there fuming. This was it. We were done. No more secrets, no more stupid Right & Real Church. I was over him. And I didn't care how sweet his smile was or how sparkling his eyes were or how my body melted under his touch. I didn't . . . really, I didn't.

Dammit.

I'm not proud of it, but I didn't move. I stayed there, my skin absorbing the sweaty odor of all those guys, my ears assaulted by the gross things they said about a couple of girls they thought were hot, and my legs going numb.

Finally, about the time I thought I'd either pass out or find a pen in one of the random sweatshirt pockets and stab myself in a major artery, they left. I heard the door clang shut behind them, cutting off their voices, and when I moved all the coats, I discovered I was in total darkness. Great. Since when did the guys do what the sign by the door said?

Last one out, turn off the lights.

I struggled to get up, massaging feeling back into my legs. As I tried to get my bearings and figure out a path to the door where I wouldn't get killed by dumbbells or trip over a treadmill, the door opened and I froze.

"Bro! I forgot my sweatshirt," I heard Josh yell back toward the gym. "Meet me at the car."

He flipped the switch, and light flooded my eyes so I was temporarily blind. By the time I could see, Josh was standing over me. "Jamie, you're the best. I'll make it up to you tomorrow night. I'll take you somewhere nice. I promise." Before I could say anything, he'd scooped me up, giving me a bear hug and a kiss on the forehead. "Thank you so, so much. You're the one person I can count on in my life."

He set me down and sprinted after Derrick.

I HAD FIRST NOTICED THE REGIS DELUXE MOTEL when I'd gone to the Coffee Klatch on Saturday, because it was only a few blocks away, on dicey Sandy Boulevard. Ever since I'd moved in, I'd been haunting the little café, avoiding my dingy, cold room, stretching a cup of overpriced black coffee out as long as I could.

I did my homework on one of the couches, and every once in a while, when I thought I could spare an extra two dollars, I'd surf the web for fifteen minutes and answer e-mails, IM'ing Krista and Liz so they wouldn't ask why I was never online anymore. I'd already told them my cell was broken and Dad said I'd have to wait until next month to get a new one because then I'd be eligible for a free phone if he signed me up for a new contract. I'd totally made that up, but they bought it because it's not like they were keeping track of how long it'd been since I'd gotten my last one.

The cute guy, Trent, who had leapt over the counter to get my coffee that first night I'd gone into the café, worked the morning shift, and so I started dropping in before school too. It wasn't like I wanted to date him or anything, because I had Josh, but he was funny. And he had those floppy bangs I was a sucker for. I could imagine myself pushing them out of his eyes for him, which I knew was totally wrong, but still . . . The real bonus was Trent didn't know anything about me, which made him safe to talk to. I was anonymous at the Coffee Klatch.

On Friday morning I sat there sipping my lukewarm coffee and filling out job applications for fast-food places. I'd already turned in about a dozen apps to the stores at the mall, but every place I'd tried told me they didn't hire in February. Fact was, they were laying people off. It was going to be fast food or nothing. At least I'd get discounted meals.

Trent came over to clear the table in front of me. "I'm starting to think you're homeless," he said.

I'd been kind of dozy, but that woke me right up. After five days of living in the skanky motel, I was still too scared to undress in my room in case someone broke in, so I'd been showering after dance class instead. I'd put a bunch of mousse in my hair this morning, but instead of the cool bed-head look I was going for, it was just flat and greasy. The hour I'd spent as the filling inside a stinky wrestling-mat burrito yesterday hadn't done much for it either. I probably did look like a street person.

"I have roommate issues," I said.

"Been there."

Trent had an old-fashioned movie camera tattooed at the base of his neck, which I hadn't seen the first time we'd met, and I'd been meaning to ask him about it, but before I could, he said, "Are you seriously thinking of working at Rotten Ronnie's?"

I looked at him blankly and he tapped the job application in my lap. "The Golden Arches doesn't seem like your style."

"Yeah, well. Not a lot of choice this time of year."

"True. Plus there's the bonus of the outfit they give you. Mustard gold polyester. There *is* something to be said for a girl in uniform." He made the hourglass shape with his hands. "Oh, yeah. Hubba hubba. Plus, free Whoppers."

"That's Burger King."

He smirked, and I saw that sexy oh-so-slightly-crooked tooth again. "I know," he said. He stacked a few dishes onto a tray. "Taco Hell is always hiring."

"Ugh, that assembly line? Slapping refried beans onto tortillas?" I said. "I so could not do that."

"Snob." He grinned. "You can't get a job anyway."

"Why not?" He probably thought no one would hire me because of my hair issues.

"You'd miss me too much," he said.

I couldn't stop my smile. Some actress I am.

"I'd love to stay here all day and fascinate you with my titillating conversation," Trent said, "but duty calls."

As he leaned across me to pick up the tray, his knee touched my leg so lightly I wondered if I'd imagined it. A little zing went all the way through me, regardless. And yeah, I'll admit it. I watched him walk away, thinking about touching his tattoo the whole time. But at least I felt guilty about it.

After he left, I was kind of bored, and the café was slammed, so to keep myself from falling asleep, I ditched the applications and grabbed a bunch of dirty mugs.

"Don't make me fall in love with you," Trent said when I dumped them off at the busing station.

I managed to suppress my smile this time and grabbed a tray. I was hoping he would think I didn't hear him, but I was pretty sure my pink face gave me away. After we finished clearing, another rush of people came in for their morning fix and Trent had to help behind the counter. I grabbed a rag and started wiping down the tables, but they looked way worse than when I started because the cloth was cold and wet, and it smeared everything around.

"Ummm . . . that's the floor rag," Trent said, taking it from me after he'd served everyone.

"Oh, sorry. I was just—"

He grabbed my arm dramatically and pulled me in close. "No one will ever know," he whispered into my ear. "I'll take your secret to the grave."

"My hero," I said, playing along. But then I realized exactly how close we were standing to each other and how shallow my breathing had become, and I broke away from him, grabbing a stray spoon off the floor.

"How come you always talk like you're in a movie?" I asked, trying to make my voice sound casual. "I bet you watch those old black-and-white ones on TV late at night. Or I know! You want to be an actor."

He took the spoon from me and held it up like a microphone. "No. And no," he said. "I like art films and action movies, the occasional rom com, and even the ones that make you cry, but not old black-and-whites. And I'm strictly behind the camera."

"Really? Cool. I want to be an actress."

We stood there grinning at each other so long, we whizzed right past *this is so awkward getting to know you,* sailed directly through *goofy but having fun,* and landed at *I should leave now because I have a boyfriend.*

"I better go," I said.

He shoved the spoon into his apron pocket and brushed back

his hair. "Yeah, I need to make more coffee or whatever it is we do here."

I gathered up my applications, trying to smother a smile the whole time. This was totally wrong. Josh trusted me. And he should. I was completely trustworthy. I told myself I'd been under a lot of stress the last two weeks and so I was just having a bit of fun. Besides, if Trent was into filmmaking, then he was probably a lot like all the theater guys . . . a harmless flirt.

I used the bathroom before leaving, but still couldn't do anything with my hair. When I came out, Trent was waiting for me.

"Here." He held out a tall paper cup with a lid. "Mocha."

"Oh, I don't—"

"On the house. For helping out."

"Thanks." I took the hot cup and passed it back and forth from hand to hand. Like the first time he'd given me a free drink, I got all teary. What was wrong with me? But it was so sweet, I couldn't help it. Trent stared at me, his head tilted until I couldn't stand it anymore.

"What?" I asked. "Why are you looking at me like that?"

"I'm trying to decide whether to ask you out on a date or offer you a job."

"Oh, a job!" I said. "I want a job!"

Trent whirled around and squatted down to look under a table. "Did you see that?" he asked.

"Ummm? What?"

He stood up. "That was my ego scurrying for cover."

I laughed. I couldn't help it. He'd made me giggle more this morning than I had in weeks. "Oh, sorry," I said. I tried to force down my smile. "I mean, a date would be . . . ummm . . . I just . . . I really need a job."

"Fine. Break my heart," he said, all business. "So the deal is this: I need another person for the weekday morning shift. You up for it?"

"Can you do that?" I asked. "Just hire me?"

"OF COURSE I CAN," he said in one of those deep movie-announcer voices. "I AM THE SHIFT MANAGER!"

I just shook my head at him. He was crazy.

"Besides," he said in his regular voice, "today's Becky's last day. She quit without notice. Pay's not great. Minimum wage plus tips. But you never have to ask customers to supersize their drinks."

"When do I start?" I asked.

"You can train this afternoon with our other manager, Amanda," he said. "Come back at four thirty, okay?"

"Yeah. Definitely. I'll be here," I said.

"DON'T BE LATE," he said in his shift-manager voice.

"I WON'T!" I answered back.

Finally something was going my way.

As if I didn't have enough to worry about, Krista was driving me insane about getting in to drama school. Now that she knew she was going to New York for sure, she was dying to make some concrete plans. The whole admissions letter thing gnawed at me constantly already, without her bugging me too.

At morning break, I went to the lab and signed onto a computer. The drama school's website had an eight-hundred number, so I called them from the pay phone by the gym. I got connected right away to a guy I knew named Stevie. He was a student at the school and worked part time in the office. We'd met when I'd gone to New York to audition last fall.

"Sorry," Stevie said. "I can't tell you over the phone."

"I just want to know if you sent out the letter already," I explained. "The only reason I'm asking is because I had to move suddenly, and so if you did, I probably won't get it."

"Well . . . ," he said, "since you bought me that cinnamon roll when you were here, I guess I can tell you that. But nothing else." I didn't actually remember buying Stevie a pastry. He must've mixed me up with one of the other girls who was there to audition when I was, but I didn't correct him. His fingers tapped the keyboard. "Yeah . . . okay," he said. "We sent the letter last Monday. Give me your new address. I'll mail you another copy."

"Ummm . . ."

Crap.

I didn't know the address of the motel. And even if I did, could I get mail there? I told him I'd have to call him back. Today was Friday. If a letter was sent from New York on Monday, it had probably been delivered already, but maybe not. It might come today. And if it did, I intended to be the one to get the mail.

Our school is super diligent about keeping us from skipping, so they take attendance at the beginning of every class, but I figured the afternoon was my best chance for stealing my mail because my dad would be at work, so I decided to worry about getting in trouble later.

Mira had quit her job as a dental assistant right before the wedding and might be home, but I could probably run faster than her if I had to. Was it a federal offense if I tampered with my *own* mail, but it was in someone else's box? I hoped not. What I actually hoped was I wouldn't get caught.

I parked three houses from ours and pulled my pink fleece hat as low as I could, trying to hide my face. Then I strolled casually down the street. We lived in a nice neighborhood, or at least, I used to live there. The ranch-style houses with two-car garages probably looked alike back in the seventies when they were built, but after all these years, people had personalized them with paint and new doors and fancy gates. Some yards were ragged with weeds, but my dad kept ours immaculate.

It was one of those clear, sunny February days, where the sky is such a brilliant blue you can't believe it's not summer, but the wind is so cold you think you'll cry from the pain in your frozen ears. Even with the hat, I had goose bumps on my scalp.

When my dad and I had moved into this house, right after he got custody of me, one of the things I loved most was the designer mailbox—flat on the bottom, but with a domed top. The previous owners had decorated it like a ladybug, bright red with black spots. And they'd painted long eyelashes over the blue eyes. I loved getting the mail every day, and if I was outside playing when the mailman came, I would insist he stick our letters inside it so I could take them out. Every summer, Dad and I would get the paint out and touch her up, making her shiny and new again.

After glancing at the house and not seeing anyone, I turned to open the ladybug, but she was gone. In her place stood a gray metal mailbox. It wasn't your standard one, either. It was the kind with a tiny slot for the mailman to stick the letters through, and the owner had to open it with a key.

I stood there staring at it, the icy wind whipping at my face. I swear to God if I'd had a bat, I would've bashed that mailbox into the ground. Instead, I ran back to the Beast, slammed the door, and revved the engine. The tires screeched as I raced back toward the motel, anger pulsing through me right down to the gas pedal.

I skipped the rest of my afternoon classes and holed up in my room, clutching my knees to my chest, rocking back and forth, my mind spinning with crazy plans of sneaking into Dad's house to find my mail. Eventually, though, I had to let the idea go because I was due at the Coffee Klatch for my training.

MY STOMACH FLIP-FLOPPED AS I WALKED THROUGH the deserted café. I'd never had a job before other than acting because my dad said he wanted me to concentrate on school. Behind the counter, a girl stood on a stepladder, adjusting what looked like a video camera suspended above the espresso machine.

"I'll be right with you," she said. Her straight black hair hung in a sheet around her face, and she swept it back like a curtain with one hand while trying to keep her balance and maneuver the camera angle all at the same time.

"I'm here to see Amanda."

She blew a strand of hair out of her face. "I'm Amanda. What can I do for you?"

"Oh, okay. I'm Jamie."

She gave me a blank look.

"Trent hired me for the morning shift? He said to come here at four thirty for my training."

She let go of the camera. "Trent hired you? Figures."

"What?" I asked, confused by her pissed-off tone.

"Trent never hires ugly girls," she said, climbing down.

I wasn't sure what to say to that.

"Well, come on." She folded up the ladder and walked off. I hurried around the counter, following her into a supply closet where the odor of coffee was so thick, it was hard to breathe.

"I haven't got time to train all Trent's new girlfriends," Amanda said, "so when Jezziray comes in, she'll show you how to make the coffee. In the meantime, study this." She handed me a fat red binder. "You can sit at one of the tables unless we get busy."

"Ummm . . . okay. Thanks." *All Trent's new girlfriends?* So I was right. He was just a flirt, and I didn't have to feel guilty about joking around with him at all. For some reason, that made me disappointed instead of relieved.

Jezziray didn't start until five o'clock, and I'd had such a long day, that by then I was having to tickle the roof of my mouth with my tongue to stay awake. I tried to hide my surprise when I met her because she looked almost identical to Amanda. They had to be related, but neither of them said anything about it, so I didn't either. You couldn't mix them up, though, because Jezziray had a silver stud in her tongue that clicked against her teeth when she talked.

After she'd walked me through the process of making coffee in the big urns, she said, "Just don't forget to put the used grounds in the compost, not the garbage."

"Okay. Thanks." I stood there.

"That's it," she clicked.

"Right. I guess I'll go read the manual some more, then."

She shrugged like, *whatever.*

"Oh, I do have one question." I pointed to a red *X* made with tape on the floor by the cash register. "What's that for?"

Jezziray clicked her tongue stud and pointed at the camera. "That's so you know where to stand if you want Trent's stupid webcam to get a good view of you."

"We're on the web?" I asked. "Live?"

She shook her head. "No, not live. He got in trouble for that with his uncle."

"His uncle?"

"Mr. Schubert? He owns the place?" she said like I was stupid. "Anyway, Trent has this lame site where he puts up videos he calls 'Coffee Clips.'"

"Why?" I asked.

"Because he's a weirdo," she said. I must've looked worried, because she explained, "He's a filmmaker. He's going to NYU in the fall. We're just one of his projects."

"Oh." He'd told me he was interested in being behind the camera, but aside from the sweatshirt he'd been wearing the day we met, he'd never mentioned being accepted at NYU. Very impressive.

What looked like an entire junior high girls basketball team pushed through the door, hugging each other and singing "We Are the Champions" off-key. I moved out of the way so Jezziray could serve them and went back to studying the manual. As fascinating as the recipe for an Americano was, my mind kept wandering to the fact that Trent was moving to New York too. It wasn't like it mattered anyway. First of all, I hardly knew the guy. Second, there was Josh. And third, I didn't even know if I'd get to go to New York.

After I finished my "orientation" at six o'clock, I stayed at the Coffee Klatch drinking coffee samples and eating free stale croissants until seven, and then I drove over to the school to pick up Josh. He'd slipped me a note saying Derrick was going to the Friday Night Mixer, but he'd talked his dad into letting him go to the basketball game. Somehow watching guys chase a ball up and down the court didn't exactly seem like he was making it up to me for stuffing me behind the mats, but luckily for him, he had other plans for us.

The waiter gracefully set a plate mounded high with golden halibut and chips in front of me. "I could get used to this dating in secret," I told Josh.

We'd driven up the Columbia River Gorge to have dinner at the Multnomah Falls Lodge, a fancy place with white tablecloths, twenty-dollar entrees, and candles. Josh cut into his steak and smiled. Behind him, the fireplace crackled, and soft jazz poured out of the speakers.

"I thought you deserved something special after being so nice about the weight room," he said.

I actually was still kind of pissed about that, but maybe something decadent and chocolate would soften my mood. The restaurant was empty except for us because in the winter they closed at eight and we hadn't even gotten there until seven forty-five. The waiter had told us they had lots of cleanup to do, though, so to take our time, but I guess he didn't mean it because he brought the bill without asking if we wanted dessert.

"We should climb the falls," Josh said when we got outside.

The wind tore at my scarf, biting into my skin, but you can't go to Multnomah Falls without climbing at least to the bridge. Even in February. Trekking up to the bridge looks deceptively easy, I guess maybe because it's only about a third of the way to the top of the falls, but the trail is still uphill, and I was seriously stuffed. The path was paved, though, and Josh had his little flashlight, so we weren't in total darkness. He took my hand in his, and we started up through the trees, zigzagging our way along.

"How are you doing, Jamie?" Josh asked.

"Fine. But don't go too fast because these boots are kind of slippery."

"No, I mean, do you have enough money to get by?"

"Oh, that." There was so much stuff I wanted to tell Josh, but tonight I needed to pretend things were normal. "Can we not talk about it?" I asked him. "I don't want to think about anything except what a nice time we're having."

He squeezed my hand. "You got it."

"Ohhh! Look," I said. "A make-out cave." It wasn't really a cave, although I was willing to bet a lot of couples had made out in it. It was more of a large depression in the side of the stone cliff big enough for two people to crawl into and sit down. "Come on."

The ceiling was low, and we had to hunch down to get inside. We sat on the cold dirt floor, cuddled together. Josh's breath was warm on my face, and his lips even warmer. I pressed myself against him. Josh pulled me onto his lap facing him, our bodies fitting together like puzzle pieces.

I ran my hands through his short, prickly hair, kissing him deeply. I began to slide into that safe, comfortable place being close to Josh always took me to. It might've been comfy, but it was exciting too, and after a while we had more clothes on than either of us wanted. As the heat rose between us, I slipped out of my coat and he wrapped his around me. He'd pulled his gloves off and his hands worked their way under my sweater, hot against my bare skin. He'd just undone my bra when his phone beeped.

"Ignore it," I said, running my tongue over his ear.

"Can't," he mumbled, shifting so he could get it out of his pocket. I bit his lower lip gently. "Jamie, stop it. . . . I need to see." He moved his body so I fell off his lap onto the dirt floor.

Annoyed, I stepped out of the cave and fixed my bra while he read his stupid text.

"Shit. Oh, shit!" he said. "Come on!" He grabbed my hand and dragged me back down the path.

"What's wrong?" I asked, panting from the running. Or maybe the kissing. But probably both.

"It was from Derrick," he said. "Dad went to pick me up at the game, and I wasn't there."

"What time is it?" I asked.

"After ten."

Crap. We'd really lost track of the time.

"You better drive," I said. I handed him the keys. "What are you going to do?"

"I don't know," he said, tearing out of the parking lot before I had my door closed.

Even if Josh sped, it would probably be thirty minutes, minimum, back to the school. Maybe longer. We threw out ideas along the way, but all he could come up with was that someone gave him a ride home and he'd texted his dad to let him know, but it must not have gone through.

"That's pretty lame," I told him. "By the time you get home, it will be almost eleven, and the game ended at—what? Nine thirty?"

"Do you have a better idea?" he snapped.

"No . . . sorry."

He stopped the car about a block from the church compound and sprinted off without even kissing me good-bye.

"Thanks for dinner," I muttered as he ran away.

On the drive back to the motel, so many emotions bubbled up in me, I felt like a pot of simmering soup. On one hand, we'd had a really romantic meal and a lot of fun in the cave. On the other, I knew Josh had made such a big effort only because I was still kind of pissed about him making me hide the day before. He'd tried to make this secret relationship sound fun, but actually it really sucked. I should've listened to Krista and Liz when they told me not to do it.

But I was in too deep now. In my heart, I knew Josh was trying. He really was. And I couldn't ask him to risk his scholarship or make Derrick lie for us. College was the only way Josh would ever get away from the R&R, and if there was one thing I wanted for him, it was that.

In the parking lot, I set the car alarm and braced myself to face the stinky, dim staircase. Stub was on duty at the front desk, playing solitaire on the computer when I came in though, and I figured I could scream if I needed help. Not that he'd come running the other night or anything.

"Hey, Stub," I said.

He glanced up briefly from the computer. "Son of a bitch," he said in his sultry voice. "I lost again."

I nodded, commiserating, but his eyes were back on the screen. I braced myself for the run to the top of the stairs. No one had bugged me all week, but I was still nervous about that guy from the first night. I'd carried pepper spray in my purse since I was about twelve, but before now, I'd never bothered to take it out. Tonight I clutched the little cylinder in one hand, my room key in the other. My purse was slung over one shoulder, and it thumped against my hip as I ran up the stairs. I had just jammed my key into the sticky lock when possibly the biggest man I'd ever seen came out of the room next to mine, casting a shadow over me.

"Hey," he said.

I kept my head down like I hadn't heard him. He had that same deep, scary voice from the other night. Not the guy who had been trying to break in, but the one who had scared him off.

"I been waiting for you," he said. "Stub told me you in that room now. I wanna talk to you for a sec."

I knew I was the only one in the hallway, so I tried to look up at him like I wasn't terrified, but I could barely lift my head. He resembled every scary inmate in every prison movie ever made. I decided that just because he wanted to talk to me didn't mean I had to talk to him, and I tried to turn the key, but my hand shook so badly, I accidentally pulled it out of the lock and dropped it.

"Hey, chill, girl. I ain't gonna hurt you," he said. When he bent over to pick up the key, I saw his bulging biceps was bigger than my thigh. If I hit him with my purse, would it knock him down long enough for me to run away?

"I just wanna talk to you," he said, handing me the key.

"Okay," I whispered, my left hand clutching the pepper spray.

"I'm LaVon. Who're you?"

"Ja—Jamie."

"What're you doing here?"

"Ummm . . . I rented this room."

"Yeah, I got that," he said. "You a runaway?"

"No. I'm . . . just . . . I'm on my own." I checked over my shoulder to see if I had a clear shot at the stairs in case I needed it.

"Yeah, well, this ain't a place for a little girl like you. You get me?" he asked.

"Yeah. . . ."

Perspiration dripped under my armpits.

"I advise you to go home to Mommy and Daddy," he said.

"I can't."

"Okay. Whatever." He shrugged. "Your funeral. But in the mean-time, bang on the wall between us if anyone fucks with you. I'll take care of it."

He reached for my hand, and I jerked it away, swallowing back the rising scream when I realized he was only going for the key.

"You see what I mean?" he said. "You about to have a heart attack just talking to a nice brother like me. You radiate victim, and that's gonna get you into all kinds of trouble."

"Sorry," I mumbled.

"That pepper spray shit in your hand ain't gonna save you," he said, "'cause you'd probably drop it. Relax. I'm trying to help you with the door, man."

"I'm . . . I'm sorry," I said again. I tried to look him in the eye, but he was wearing silver wraparound shades like all the rappers on MTV.

He shook his head as if he didn't know why he'd bothered. Then he turned the key in the lock and pulled it out, handing it to me. "I'm goin' straight," he explained, "so 'cept for game nights, I'm in by ten."

"Game nights?" I asked.

"Got me a job hawkin' beer at the basketball games at the Rose Garden," he said. "The Blazers suck this season, but people still like beer."

"Oh."

"Knock on the wall if you gotta go out at night," he said. "I'll walk you downstairs."

"Thanks . . . uh . . ."

"LaVon."

"Thanks, LaVon."

"No problem, Ja—Jamie," he said. Before he walked off, he smiled a big wide Cheshire Cat grin at me and shook his head again like he didn't think I'd survive the night. I tried to smile back as if I were totally confident and he didn't know a thing about me, but I think my attempt was pretty pathetic. I slipped into my room, locked the deadbolt, put the chain in place, and collapsed onto my cot. A shudder escaped, and for a second, I couldn't tell if I was going to laugh or cry. And then I did both.

KRISTA HELD UP A VINTAGE NINETEEN-FIFTIES tangerine-colored coat. "Yes?"

"For you?" Liz asked. "Or the show?"

"Me." She undid the gold buttons, and when the coat fell open, we saw it had an intricately embroidered lining. "Very nice." She slipped it on.

"Definitely," I said.

Krista twirled in front of the thrift store mirror. "I think so too," she agreed.

Technically, we were spending our Saturday morning hitting all the downtown vintage shops for scarves and other accessories for *West Side Story*, but so far, all Krista had bought was stuff for herself. She took the coat off and slung it over her shoulder.

"Okay, sorry, Jamie," she said. "Didn't mean to interrupt you. Tell us more about your hot date last night."

I shrugged and ran my hands over a lime green lambs wool sweater. I'd already dished about the romantic restaurant, and I didn't want to tell them how the night ended.

"I told you," I said, "we had a really nice dinner and then we went for a walk up to the bridge."

They looked at each other and then grinned at me with big, knowing smiles. "So why are you blushing?" Liz asked.

"What? I'm not." I felt my face go a deeper shade of red. The softness of the green sweater I'd been touching had reminded me of the cave and how good Josh's hands had felt against my skin. I was totally busted. I laughed. "Nothing else . . . well . . ." I couldn't keep back the smile.

Liz and Krista gave each other another look and then they posed with their hands on their hips and their eyes wide. I knew what was coming. Every time one of us had boy gossip, we would break into that song "Summer Nights" from the musical *Grease*. Usually we were safely ensconced in one of our bedrooms but being in public never, ever deterred my friends.

"You guys, don't!" I said, laughing. But it was too late.

"Uh well-a, well-a, well-a huh," Liz sang at full volume. "Tell me more, tell me more . . ."

"Was it love at first sight?" Krista joined in.

"Tell me more, tell me more . . ."

"Did he put up a fight?"

They skipped all the rest of the lyrics and just kept singing the "tell me more" part.

"Tell me more, tell me more," Liz sang. "How much dough did he spend?"

"Tell me more, tell me more. Could he get me a friend?" Krista asked.

I ran down the aisle between the musty clothes, giggling and trying to get away from them, but it encouraged Liz, and she danced after me, just like the Pink Ladies in the movie.

"Tell me more, tell me more," she belted out.

I was laughing so hard, I wasn't watching where I was going. I careened around the end of a tall shelf in the household section and almost ran smack into a wiry lady with gray hair and a name badge that said FRIEDA. She glared at the three of us as Liz and Krista crashed into me.

"This isn't a playground, girls," she said.

"Sorry," we mumbled.

We followed Krista up to the counter, where she paid for her coat, our heads down so Frieda wouldn't see us laughing. Then we burst out onto the sidewalk, cracking up so hard, purple mascara tears ran down Krista's face.

"You guys are so bad," I said, shoving them.

"Us?" Krista demanded. "Your face was bright red!" She put her arm around my shoulder. "I bet you and lover boy never even made it past the cave."

I raised my eyebrows. "I'll never tell."

"Does he still respect you?" Liz joked. "Do you think he'll call? Did he kiss you good night on your front porch until your dad blinked the lights?"

My face fell. I tried to shake it off, but they noticed immediately.

"What's wrong?"

"Nothing," I said, forcing a smile. "Come on. We still have lots of stores to check out."

Krista grabbed my shoulder and turned me to face the two of them. "What happened when he took you home?"

"Nothing."

They stood there, waiting.

"Fine," I said. "He didn't take me home, okay? We were in my car anyway."

"And?" Liz asked.

"And . . . and we lost track of time, so we were really late, and Derrick texted him to say his dad knew he hadn't gone to the basketball game, and . . . well . . . Josh made me drop him off a few blocks from his house, and he just ran off. That's it. No big deal. We were late. . . ."

All morning I'd told myself that if I wanted to stay Josh's girlfriend, then that was how it was going to have to be. Sometimes I might have to hide behind a pile of smelly mats. And from time to time, maybe he'd have to run off without saying good-bye or pretend he didn't see me in the hallway. We had to protect his scholarship at all costs, didn't we?

"So why are you so upset, if it didn't matter?" Krista asked.

"I'm not," I said.

"This secret thing is bullshit," Krista snapped and walked off.

Liz and I hurried after her. "I know," I said, "but—"

"But nothing, Jamie," Liz told me. "You're worth more than that."

The rest of our shopping trip was a bust, and after an hour, we'd given up and I'd taken Krista to her dad's and dropped Liz off at home, saying I'd see them on Monday. I'd slacked off in school for the last two weeks, and the homework had really piled up, so back in the motel, I got out my English notebook to review the essay assignment and get started. Half an hour later, I hadn't done anything because my mind kept wandering to money. I tore out a clean piece of paper from my binder, drew a chart, and filled in how much I might earn at my job, versus my expenses. I could tell right away that without picking up extra shifts at the Coffee Klatch, I'd be broke within four weeks. Crap.

One minute, I was calmly strategizing, thinking about what a great story my teen hardships would be on late-night television someday, and the next, like a pot of water coming to a slow boil, starting right down in my gut, this huge surge of fear and pain pushed its way up through my chest, slamming against my heart and into my throat. In a split second, I went from a girl with a plan to a gasping and sobbing mess. Tears streamed down my face, and my chest heaved as I struggled for breath. My body shook, and I pulled the comforter up to my face, burying myself in it, trying to muffle the sobs. I banged my fists against the pillow. I couldn't do this on my own.

I wanted to eat dinner with my dad every night, not live on pizza pockets from 7-Eleven. Everything was such a mess. I ached for my old, easy life. No one else had to deal with this crap their senior year. Krista hadn't eaten a Happy Meal in years. I'd had three this week. If it was only food I had to pay for, I might survive, but there were all the things you don't think of, like toothpaste, shampoo, and washing my clothes downstairs in the laundry room, which cost about a million quarters.

I rocked on the wobbly cot, the tears giving way to anger, and I wiped my face on the comforter, leaving big streaks of black mascara. Why had Dad fought so hard for me back in third grade, only to abandon me now? Deep inside, I knew it wasn't me, and he'd been brainwashed, but that didn't change the fact he'd dumped me for Mira and the church.

"Dammit!"

It was that stupid church. If you could call it that. It was a cult. I bashed my fist against the wall and tossed aside my stupid financial plan. I kicked at the thin mattress, ripping it off the little cot and flinging it across the room. It smashed into the lamp, knocking it off the dresser, and the bulb shattered. LaVon's door opened. I heard his footsteps in the hallway and then a light tapping knock.

I stopped, frozen.

"Hey, Jamie," he said, "you okay?"

I didn't answer.

"I know you're in there."

I still didn't say anything.

"Want me to break down the door?" he asked. "I can, you know."

"I'm fine," I said. "Just leave me alone."

I could tell he was still standing outside, listening. After a minute he walked away and his door shut. I grabbed my purse and shoved at the boxes, tumbling them to one side. Once I could get out, I squeezed through and ran down to the parking lot.

I should have gone somewhere to cool off, maybe walk around the mall or something, but the anger boiled up inside me, and I couldn't be rational. I drove too fast through the narrow side streets of my old neighborhood and screeched to a halt in front of our house. He could not do this to me. I wanted an explanation. A compromise. Something. The Teacher wouldn't let me sign the Pledge now, but I refused to accept this as our new life.

I ran up to the front door and just barely managed to keep myself from barging right in. Instead, I rang the bell. When no one answered, I began to knock. Movement in the front window made me look up, and I saw Mira step back behind the drapes.

I banged on it harder. The rage I'd been suppressing climbed to the surface, and I was almost surprised I wasn't strong enough to knock the door in. I had to see my dad face-to-face. If I could look him in the eye, I knew he couldn't turn me away. Since he wouldn't answer, I tried using my key, but they'd obviously changed the locks.

Frustrated, with fresh tears sliding down my face, I ran around to the back of the house, but that door was locked too. I kicked hard at the old plastic pet door the previous owners had installed, and I heard it crack. I kicked it again, and again, not satisfied until it splintered and fell off.

And then I heard a voice coming through the hole. "If you don't leave," my father said, "we'll be forced to call the police."

"Oh, really?" I dropped to my knees and yelled into the pet door. "What will you tell them? Will you say you kicked out your seventeen-year-old daughter because you joined a goddamned cult and they told you she's a sinner? Maybe you'd like me to tell them how I slept in my car because I didn't have anywhere to go?" I thumped on the door for emphasis. "Are you listening, Dad? I never thought of you as a coward, but if you won't come out and talk to me, then I guess I never knew you."

A murmur of voices floated out to me, and I stopped to listen, but then it was silent.

"Who do you think would be in trouble with the police?" I shouted. "Me? Or you?"

He still didn't answer.

"Somehow," I said in my most patronizing voice, "I don't think you can legally kick me out, but it's not like I'm a lawyer or anything, so I can't exactly take that chance and turn you in, can I? I mean, the last thing I want is to be sent to live with dear old Mom. Sounds fun, but I think I'll pass."

Silence.

By now the tears had dried up, replaced again with the white-hot anger. I pounded on the door with both fists to make sure I had his attention. "But, hey, Dad? Don't worry about me because I'm not on the street anymore. Nope, I'm living it up in a luxury motel now. You know, the kind that rents by the week? Hell, they probably rent by the hour. Hey, maybe I can turn a few tricks to earn money to pay for food. That's a great idea."

I remembered my drama school letter. "And I want my mail!" I screamed, the frame of the pet door pressing into my face.

Still nothing from inside.

Then I heard the whir of the electric garage door opening, and I jumped up and ran around to the front of the house in time to see my father's car back out into the street and drive away, my dad looking straight ahead and Mira beside him in the passenger seat where I used to sit.

I had parked right in front of the house, and when I got back into the Beast, that plain, gray mailbox sat there taunting me. Daring me.

"I HATE YOU, YOU GODDAMNED FUCKING MAIL-BOX!" I screamed.

I gunned the motor, swerved up onto the sidewalk, and bashed into it with my front bumper. The wooden post snapped in half. I jerked the gearshift into reverse, backed off the curb, slammed into drive, and tires squealing, tore off down the road. In my rearview mirror, I saw the mailbox lying in the street. I did a U-turn without checking for cars and raced back toward it. There was a loud thump as I flattened it with the Beast's enormous tires. I sped away from the scene of the crime, still angry, but also feeling a tiny bit of satisfaction.

I USED A KLEENEX TO WIPE OFF THE HANDLE OF the pay phone in the motel lobby. I'm normally not afraid of germs, but who knew what the sleazy people in this place had. I put my quarter in and dialed the after-hours number on the business card.

"Kennedy, Hyatt, and Jovanovich," said a chirpy voice.

"Ummm . . . may I speak to Dr. Kennedy?"

"I'm sorry, this is his answering service. If you give me your number, I can have him call you back."

"But I'm at a pay phone," I said. "And this is really important."

"If this is a medical emergency," she said, "you need to hang up and dial nine-one-one."

"It's not that," I said. "It's more mental health related."

"I understand," she said. "Give me your number, and if he can't call you back within five minutes, one of his associates will phone you."

I gave it to her and hung up. About two minutes later, the phone made a sort of weird half ring, sounding like a dying cat. I grabbed the receiver.

"Hello?"

"This is Dr. Kennedy. With whom am I speaking?"

"Oh, thank you so much for calling back. My name is Jamie Lexington-Cross, and Richard Cross is my dad. He's one of your patients, and he needs your help."

"Hello, Jamie," he said in a calm, almost monotone voice. "Jamie, is this a medical emergency?"

Why did everyone keep asking me that?

"No," I said. "It's just . . . well, he's gotten mixed up in a cult, and I was thinking maybe if he talked to you—"

"I'd like to help you, Jamie," he said. I wished he'd quit using my name in every sentence. It made me feel like a dog. "But I'm afraid your dad isn't one of my patients anymore."

"Well, I know. But the estate will pay you, if that's what you're worried about."

"Jamie, it's not the money. It's the fact that your father told me, in person, he was through with therapy and he no longer needed my services."

"But he does," I said, desperation rising in my voice. "He really, really needs you. Didn't you hear what I said? He's gotten sucked into a cult."

"I understand, Jamie," he said in that stupid soothing voice. "Perhaps you should call the police if you think he's in real danger."

"The police? I can't call the police. What would I tell them?"

"I don't really know, Jamie," he said. "I'm sorry I can't be of more help. But—"

"Oh, forget it," I said, slamming down the phone.

I immediately felt bad for being so rude, but he'd made me so mad. That fake caring voice when he wouldn't do anything to help. And

I couldn't call the police, or they'd ask me a bunch of questions and then I'd end up at a strange new high school in Los Angeles. Plus, I wasn't totally certain the church had actually broken the law.

I slumped against the wall, too tired to think anymore. After a while, I went upstairs and collapsed on my bed. For the rest of the evening, I sat in my room in a daze, memorizing the ingredients for each drink at the Coffee Klatch.

All night people staggered up and down the hall. Pulsing music from a party beat against the paper-thin walls, and drunken voices echoed through the ductwork. About midnight, things suddenly got louder, and I could pick out two guys having an argument.

"How many times do I have to tell you not to scam on her?" a man yelled.

"Shit, she was talkin' to me. I can't help it she thinks I'm so damn good-lookin'," the other guy said.

There was a loud thump, which sounded a lot like a body hitting the wall. "Ain't so good-looking now, are you, asshole?"

Then a woman screamed, "Look what you did. I'm gonna kill you!" Another body hit the floor, followed by more loud voices. "I'm calling the cops."

About time.

Someone crashed into my door, but I'd barricaded myself in with the boxes earlier, and I took deep breaths, trying to stay calm. The fight moved away from my room, down the hall. Over the grunts and groans from the two men, several people swore, and others cheered them on.

"Ooohh. Good one."

"Sick. That's a lotta blood, man."

Even with all the shouting, I could hear LaVon pacing in his room.

I wished he'd go out and stop them. One glare from him would've frozen any of the skinny guys I'd seen living in our building. The thumps worked their way back down the hallway toward me again. And then, in a low voice, right outside my door, I heard one of the men say, "I got worse than that wuss knife in my pocket, you son of a bitch. Don't make me kill you."

LaVon banged on my wall. "Jamie! Get your ass down on the floor."

"What?"

"Get down," he yelled.

He had to be kidding. The carpet was so sick and mangy. Plus there was glass in it from the broken lightbulb. And then I thought of all those TV shows I'd watched where gunfire broke out and the safest place was the ground. I threw myself facedown onto the disgusting brown shag rug.

I lay there, shivering. Outside my door, a woman spoke in a low, soothing voice. "Come on, Jake, baby. . . . He's not worth going to prison for," I heard her say. "Give me the gun, baby. . . ."

My heart pounded hard against the floor, and I prayed I wouldn't die in this disgusting place. I wondered if my dad would be sorry then. Everyone heard the sirens pierce the night at the same time, and suddenly the shouts gave way to running footsteps. By the time the police got to our floor, it was as quiet as a morgue. I was just glad no one was going to end up there.

I was still lying facedown on the stinky carpet, shaking, when someone started pounding on doors calling for people to come out. I don't think anyone did, because the knocking and voices seemed to keep moving toward my end of the hallway.

Someone banged on my door. "Open up. Police."

I didn't know what to do. How could I be sure they were really cops?

"Open up," shouted the voice again.

No one else had bothered to answer. Why should I? I heard LaVon's door open.

"Hey, come on, man," he said. "There's just a girl in there, and you're probably scarin' the shit outta her. You can check with Stub—he'll tell you."

"Well, if it isn't LaVon Mitchell," said a deep voice. "Staying outta trouble, I hope."

"Always."

"Don't know nothing about this fight, do you?"

"That's right," LaVon said.

"But it happened on your floor," countered the voice. "Sure you weren't involved?"

"Man, don't bust my balls." LaVon sounded relaxed and calm, but I wasn't sure if he should be. The cop seemed serious. "I was in my room reading a book," he said. "Besides, we both know if I was involved it woulda been over before you was called."

"Real tough guy, aren't you?" asked the cop. "Maybe we should talk about it at the station."

"You're in charge, man," LaVon said.

"That's right, and don't you forget it."

"Should I get my coat?" LaVon asked, "or are you just gonna harass my ass some more?"

By now I had pressed myself up against the pile of boxes, trying to hear better.

"I don't like your attitude, Mr. Mitchell," the officer said.

"Likewise, man," LaVon sneered.

I couldn't let LaVon get in trouble after he'd been so nice to me. Sure, he had terrified me too, but still, I owed him for offering his protection. I shoved the boxes out of the way and threw open the door.

"He wasn't involved. I'll swear to it. I heard him pacing in his room the whole time."

The policeman closest to me looked like one of those stick-figure drawings. His hat sat too big on top of a thin face, and the utility belt around his waist weighed him down. He grinned as he ran his eyes up and down my body.

"Well, aren't you a nicer sort than we usually get around here," he said.

Panic flushed out the adrenaline when I realized I'd given myself away. What if they took me in for being underage? The officer's leer sent shivers through me.

"He didn't do anything." I gulped back tears.

"All right, don't snivel," Stick Figure grumbled, looking away. "We're not taking your pal anywhere. We were just talking."

The other officer stood back by the stairwell, a bored expression on his squashed Muppet-like face. "Okay. Enough already, Jenkins," he said to Stick Figure. "Let's go. We're missing the basketball game."

Jenkins shook his head sadly. "It's not like the Blazers can even find the hoop," he said. As they disappeared into the stairwell, their laughter floated back up to us.

"You didn't have to do that, you know," LaVon said. "They were just messin' with me."

"Oh."

"But thanks, anyway."

"No problem," I said, my voice still shaky. "How come you're not at work?"

"Road game. They're listenin' on the radio," he explained. "You hungry?"

I actually was. I'd gotten two bean burritos for ninety-nine cents at the corner store for dinner, but they were a distant memory. "Ummm . . . I guess."

"Come on in," LaVon said.

Obviously I wasn't as good of an actress as I hoped because he read me like a dog-eared paperback. "Leave the door open if you're so chicken," he said.

Against my better judgment, I closed it behind me.

LaVon's cell was exactly like mine—tiny, with a single bed and a thin mattress. At the foot of the bed, a giant mountain bike hung from a hook he must've screwed into the ceiling himself. In the corner he'd set up a folding table, and on it was something that looked like a single burner of a stove. There was a pot bubbling away on top, and as I stepped closer, I got a whiff of garlic and spices.

"What's that?" I asked.

"Vegetable curry."

"I mean, that little stove thing."

He smiled. "Ain't you ever seen a hot plate before?"

"I guess not."

LaVon also had a toaster oven, a George Foreman grill, and a silver bowl thing that was plugged into the wall with a little wisp of steam escaping from it. He took the lid off, and inside was white rice, which he scooped into two chipped bowls. He topped them with the yellow curry, and then I watched in amazement as he chopped bright green onions on a tiny cutting board and sprinkled them over the food, followed by a handful of crushed peanuts.

"Wow," I said. I took the beautiful food from him. "It looks like it's from a restaurant."

"You eat with your eyes first," he said, waving at a folding chair. "Go on, before it gets cold."

LaVon sat on the bed and began to shovel in his food. I scooped up a forkful and blew on the hot rice. My stomach rumbled as I took my first mouthful. The spicy curry burned my tongue, but was immediately soothed by the sweetness of coconut milk and the bite of fresh green onions.

"This is fantastic. Where'd you learn to cook like this?"

"Inside," he said.

I'd watched enough TV to know what he meant, but I asked anyway. "You mean . . . jail?"

He looked directly at me, challenging me. "Yep. You got a problem with that?"

15

I CONCENTRATED ON MY FOOD TO KEEP MY MIND from wandering to what possible activity had landed LaVon in jail. The vegetable curry tasted so good, I could hardly get it into my mouth fast enough. I couldn't believe my luck. For the last two weeks I'd eaten bargain food, but this was the second night in a row I'd gotten a really yummy meal.

"Have some more," LaVon said when I'd scooped up the last bite. He took my dish and ladled curry over rice. I guess he could tell I'd been about to lick the empty bowl.

"Thanks," I said between mouthfuls. "I didn't know they ate so good in jail."

He laughed. "What? You think they taught me this in the kitchen?"

"Ummm . . ." The blood rushed to my face. "Well . . . you said . . . I mean, I thought—"

"The TV room, man," LaVon said. "You know, Emeril Lagasse . . . BAM! And my main man, Vegetarian Vic. They taught me everything I know."

"Oh . . . the Food Network?"

"Exactly." He faced me from his seat on the sagging cot. "What's your story?"

I chewed, debating. Sure, LaVon could turn me in to the cops, but somehow I didn't think he played by society's rules.

"Kicked out," I said.

"Drugs?" he asked.

I choked on my rice. "No. Do I look like a druggie?"

"Can't never tell." It seemed like he was eyeing me, but he had on those sunglasses again, so I wasn't sure. "Especially skinny girls like you," he said. "Speed, coke—"

"I do not do drugs."

I was not my mother.

"And I'm not skinny," I said. "I'm a dancer. I'm fit. There's a difference."

He held up his hands in surrender. "Okay, chill."

I ate a couple more bites before speaking again. "My dad joined this church, and I didn't want to, so he kicked me out. I'm going to help him get away, though."

"How?"

"Well, I'm not sure exactly, because he won't talk to me. But I've been sending him a lot of letters and printouts from the Internet about cults and stuff."

"How's that working for you?" I could tell he didn't think much of my attempts.

I shrugged.

"And your mom?"

I got the feeling LaVon would understand Mom's drug habit, and I considered telling him the truth, but I'd just met him, so instead I said, "My mother's out of the picture."

He nodded.

"Can I ask you something?" I said.

"Go for it."

"Why do you wear sunglasses inside?"

"Don't want to ruin your appetite."

"What?"

He shrugged and slipped off the shades. A jagged, pinkish-white scar ran under his right eyebrow and down across his eyelid. It looked all bumpy and gross, like a chewed up earthworm, but also like it was an old injury.

I couldn't help it, I gasped. "How did it happen?"

He put the glasses back on. "You don't wanna know."

I decided he was probably right. He took our empty bowls and washed them in the tiny bathroom sink, and when he was done, he lifted the tablecloth and revealed a small fridge like the one in the corner of my room. He took out two candy bars and tossed one to me.

"My downfall," he said.

"It's good for you," I joked.

He shook his head. "Bad for me. Bad for mankind."

"How is chocolate bad for mankind?" I asked.

"Slave labor," he explained.

"What do you mean?"

"Man, I'm tellin' you," he said, his voice getting louder as he got revved up, "it's pathetic. The farmers who grow the cocoa beans don't get nothin'. It's like not gettin' paid at all. They can't even afford to live in poverty like you and me," he said. "You gotta buy organic, fair-trade chocolate if you wanna sleep good at night, but I can't afford that shit."

How did he know this and I didn't? I ripped open the candy bar, but I felt kind of bad doing it. "I had no idea."

"No one does, man," he said, shaking his head sadly. "No one does."

We sat there eating in silence. I didn't know about LaVon's chocolate, but even with the guilt factor, mine tasted delish after the spicy curry.

LaVon probably wanted me to tell him more, but the truth was, I couldn't. It was past midnight, and after that morning's shopping with Krista and Liz, and the fiasco at my dad's, plus the scrumptious food, I thought if I didn't get back to my room right away, I'd fall asleep in his chair.

"I better go," I said. "Thanks for dinner."

"I'll give ya some leftover curry, if you want," he said. "You can heat it up downstairs in Stub's microwave for a buck. You got a fridge, right?"

"Yeah, but it smells super bad. I am soooo not using it."

"What? Like old food?"

"I don't even want to know. My whole room stinks. The bathroom's so ripe I can hardly use it. You're lucky yours is so nice."

"Like hell I am. This place smelled like there was a dead body under the bed when I moved in. Did you clean yours?"

I stood, stretching. "I wanted to, but I keep forgetting to buy some Lysol and rubber gloves."

LaVon took a white bottle, an orange box, and a scrubber pad from under the bed. "That chemical shit'll kill you anyway. Baking soda and vinegar is all you need to clean a bathroom."

"Ummm . . . okay." I took them from him. "How exactly do I use them?"

LaVon burst out laughing, and I blushed.

"Girl, you don't know nothin', do you? Ain't you ever cleaned a toilet?"

I shook my head. He reached out and grabbed the stuff back from me. "Never mind," he said. "I'll come over in the morning."

"Oh, you don't have to clean my bathroom."

This time his laughter came all the way from his belly. I was so glad I could amuse him.

"I ain't gonna touch your dirt," he said. "You are. But I'm gonna show you how to do it right." He opened the door. "Go on, now. I need my beauty rest."

He watched me walk down the hall and hesitate outside my room. I had accidentally left it open while we talked with the police earlier.

"What's the matter?" he asked.

"Nothing . . . The door was open. . . ."

"Scared someone's hiding under the mattress?" He stepped past me and looked under the cot. "Anyone hiding under there?" In a falsetto, he added, "Only me, an ax murderer."

"Very funny." He started to leave. "Ummm. What about the bathroom?"

He stuck his head inside. "All clear." His amusement vanished when he got a whiff of it, though. "Smells like a Dumpster in there."

"I know. Thanks. And for dinner too," I said, letting him pass.

"No prob."

After he was gone, I locked the door and crawled into bed in my clothes.

The next morning I woke up because someone was rapping lightly on my door. "Maid service," LaVon called, and his laugh rumbled through the walls.

126

I staggered out of bed and undid all the locks. "What time is it?"

"Time to clean up this shithole." He grinned.

With all my boxes, plus the two of us, there was hardly room to turn around in the tiny room, let alone clean it, so we stacked everything out in the hallway and left the door open to keep anyone from messing with my stuff.

"You got a lot of crap," LaVon said.

"Everything I own."

"How much of it you actually use?" he asked.

I shrugged. "So far only the clothes. I don't have a place for CDs and books anyway."

"If you don't unpack it in six months," he said, "you never will."

"Well, hopefully I'll have my own apartment and be in New York by then. I'm going to drama school." At least I hoped I was.

"What? Like you gonna be a movie star?"

"Maybe. Or on Broadway."

"Hmmm . . . not a life I'd want," he said.

"Why not? Would all the fame get to you?" I asked.

"I've had enough of people pryin' in my life to last me till eternity," he said, his voice kind of sad.

"Oh, well. Not me. Bring it on."

He smiled and shook his head at me. I wasn't sure if I liked that habit much, but what could I do about it? He opened my bathroom door and coughed dramatically.

"Man, girl. How do you breathe in here? This is nasty."

"I know," I agreed.

LaVon showed me how to wet down the tiny shower stall and then scrub it with baking soda. The white powder turned a dingy gray as he stood over me, watching, making sure I scrubbed hard enough.

"That is foul," he said. "I can't believe you used it like that."

"Only when I had to. I usually take a shower at school."

He gave me his signature look of disbelief. "You real desperate to shower in the locker room."

"No kidding."

I guess I'd passed some sort of test last night, like I'd proved I wouldn't freak out too much over his eye, because today he wasn't wearing his shades. In the harsh bathroom light I noticed little crow's-feet around his eyes. LaVon was older than I'd thought, but I still wasn't sure how old.

I rinsed off all the gritty baking soda and then he made me do it a second time because he wasn't satisfied. While I scrubbed, I sang a piece I'd been working on with my voice teacher, Betsy. I hadn't had any lessons lately because she'd taken a three-month singing gig at a casino in Vegas. I missed working with her, but at least I didn't have to make up some reason about why I was going to have to quit. If I told her I couldn't afford the lessons, she'd probably offer them to me for free, and I couldn't accept that. She needed to make her living.

"Nice song," LaVon said. "What is it?"

"It's called 'Poor Wand'ring One.' From the operetta *Pirates of Penzance*," I said.

"You sing good."

"Thanks."

The tiles weren't exactly sparkling when I was done, but you could see they were yellow instead of brown. After that, I scrubbed the sink and then the floor, which was so gross around the toilet I literally gagged and had to run into my room and stick my face out the open window, gulping for air.

"Don't forget the toilet bowl," LaVon said, ignoring my theatrics.

I went back to the bathroom and looked at the brown-stained toilet. "But I don't have a brush."

"What's wrong with the scrubber pad?"

"Ew! I'd have to put my hand in there."

"What're they made of?" he asked. "Gold? It ain't gonna kill you."

"No way," I said. "I'll buy a toilet brush at the dollar store."

"Your dollar," he said.

The vinegar was for cleaning the faucet and the mirror, and LaVon had provided an old T-shirt to use as a rag. Wiping it down almost made it worse, though, because the faux chrome flaked off the faucet. The mirror had those brown age splotches all over it, so it was still hard to see my reflection, but knowing it was all germ-free made me happy.

LaVon surveyed my work. "Better," he said.

After that, we cleaned out the refrigerator and plugged it in. LaVon went and got a small dish from his room and put some baking soda in it and told me to keep it in the fridge.

"What's all this crunchy shit in your carpet?" he asked.

"Glass. I broke the lightbulb in the lamp."

"Oh, yeah," he said. "I heard you freakin' yesterday."

"Yeah . . . well . . ." I felt myself blush.

"Go to the front desk," he said, "and tell Stub you want the vacuum cleaner."

"Okay."

I lugged the dust-encrusted monstrosity back up the stairs, the long hose winding itself around me like a snake and tripping me more than once. When I finally got to my room, I found LaVon scrubbing the filthy window with crumpled newspaper. The strong smell of vinegar wafted out to meet me.

"This ain't coming clean," he said, "so I guess you won't be able to enjoy the stunning view of the parking lot after all."

I laughed, then unwound the power cord and plugged it in, but I couldn't see any way to turn the vacuum on. LaVon tossed the newspaper in the recycle bag he'd started for me and said, "You like watching paint dry too?"

"What?"

"That vacuum cleaner ain't gonna work by magic."

"Well . . . I ummm . . ."

Comprehension dawned across his face.

"No fucking way." He laughed. "You ain't never vacuumed before neither?"

I shrugged. "My dad's kind of a crappy housekeeper, so my grandpa hired us a maid to come in once a week," I mumbled.

"Man, I been meaning to get me one of those," he said. "You think they take fifty cents an hour? That's 'bout what I can afford."

When I didn't respond, because, really . . . I was too embarrassed, he nudged my shoulder and said, "I'm just teasing ya. Don't be so serious." He stepped on a round button I hadn't noticed and started running the vacuum up and down the threadbare carpet. "It ain't brain surgery," he said, moving out of the way so I could try it.

I pushed it across the carpet and for about thirty seconds there was a satisfying clicking sound of glass being sucked into it, but then a thread from where the rug was worn through caught in the vacuum and the motor made a high whining sound. Before I could decide what to do, the room filled with a burnt rubber smell. LaVon pulled the plug out of the wall without bothering to turn it off and gave the string a yank, ripping it loose.

He surveyed my carpet. "Good enough," he said.

I started to take the vacuum downstairs, but he said he wanted to use it and took it to his room. After lugging my boxes back into my room, I sat on the cot breathing in the quickly fading scent of vinegar and burnt rubber. A minute later, LaVon tapped on my door and handed me one of those curly lightbulbs.

"Don't bash this into the wall," he said. "These ones got mercury in them, and I don't want to have to identify your body."

"Thanks. Hey, aren't these environmental ones really expensive?" I asked.

"Kinda, but they'll last a long time."

I reached for my purse.

"Don't worry about it," he said. "I got a two-pack. I only need one."

"I really appre—"

"It's all good."

He shut the door behind him.

Maybe it wasn't all good, but it wasn't all bad either.

16

I TRIPPED OVER AN EMPTY MILK JUG, AND TRENT reached out and steadied me, essentially keeping me from falling right on my butt. A little zing of electricity went up my arm.

"You might want to wear other shoes tomorrow," he said.

"Yep." I looked down at my favorite pointy-toed boots, now splotched with coffee. My feet killed me already, and it was only seven-thirty. A café was no place for anything but comfortable shoes. My white cashmere sweater had a pink syrup stain on the sleeve and was damp with sweat. Chocolate milk splatters covered the left leg of my pale blue jeans too, in spite of the black apron Trent had given me. Why hadn't I noticed the other employees wore dark clothes and short sleeves? The worst part was I would have to go to school like this.

"Jamie? Did you make the decaf yet?" Trent asked.

"Uh . . . I'm doing it now."

"You're going to have to move faster," he said, all business. He squirted whipped cream on a mocha while taking a swig of his own quadruple espresso at the same time.

"Sorry."

Trent had been kind of annoyed when I'd shown up and didn't know how to make any of the espresso drinks. "Damn it," he'd said. "I knew I couldn't trust Amanda to train you. She's still mad because I wouldn't take her to the prom."

"Is she your girlfriend?" I asked.

"Not anymore," he admitted. "Too high maintenance."

"You or her?"

He smiled. "Me."

The fact she wasn't his girlfriend was a relief, and it totally shouldn't have been. Especially since I needed to concentrate on my job, not Trent's love life. There were at least six impatient people in line, and we'd run out of decaf in the big urn because I'd forgotten to start it. How anyone could live without caffeine this early in the morning mystified me, but apparently the guy who was complaining to Trent could.

"I thought this was a coffee shop," he sniped.

"I'll make you a drink on the house," Trent offered. "What's your poison?"

"Double decaf soy latte," the guy said, perking up at a free drink.

A girl with black dreadlocks and a nose ring dumped a pile of dishes onto the counter. "All the tables are dirty," she told Trent, and she huffed off.

"We've got a new girl," Trent called after her. "Give us a break, and I'll give you a cinnamon roll."

She waved her hand at him like, *forget it.*

I flushed. "Sorry."

"She's a regular," he said. "She'll get over it. I'll handle the counter, and you try and clear some tables."

I grabbed a rag and ran it under hot water, feeling totally stupid for not having thought of it myself. Trent was going to be sorry he hired me if I kept screwing up. All last week when I'd been sitting here doing my homework, he and the girl I'd replaced had made it look so easy. They'd kept the line moving, and most of the time the tables had been clean and shining. Now everything was a mess, and I kind of knew it was my fault.

There was one other morning employee at the Coffee Klatch besides us, but she handled the food. Mishka, whom I hadn't officially met yet, hid out in the back washing dishes and making soup and baguette sandwiches for lunch.

Both Trent and Amanda were kind of young to be managers, and when I'd asked him about it while we prepped to open, he said, "Nepotism. At least for me. Amanda's just hot." He saw me grin and raise my eyebrows like, *oh, really?* and he realized what he'd said. "Not that *I* think she's hot. I meant I got the job because my uncle owns the place and my cousin Ian manages it. Amanda got the job because *Ian* thinks she's hot."

"Oh, right," I said, nodding, but I'd actually been thinking, *God, why does his hair have to look so silky and fall in his face like that?*

After the decaf guy left with his complimentary five-dollar drink, Trent filled the milk and cream carafes, and I rinsed out the empty jugs for recycling.

"Okay," Trent said. "Time for speed training."

"What's that?"

"Like speed dating. You ask me as many questions during this lull as you can, and I will train you into Super Barista Chick."

I actually had a lot of things I wanted to ask Trent, but none of them had to do with my job. I wanted to know if he ever made any short films. And did he use local actresses in them? And was he really moving to New York next fall? I settled on the third one.

"I heard you're going to NYU," I said.

"Okay, first of all—not a question." He handed me a container of cream to stick back in the fridge. "Second—doesn't have anything to do with your job," he said. "But, hey, I'm always willing to talk about me."

"So, are you going to film school?"

He let out a defeated sigh. "We'll see. I already deferred it one year for lack of cash, and I don't know if I'll have it this fall or not."

He told me a little about the scholarships he'd gotten and how they weren't enough, and then he showed me how to make a few drinks, but both of our moods had sunk. I didn't mention my New York dreams. We were pretty much in the same boat. No money. And it depressed me too much to talk about it.

I was still thinking about how unfair it all was while I scrubbed the tables and Trent made the drinks for the next rush of customers. As soon as I finished clearing, I went back and checked on the coffee. I decided to empty the steaming grounds so we'd be ready to make more, but they were way hotter than I expected.

"Ow! Ow! Ow!" I dropped the basket, dumping the grounds on the floor in a soggy pile.

"You okay?" Trent asked. "Did you burn yourself?"

My fingertips felt like I'd dipped them in hot oil, but I didn't want to admit it. "Sorry. I'll clean it up."

"Hang on." He took my right hand in his and wiped the grounds off with a rag. He held it up and examined it, then started kissing the tips and making loud smacking noises. "That'll make it better."

"Ooohh, yuck, boy germs," I said to hide my embarrassment, and tugged my hand away. After that, while I was scooping up the mess, I had a stupid grin on my face, which seemed to be a permanent fixture around Trent.

"Oh, crap," I said. "I accidentally threw the grounds in the garbage instead of the blue bin. Should I scoop them out?"

"Definitely," he said, nodding, making a very serious face. "I need you to pick them out one ground at a time. Otherwise I'll probably have to fire you." He laughed, and I shoved his shoulder.

"Excuse me. Hello?" said a woman at the counter. "I'll have a double skinny latte." She was so thin I wanted to slip her a full-fat drink.

"Coming right up." Trent waved me over to his side. "Watch and learn, Jamie."

I made a big deal over his technique with the foam, pretending to take notes. "If I'm going to be Super Barista Chick, I need to know what I'm doing," I said, and he rolled his eyes.

I actually did try to concentrate on the drink and how he made it, but I kept sneaking looks at Trent the whole time too. It sounds pretty cliché, considering where we worked, but his eyes really were the color of dark, rich coffee. Or maybe melted chocolate.

After the woman was gone, Trent said, "You think you can handle the counter? I have to check in with Mishka about the lunch menu."

"Sure." I hoped I sounded confident.

"Yell if you need me. And could you fill the straws and napkins while I'm gone?"

"Will do, boss."

He was totally nice, but I still felt kind of dumb because he had to tell me everything. Maybe I wasn't cut out for a restaurant. I put more napkins in the basket and got out a fresh box of straws. I was thinking

I was pretty smart for refilling the brown sugar all on my own when LaVon walked in and the strangest thing happened.

The Coffee Klatch is not that big of a place. About a dozen people were sitting around, and a low hum filled the room. But when LaVon stepped through the doors, everyone looked up and the conversation totally died. Only for a beat, though. Then it started right up again. Except for two girls who gave each other frightened looks and grabbed their cups and scooted out as soon as he had passed them.

Their reaction kind of pissed me off because it was so obvious they thought he was here to rob us or something. He *was* big and scary-looking, though. I'd have to give them that. Also, it was overcast and raining outside, but he had on his wraparound shades to cover his eye, which probably looked suspicious if you didn't know him.

"Hey, LaVon," Trent said from behind me.

"Trent." LaVon lifted his chin hello. If he'd noticed everyone's reactions, he didn't let it show. "I came to check out the new girl."

"We only hire the finest," Trent said.

"Hi, LaVon." I hoped I wasn't blushing over Trent's comment. "You came to see me? How did you know I worked here? Did I tell you? The muffins are really good. Whole grain with blueberries."

LaVon laughed. "Girl, you had too much coffee this morning."

He was probably right. "What can I get you? I think I can make a mocha now, and probably a latte too."

"Load me up with organic hot chocolate," he said, handing me a stainless steel travel mug.

"Sure. With whipped cream?" I chirped.

"Hell, yeah, I want whipped cream," he said. "Do I look like I'm on a diet?"

That totally cracked me up. We joked around while I steamed the milk and then LaVon took his drink to go.

"How do you know that guy?" Trent asked after he was gone.

"Lives in my neighborhood. Why?" I heard something challenging in my voice.

"No reason," Trent said. "He comes in here every day. Usually later, though. He seems okay, but still . . . he makes me nervous. He's one scary-looking dude."

I shrugged. "He's a great guy."

"If you say so."

"I do," I said.

But I wasn't totally sure. I couldn't really argue with the fact that the way LaVon carried himself and wore sunglasses inside made him intimidating. And he'd been nice to me, but he'd also been to jail for something. I couldn't remember his last name, but once I found out what it was, I intended to look him up on the Internet, because my curiosity was killing me.

As I wiped down the counter, I asked myself, *Would I have been as afraid of LaVon if he'd been as big and worn those shades, but was white?* I liked to think so, but . . . the truth was, and it seemed so . . . weird and . . . I don't know . . . embarrassing, I guess . . . to admit it even to myself, but I was worried those two girls were more like me than I wanted anyone to know. Maybe they *were* afraid of him because he was black, and maybe . . . maybe I was too. Or African American. I wasn't even sure what words to use, which made me acutely aware of the whole race thing too.

Trent snapped me out of my contemplations by asking me to mop behind the counter before I left for school. I rolled the yellow bucket out of the storage closet and gave the floor a quick swipe.

"Ummm . . . Cinderella?" he said.

"Yeah?"

"Not to be critical . . ." He was smiling, but my stomach sank. I knew I'd done something wrong. Again. "Next time, maybe sweep before you mop, okay?"

I looked at all the dirt, crumbs, and coffee grounds floating in the water, which had been clean when I started. "Oh, man. I am never going to reach Super Barista Chick status," I said. I glanced up at the clock. "Should I change the water?"

Trent took the mop from me and leaned on it, grinning. "I'll do it, but you'll owe me. You better get going, or you'll be late for school."

"Yes, Dad," I said.

We were laughing as I left, but when I'd jokingly called him *Dad,* it sent a little ping into my heart like I'd been shot by a BB gun.

I'd called Krista from the pay phone and told her she'd have to get her own ride today because I'd overslept, which of course was a lie. I didn't want her to know about my job—she'd say I wouldn't have time to work and be in *West Side Story* too, and I didn't want to think about that until I had to.

She came running up to me before first period for a hug. "Ooohh! You smell like coffee." She stepped back and checked out my stained sweater, jeans, and boots. "My God, Jamie. What happened to you? You look like you got in a fight at Starbucks."

"Something like that," I said.

My first two classes went by in a blur, and when I got to English, Mr. Lazby told me to stop by the office after class because I had a message. I needed to change for dance and didn't want to be late, but I was hoping maybe my dad had finally dropped off my mail. The balls of my feet ached with every step, and my arms felt rubber bandy from lifting milk, and mops, and coffee, but in my pocket was a wad of ones. Trent had given me my first tips before I left.

"This is for you, hon," Mrs. Monroe said, handing me a large manila envelope when I got to the office. Her bright orange fingernails looked like carrot sticks stuck to the ends of her fingers. "Your dad left it for you."

"Thanks."

The envelope was filled with mail. Unfortunately, the bulk of it was all the letters I'd been sending to my dad. And none of them were opened. As I walked toward the locker room, I searched through the rest, looking for my letter from RAC, but it wasn't there. Instead, I found two drama school flyers for programs I hadn't applied to, a letter from *Seventeen* magazine asking me to renew, the new issue of *Dramatics,* and a change of address form with a sticky note stuck to it that said in my father's handwriting, *Please use this.* Yeah, well . . . it wasn't like he had a mailbox anymore anyway. I couldn't help grinning a little.

I guessed the letter hadn't come yet, but at least it seemed likely he'd drop it off when it did. That was something. The warning bell rang, and I headed for the locker room. I had shoved almost everything back into the envelope when a letter fell out of *Dramatics.* I stopped, staring at the New York postmark. Around me I heard running footsteps of kids hurrying to class, and I picked it up and moved out of the way, leaning against a block of lockers. Carefully, slowly, afraid of what I'd find, I tore open the thin letter from the Redgrave Actors Conservatory.

"YES!" I screamed.

I was going to New York City to be an actress. Nothing could stop me now. I had to find Krista and Mr. Lazby. I was on my way to the Big Apple, baby. And if I could make it there, I could make it anywhere.

The halls were almost empty now, but a few stragglers turned and looked at me. I waved the letter as I ran past them toward the art room. *I got in! I got in!* thumped my feet as I ran. I skidded to a stop in front of the open door to Mrs. Steen's art room and peered in. Krista was sitting at a drafting table, a piece of charcoal in one hand, her tongue sticking out just a little between her bright purple lips.

This period was Advanced Independent Study, so there were only four other kids in the room. Mrs. Steen was standing on a chair stapling drawings to a bulletin board. As usual, she had four pencils stuck in her graying bun, plus a pair of glasses on top of her head and another pair dangling around her neck on a chain.

Krista looked at me as I sidled up next to her with a huge grin on my face. "You got in!" she said, before I could tell her. She dropped the charcoal and threw her arms around me.

"Come with me to tell Mr. Lazby?" I asked.

"Definitely!" she said. "Mrs. Steen? I need to run over to the costume shop for a few minutes."

Krista's independent study project was designing the costumes for *West Side Story,* so Mrs. Steen told her it was fine to go. When we got to the theater, we found Liz sitting at Mr. Lazby's desk downstairs in the drama room, working on her English essay. She'd taken dance with me for the first half of the school year, but after a while, the lameness of most of the other students got to her, so she'd begged her guidance counselor to let her be Mr. Lazby's teacher's assistant, and now she babysat his beginning drama class for him.

"Hey," I said. "Mr. Lazby in the costume shop?"

"Of course," she said.

Around the drama room, the first-year students were paired up, studying scripts and practicing lines for some scene they were probably going to do in class. Liz's sister, Megan, was in the corner with a tall, skinny boy. She waved at us, and we waved back.

"Come on," I told Liz.

"What's up?"

Krista grabbed her arm and pulled her along. "You'll see."

"You must have good gossip."

"Better than that," I said.

She followed us down the dim hallway to find Mr. Lazby. He was sitting at his sewing machine, leaning back in the swivel chair and talking on the phone. "Hang on a sec." He covered the receiver with his hand. "You got in, didn't you?"

I nodded, a grin splitting my face. He murmured something into the phone and hung up. Then he heaved his large body out of the chair, sending it flying back on its wheels, and scooped me up into a big hug.

"Wait? What happened?" Liz asked.

"I got into the Redgrave Actors Conservatory," I said, although I think it sounded more like "mmhhmlphl . . ." because Mr. Lazby was squishing me with his hug.

"Start spreading the news," Krista sang, and we all joined in, picking up the next line of the song together. "I'm leaving today. . . ."

Mr. Lazby added a walking bass line to jazz it up, and Liz and I started improvising a dance number. Krista can't dance, so she made fun of us, hamming it up by exaggerating all our movements.

"I want to be a part of it, New York, New York," we sang together.

Liz and I grabbed Krista and spun her around until she was so dizzy she fell on the floor laughing. Then we danced around her, each trying to outdo each other. Near the end, when the song really gets going, Liz and I pulled Krista off to one side and belted out the climax while Mr. Lazby took center stage, pretending he had a hat and cane, and doing a little soft-shoe number. We all finished together, throwing our arms out in front of each other, "New Yorrrrk! New Yorrrrk!"

Mr. Lazby sank into his chair, slightly out of breath, while the three of us collapsed onto the concrete floor of the costume shop, laughing our asses off.

"Liza Minnelli's got nothing on us," Krista said.

"Can I read your letter?" Mr. Lazby asked.

"Sure." I handed it to him, and we all crowded around, reading over his shoulder. I read the "Congratulations" part about five times before I kept going all the way to the end. Which is when I saw the sentence that sent my heart plummeting.

To reserve your spot in our fall term, please send a $500 deposit within thirty days.

LAVON HAD MOVED HIS SEAT ALL THE WAY BACK in order to cram himself into the Beast, and so far, he'd refrained from commenting on my driving, but if he thought I didn't notice his hands clutching the sides of his seat, he was sadly mistaken. I forced myself to concentrate more on the traffic and less on our destination.

"Tell me again why you're draggin' my ass 'cross town?" he asked.

"Well . . . last time I went over to Dad's, he wouldn't open the door for me, so I thought I could stand off to one side and you could knock. And then when he opened the door, I could ask him for the title to the Beast."

My plan was to sell it and use the money for the down payment on my tuition. I didn't know why I hadn't thought of that the very first day Dad kicked me out. The Beast was five years old, but it was a Lexus. It had to be worth a lot. I could probably even get a new, smaller car, and an apartment. LaVon's laughter rocketed through the SUV, bringing me back to reality.

"What?" I asked him.

"You think," he said, "your old man's gonna open the door to me? You're crazier than I thought."

Anger flared up in me. "My dad's not a racist."

"Chill, girl. I never said nothin' about him being no racist. But have you looked at me lately?"

We'd stopped at a light, and I glanced over at him. "Ummm . . ."

"Hell," he said, "if I came to my *own* door, I'd call the cops. You don't have to be no bigot to be scared of me."

I sighed. "Yeah . . . okay. You're right. I'm an idiot." I'd thought about asking Krista to come along to knock on the door for me, but I would've had to explain way too much. "I've got it," I said, a new idea forming. "You lurk in the bushes and when he sees you, I'll say you've been following me. He'll have to let me come inside then."

"Next plan."

I slumped in my seat as I turned down my old street. "You wait in the car and then I give you a ride to work afterward like I promised?"

"There ya go."

I pulled the Beast up to the front of the house. Maybe having LaVon go to the door wasn't a good idea, but it might not hurt to have him seen in the passenger seat. If nothing else, it might pique my dad's curiosity.

"They got a new mailbox," I muttered as I opened my door.

LaVon put his window down and pulled a pack of cigarettes from his pocket.

"Could you get out?" I asked. "I don't want you stinking up my car if I'm going to try and sell it."

"Fine. I'll stand outside and freeze my ass."

"I can't believe you smoke anyway," I said. "I thought you were some organic-eating, bike-riding health nut."

LaVon shook his head. "Girl," he said, "you don't know nothin'."

"What do you mean?"

145

"I mean, I'm doin' the best I can to leave the booze and herb alone," he said, all his usual humor gone. "I don't need you ridin' me about smokin'."

I could tell I'd stepped over a line, and I started to apologize, but LaVon stopped me. "Go get your title, and let's get the hell outta here."

"Okay . . . sorry."

It was almost six o'clock, but my dad kept his car in the garage, so I couldn't tell if he was home from work or not. A single light flooded the porch, but the rest of the house was dark. I stood in the street, leaning against the SUV, taking deep breaths and trying to work up my courage. I would take LaVon's advice this time and chill. I wouldn't yell or scream or do anything crazy. I wouldn't even bring up the church. I'd just ask for the title and go.

As I came around the back of the Beast and stepped up into the yard, I tripped right over one of those "Vote for so-and-so for mayor" signs that my dad always lets people put up in the yard because he can't say no. As I righted it, I saw it wasn't for any political race.

CENTURY 21
FOR SALE

LaVon stood leaning against the front fender of the Beast, his cigarette glowing in the dark.

"The house is for sale," I said.

"Yeah? So?"

"Why would Dad sell the house?"

"Go ask him."

Duh. I ran up the walk and knocked on the door. When no one answered, I rang the bell a couple of times, but nothing happened. Right in the center of the window, a slim gap in the curtains let a bit of light out from the living room onto the rosebushes. If I could get close enough, I might be able to see inside.

I pushed a shrub out of the way and stepped into the flower bed. Dead leaves crunched under my feet, and branches scraped at my neck and face as I slid along the big front window. I protected my hand with my sleeve and moved a thorny stem out of the way. It snapped back as soon as I let go and caught on my coat until I yanked myself free.

I was close enough now to see through the opening, and I cupped my hand around my eyes to peer inside. On the floor sat the green-shaded reading lamp from my dad's study. It cast a faint light over the room . . . the very *empty* room. They had already moved out. My dad was gone, and I had no idea where.

I couldn't take it in. He'd not only kicked me out, but totally abandoned me. I think I actually thought one day my dad would wake up and snap out of it and everything would go back to the way it was. But he was gone. Moved away. Just like in those nightmares I used to have at camp.

I'd thought I was alone before, but now I knew I was. I sank down, my legs weak, the tears falling before I hit the ground. I sat there, hugging my knees, the smell of damp earth reminding me of other bushes where I'd hidden to cry so many times.

During those long seven weeks after my mom's shoplifting arrest when I'd lived with my grandpa and my dad wasn't allowed to visit me because Mom had filed a totally false abuse complaint against him, the feeling of being abandoned by my parents never went away. All I could do was wonder where my dad was or why my mom hadn't come to get me. More than once, tears had driven me outside into the backyard, where I'd crawled into the boxwood hedge to cry so my grandpa wouldn't see me and feel bad.

Sometimes I sat there, tears streaming down my face until I could hardly breathe. Other days, I'd curl up into a ball and sleep. I thought about doing that now. Letting the cold chill me from the ground up until I couldn't feel anything anymore.

"James!" I heard someone yell. My head popped up, and for a split second, I thought it was my dad. He was the only one who ever called me that. But then I heard it again and realized it was LaVon.

"Where the hell are you?" he shouted.

I wiped at my face with the sleeve of my coat. "Coming." As I stood up, LaVon strode across the grass toward me.

"I'm gonna be late to work. What you doin' in there anyway?"

"Nothing. Just . . . just looking in the window."

With a bare hand he pushed the rosebush aside so I could crawl out. "Well?" he demanded.

"They're gone."

"I figured that out. I'm just wonderin' what the hell you're doing sittin' on the ground."

"Nothing."

He shook his head. I knew it meant *this is one crazy chick.* We headed back to the Beast.

"LaVon?" I asked. "Could you maybe drive?"

"Nope. Don't got a license."

"Oh."

"Besides, it'd ruin my reputation as one of them hippies to be seen driving this gas-guzzler."

I couldn't help it. I laughed a little.

"What'd you lose your license for?" I asked, once we were back on the main road.

"Who said I lost it?"

148

"Oh . . . I mean . . . well . . . did you?"

"Kinda personal question, ain't it?"

I glanced over at him. "Is it? Sorry."

He shrugged. "DUI."

I knew LaVon went to AA meetings two or three times a week, so I wasn't too surprised, but I wondered if that's why he'd been in jail. I didn't think they arrested you for that unless you killed someone, though. Or maybe if you got caught a bunch of times.

"Hey, LaVon," I said, trying to sound totally casual, "what's your last name?"

"Why? You gonna Google me to see what I done?" he asked.

Crap. Maybe I should rethink the acting career if I was so transparent.

"Ummm . . . well . . . yeah," I admitted.

"Voluntary manslaughter," he said so low I almost didn't hear him.

The light turned yellow, and I probably would've gone through it normally, but the shock of his words made me slam on the brakes. We slid partway into the intersection, and I had to back up to get out of the way. Luckily, no one was behind us.

"Voluntary?" I asked, trying to keep the fear out of my voice.

"That's what they call it if it ain't exactly an accident, but it's not murder, either."

Oh. My. God. Did he just say murder? Murder?! What was I doing in the car with this guy? I'd let him in my room too. And eaten food with him. And stuck up for him with Trent, saying he was okay.

The light turned, but I sat there, my hands frozen to the steering wheel.

"Waitin' for a particular shade of green?" LaVon asked.

It took a Herculean effort to lift my foot from the brake and move it to the gas.

"You don't have to be afraid of me," LaVon said. "It was a bar fight. Me and this guy . . . we pretty much beat the crap out of each other."

Neither of us said anything for a while.

"I don't know exactly what happened," he said. "'cause I was so drunk I blacked out."

"Oh." What the hell was I supposed to say to that?

"Woke up in the hospital the next day," he continued. "The other guy was in a coma for about a week and then he died, so they charged me with voluntary manslaughter."

"How come . . . how come . . . you're not in prison?" I asked.

"Judge gave me five years, I did three. Out early for good behavior." He sighed. "They needed the bed too, I guess."

"Wow."

"Like I said, you don't have to be afraid of me, but I get it if you are."

"No . . . it's all right," I said. Was I seriously okay with this? Or if not okay, exactly, did I actually want to be friends with him anyway? In a way, I guess I did. He was, oddly, the one stable adult in my life at the moment, and frankly, I needed him.

"I understand addiction," I said after a while.

"Yeah, well, I was drunk, but I can't blame the booze."

"True."

Why was I reacting so calmly? Maybe I was in shock. But the truth was I'd been around alcohol all my life, so I knew what crazy things it could make you do. No, not make you, but *allow* you to do. I guess that was it. I was willing to cut him more slack than maybe Krista might, but still . . . it was a little unnerving.

As we got closer to Lloyd Center Mall, I concentrated on the heavy traffic so I didn't have to think about LaVon's criminal record.

Eventually, he broke the silence. "So what you gonna do now about unloadin' this monster?"

"I don't know," I said, glad he'd changed the subject. "Do I really need a title to sell it?"

"I know plenty of guys who'll buy it without one."

That cheered me up. "Really?"

"Yeah, really, 'cept you don't want to go down that road. They'll end up crashing it or something and then sayin' it ain't theirs, and the cops'll come after you."

"Oh. Bad plan."

"Yeah."

We drove in silence for a while. There had to be some way to sell it without a title. What did you do if you lost it, anyway? I only had about twenty-five days to sell the Beast and get the money to New York.

Heavy traffic pressed in all around me, headlights shining through the dark February night, reflecting off the wet pavement, making it hard to see, and I clenched the wheel, even though I knew it was better to try and stay relaxed when you were driving.

"Maybe I can order a replacement title on the Internet or something," I said.

"Probably."

We were still half a mile from the Rose Garden Arena when LaVon told me to pull over. "You'll get stuck in traffic," he said. "I can walk from here."

He was right, so I pulled over into the only vacant place, which happened to be a bus stop.

"James," Lavon said. He yanked at the seat belt trying to get loose. "Don't worry. Dads can't stay away from their kids for long."

"How do you know?" I asked.

"I got me a daughter."

That was the first I'd heard of her.

LaVon still couldn't get the seat belt undone because it had a child-safety lock on it. "Here. There's a trick to it," I said. I popped it open. "You've really got a daughter?"

LaVon flashed me his broad smile. "And a grandbaby."

"You're a grandpa?" I said. "My God. How old are you?"

He laughed, and as he climbed out he said, "Fifty-one."

"Really? You don't look that old."

"Girl. You got some mouth. Anyways, what I'm sayin' is in spite of your habit of actin' like a princess, I think your daddy probably raised you right, so it's likely he's got some common sense too, in spite of the church and that Mira woman. Eventually he'll stop thinkin' with his dick and remember what's important."

My laughter burst out, but then a horn blared behind me. I looked in the mirror and saw a bus descending on my bumper. "Gotta go," I said. LaVon slammed the door, and I peeled out. In my rearview mirror I saw him walking slowly toward the curb, ignoring the honking bus driver.

Fifty-one, I thought. If I'd had to put money on it, I would've said LaVon wasn't a day over forty. For some reason, the idea of him being a dad and a grandfather made me really happy. Some of the fear I'd had of him diminished too, in spite of his record. I looped around the block and crossed the freeway, heading for the motel. The only home I had anymore. I hoped LaVon was right about my dad.

AS SOON AS I GOT TO SCHOOL ON WEDNESDAY, I tried to get Josh alone to find out what he knew about my dad, but every time I saw him, he was with Derrick. The whole secret relationship thing was not working for me anymore. Scholarship or not, we really needed to talk.

That night, I got the brilliant idea of texting him from LaVon's phone. His dad wouldn't recognize the number, and as long as I kept it casual, he'd probably think it was one of Josh's football buddies. I'd told Josh I was working at the café, so my text said *DUDE! meet at coffee klatch after school 2morrow.*

As long as his brother didn't see it and think it was from one of their friends, Josh would be able to meet me there while Derrick was at wrestling.

Thursday morning, while I was changing the mop water, Trent filled my mug with whipped cream and when I took a drink, I got it all over my nose. I was busy trying to put some on his laughing face when I heard my name.

"Jamie?"

I stopped, one hand holding on to Trent's shoulder, the other in the air, reaching for his face. "Josh! Oh, hi," I said. I let Trent go and washed my hands in the sink. "Can I take my break?" I asked him.

"Sure."

I noticed he made a point of looking at the clock. It was only six fifteen, and I'd punched in at five thirty. What was Josh doing here this morning anyway? I'd told him to come after school.

"I'll be right back," I said. "It will be a mini break."

"Whatever," Trent said. "Take your time."

But he didn't sound like he meant it. I ran around the counter and led Josh over to a table by the fireplace. "I'm working, so I only have a few minutes."

"Yeah, really looked like you were working," Josh said.

He scowled over at Trent, who had his back to us while he filled the cream jug. I was sure Josh saw his tattoo of the movie camera, which was not good since one of the times Josh and I had actually been talking recently, I'd mentioned I was thinking of getting a tattoo on my ankle of the comedy and tragedy masks. Josh hadn't liked the idea much, and he'd probably like it less if he put two and two together and figured out where I'd gotten my inspiration.

"I thought you were coming this afternoon," I said, trying to change the subject and realizing too late how bad it sounded.

"Clearly."

"Josh, there's nothing going on. He's my boss."

I wasn't sure exactly who I was trying to convince.

"I have to go to Derrick's meet after school," he said. "So what's so important?"

I stared at him, not believing he didn't get it. "Well, I wanted you to come then because I thought maybe we could just hang out. You know, do homework. Joke around. Like we used to."

"Someone might see us," Josh said.

"No one cares what we do," I told him. "No one but you and Derrick, and he'll be rolling around on the mat with some other heavyweight."

That was not the right thing to say. He ran his hands over his blond flattop and glared at me. "It's too risky," he said.

"So why are you here, then?" I asked, starting to feel annoyed myself.

"Because I had to tell you not to text me, even from someone else's phone. You never know who might see it, and my dad's been threatening every day to pull us out of school. If I don't graduate, they'll take away my football scholarship."

"Yeah, I know. I'm well aware of that."

He got up to leave.

"Josh, please," I said, running after him. Luckily the café was empty, but I had the feeling Trent was watching, and I lowered my voice. "Fine. Don't hang out with me. But I need to know where my dad is. His house is for sale, and they've moved out."

"You don't have to worry about him," he said. "They made him a disciple."

"Really?"

"You better get back to *work*," he said, giving Trent another dirty look before he pushed open the door and left. It swung shut behind him, the little bell tinkling cheerfully. I knew he'd gotten his feelings hurt when he saw me and Trent messing around, and even though I didn't really enjoy being treated like a big secret, I still cared about him. I'd have to make it up to him later. At least I'd gotten an answer about my dad. The Teacher must have moved him and Mira into the compound. That was why he didn't need his house anymore. Jesus only had twelve disciples, and I knew the Right & the Real already had those slots filled. I guessed there was always room for a thirteenth, if he had a trust fund.

"Who was that?" Trent asked.

I knew the correct answer, but for some reason, I didn't want to say it.

"A friend from school."

"Didn't seem very friendly to me," Trent mumbled.

On Sunday morning, I gathered up the pile of cash I'd counted out on my bed and took it downstairs to pay my rent. I was already regretting last night's splurge with Krista and Liz. The thing was, I couldn't avoid doing stuff with them entirely, or they'd start to get suspicious.

"We thought maybe you didn't like us anymore, chickie," Krista said, when I picked them up at her house.

"You're my best girls," I told them.

"Do you think a stranger would buy us being best friends?" Liz asked, eyeing the three of us and giggling. As usual, Liz had worn black, and her hair was up in her ballet bun. All I could manage was a clean pair of jeans, my pink cashmere sweater, and high-heeled boots. Krista sparkled with glitter makeup and a ruffled gold lamé skirt, sequined high-top tennis shoes, and a silky blouse with a plunging neckline.

"Unlikely," Krista said. "Liz looks like she should be going to Carnegie Hall, Jamie is off to meet her doctor fiancé at the country club, and I'm planning to dance the night away."

We hadn't done any of those things, though. We'd seen a movie and eaten a pizza, and this morning I was acutely feeling the loss of the twenty dollars I'd spent.

A girl I knew vaguely from the laundry room was at the counter talking to Stub when I got to the lobby. Vanessa was only nineteen, but she already had a toddler, and a distinct baby bump showed under her too-short T-shirt. Her boyfriend was in jail, serving three months for resisting arrest. I didn't even want to know why he was being arrested at the time. She'd divulged all this information in the first two minutes we'd met, and so usually I tried to avoid her in case she had more depressing things to tell me.

"Come on, Stub," Vanessa said. "You can't do this."

"Rent is due by eleven o'clock on Sunday morning. If you can't pay, you have to move out."

"But I've been here for five months," Vanessa said. "You know I'm good for it."

Stub pointed to the sign that said exactly what he'd just told her. I couldn't believe she'd lived here for five months. This was only my third week, and I was already so depressed by the idea of handing over more money for rent, I could barely stand it.

Vanessa's little girl, Ruby, was sitting on the floor by the dead plant, playing in the dirt. All she had on was a disposable diaper, and it was pretty obvious it needed to be changed. I waved at her and made silly faces because I didn't know where else to look.

Vanessa saw me, and the smile she gave me was way too familiar. I'd seen my mother give people that look every time she was about to ask for a favor. I knew what was coming.

"Hey, Jamie," she said. "How you doing?"

"Oh, fine," I said, keeping my eyes on Ruby.

"So . . . LaVon said you got a job."

"I just started," I said. "I've only worked there one week."

"I'm a little short on rent this week," she said.

"Really? Wow. That's ummm . . . too bad."

Crap. What was I supposed to say? I couldn't afford to float Vanessa and Ruby. From now on, I was going to stay clear of the lobby as much as possible.

"You wouldn't be able to give me a teeny-weeny loan," she said. She made her blue eyes go all round and innocent-looking. "Would you? Just until Wednesday?"

"Ummm . . . how much?"

Behind Vanessa, Stub shook his head vigorously at me and mouthed, "Say no!"

"A hundred bucks?"

A hundred dollars? Was she crazy? She wasn't short, she was missing almost half of her rent. "Oh, I'm sorry . . . I don't have it," I said. I was kind of relieved she'd asked for so much because I really couldn't give it to her. If she'd asked for twenty, I might not have been able to say no.

"Did you want to pay your rent, Jamie?" Stub asked, coming to the rescue.

"Oh, yeah. Thanks."

I shoved the money across the counter and ran for the stairs before she could counteroffer. A couple of hours later, I went downstairs to go to the grocery store. Vanessa was loading Ruby and half a dozen black garbage bags into a dilapidated car with a broken windshield.

I thought of my dad. Countless times we'd been walking downtown together and he would hand over a buck or two to a homeless person. Then he would put his arm around me, squeeze my shoulder, and say, "There but for the grace of God go I."

Me too, Dad. Me too.

chapter 19

ON MONDAY, THE BAKER DELIVERED HEART-SHAPED scones and sugar cookies with pink frosting and arrows across them in red.

"Get a stack of gift cards ready," Trent told me as we set up for the day. "Because a whole bunch of guys woke up this morning and their wives and girlfriends gave them Valentine's gifts, and they are totally screwed because they forgot. We'll sell a ton of them."

"You're kidding," I said.

"Happens every year. Well, I only actually worked here last year, but it happened then."

I looked around the café at all the decorations that had been up for two weeks. Pink balloons, red heart-shaped pillows added to the sofas, lacy doilies in the windows. How could anyone forget Valentine's Day? Even though the weekend had gone by without a word from Josh, I'd bought him a box of his favorite cashew brittle, and I was going to stick it in his locker.

"Could you check the till and make sure we have enough ones?" Trent asked me.

I popped the drawer and then started laughing. Instead of money, he'd filled the whole thing with candy hearts. He was giving me a sexy grin, and his crooked tooth reminded me of the first time I'd met him and wanted to run my tongue over it. I really needed to stop thinking about that.

"Did you steal the money?" I asked.

"Nah. It's all underneath. But I thought maybe you'd want to take your loot out before anyone comes in."

He handed me a paper bag and helped me scoop the chalky blue, pink, and white candies into it. He held one up so I could read it. *You're special, Valentine.*

"You're a goof," I said.

"Yeah, pretty much," he agreed, and then he ate the candy.

By the time we'd cleared out the drawer, it was time to open. A guy in a gray suit was standing outside texting on his phone, waiting for me to unlock the door.

"Good thing you open early," he said. "My secretary would freak out if I didn't bring her a latte on Valentine's Day."

"You better get her some truffles, too," Trent suggested, holding up a box we'd gotten in especially for the holiday.

"You think?" the guy asked, counting his money.

"Definitely," I said.

I pressed my mouth shut, trying not to laugh, and refused to look at Trent's dark chocolate eyes or I knew I'd crack up. All morning the two of us suckered every guy who came in into buying extra goodies. We didn't really care about the café making a profit. It was more about working together as a team and a way to amuse ourselves. Two hours later, when we finally got a lull, I was beat.

"Powered by caffeine," Trent said, sucking down a shot of espresso he'd let go lukewarm.

"You and me both," I said.

He held out a box of truffles. "Here. Happy Totally-Ruined-and-Commercialized-by-Advertisers-and-Retailers Day of Love."

"Oh, wow. A box of truffles. How thoughtful," I said in a fake sincere voice. "Where did you steal these from?"

"I'll have you know," he said, whipping a receipt out of his pocket, "I paid for those. Yesterday. On my day off. I came in just to get them. In *advance*."

"Did you really?" I asked.

"Well"—he pushed his hair out of his eyes—"I was actually here to fix the Internet, but I did buy them for you."

"Thanks." I felt way more pleased about it than a girl with a boyfriend should feel. "Want one?" I asked.

"Hell, yeah, I want one," he said, imitating LaVon. "Do I look like I'm on a diet?"

I untied the ribbon, and instead of throwing it away like I should've, I tucked it into my apron pocket. We demolished the four truffles while we scrubbed down the espresso machine and counters. It looked like someone had thrown a bucket of coffee over it because we'd been working too quickly to clean up much.

"So . . . I was thinking," Trent said. "We should go out on a date."

Oh, crap.

"A date?"

"Yeah," he said. "You know . . . a date. I come to your house, bring flowers to your mom, shake your dad's hand, say 'yes sir' when he tells me your curfew. That sort of thing."

"Oh, I . . . ummm—"

"Before you say no," Trent said, "let me elaborate. I was thinking maybe we could fly to France. Have dinner at a sidewalk café. Unless you prefer Milan."

"Sounds lovely, but—"

"I know, I know. . . . You don't have a passport, right? That's okay. We could go for pizza and a movie instead. Boring, but a tried-and-true date. In fact, it might even be the definition of date. Or we could go roller-skating!"

"Roller-skating?" I asked. Now I was laughing.

"I haven't been since junior high, but I am awesome on skates. I can shoot the duck and skate backwards, as long as someone holds my hands. And there's that really cool mood lighting during couples skate. But you shouldn't wear a black shirt with a white bra because this one time, in seventh grade, this girl McKensie, she did, and when she skated under the black light, her bra glowed right through her shirt. It was actually kind of cool, but she was embarrassed. Of course, if you don't mind me seeing your bra, I don't mind seeing it either. I'm that kind of guy. Very adaptable."

He stopped for air, but by then I was doubled over laughing.

"You know," he said, after a while, when I was still gasping, "I really love it when I ask a girl out and she laughs in my face. It's very encouraging."

I think, in a way, my laughter was part hysteria because, while I was giggling like that, I was also thinking, *What the hell am I going to do?* I finally pulled myself together, but just as I was going to make myself answer him, one of the regulars came up to the counter to get a refill. While Trent got her coffee, I told myself very sternly that I had to tell him about Josh.

162

After she had taken her drink, Trent turned to me. "So, what will it be? Paris or Skate World?"

"The thing is . . ."

I have a boyfriend. I have a boyfriend. I have a boyfriend. What was wrong with me? Why couldn't I get those four words out? How hard was it to say?

But do you really have a boyfriend? asked a little voice in my head. Was Josh as committed to me as I was to him? It really didn't seem like it lately. And if I told Trent I was dating someone else, what would happen here at work? I would hate it if my job became formal and awkward every morning.

"The thing is," I tried again, "it's complicated."

"Complicated how?" he asked, but his face had clouded over and instead of melted chocolate, his eyes looked kind of like brown stones.

"Well—"

The bell on the door tinkled, and we both looked up to see a delivery guy carrying a huge bouquet of red roses. "I have a delivery," he said, "for Jamie Lexington-Cross."

"Ahhh," Trent said. "That kind of complicated."

I couldn't leave the flowers in the Beast all day or they might freeze, and I didn't have time to take them back to the motel, so I carried them into school with me. I knew lots of girls and even some of the teachers would have flowers, so no one would think much of them. Except for the fact that Josh had broken up with me so publicly. I kind of forgot about that aspect until I ran into Krista at the locker.

"Secret admirer?" she asked, eyeing the dozen roses.

"Very funny," I said.

"Seriously, did Josh send you those?" she asked.

"Yep," I said.

Liz glided up to us. "Nice flowers, Jamie." As usual, she wore black stretch pants and a tight sweater and looked like she was ready to do an improvised dance down the hallway. "What the hell are you wearing?" she asked Krista.

"You'd think by now you'd be used to her," I said. I had barely even noticed her red velvet pants and black corset laced up with a scarlet ribbon.

"Check out my new 'do," Krista said, pulling off her newsboy cap. Her hair tumbled down around her shoulders, but it was now dark purple instead of pink.

"Nice," I said. I actually liked it better. It wasn't so girly.

"So did your secret admirer give you those roses?" Liz asked.

"Would you two stop already?"

"What?" she said. "What'd I say?"

"Jamie's touchy about the whole secret admirer thing," Krista said, fluffing her hair. "I don't know why."

The really annoying thing was I had to go with "secret admirer" all morning because everyone thought Josh and I had broken up and I didn't know what else to say when my other friends asked who the flowers were from. By lunch, I was regretting having brought them inside at all. If Josh couldn't give me flowers for Valentine's like a normal boyfriend, did I even want them?

The three of us met up in the caf for lunch, and I was pawing through a box of chocolates a freshman had given Krista, trying to find the caramel ones, when she said, "Here comes your secret admirer."

"You're probably in trouble for flaunting your flowers," Liz said.

"Oh, please. He's not that bad."

They both raised their eyebrows at me, and I made a face back at them.

I felt, more than saw, Josh come up behind me. Then he whispered, "I need to talk to you. In private."

Krista and Liz both gave me told-ya-so looks.

I scooted my chair a little so I could look up at him, but I didn't stand. "Why?"

"Not here," Josh said. He crouched down and tied his already tied shoelace. I guess that was supposed to be his cover. And suddenly the whole thing just seemed really stupid to me. I couldn't even remember the last time I'd been honestly happy to see Josh. Sometimes I thought it was back before the wedding. Lately, I'd been afraid my annoyance with him was because maybe I kinda, sorta liked Trent, but in that moment, I realized it didn't even have anything to do with anyone else. Josh was just pissing me off lately. Either he loved me or he didn't.

"Just say what you have to say," I told him.

"Why are you carrying the flowers around? Everyone's saying you got them from a secret admirer. Derrick is going to figure it out."

I looked at Josh, hunched over his other shoe now, retying the lace that was so obviously fine, and I lost it.

"You know, I don't think Derrick gives a damn about us. He used to cover for us all the time, Josh, remember? We used to sneak off during fellowship meetings, and he would make up stories to tell your parents. Remember that?"

Josh was standing now, looking around the cafeteria, probably for Derrick. "Shhh . . . Jamie, people are staring."

I pushed my chair back, and it made a screeching sound against the linoleum. Josh cringed. "I don't care if everyone's looking at us.

Don't you get it? Either you're my boyfriend or you're not. Either you trust your brother to have your back or you don't. But I'm not someone you can just hide out with in a closet anymore."

By now, pretty much everyone around us had gone quiet and was looking right at us. Josh leaned in toward me and said, "Don't do this. I love you, Jamie."

"You don't act like you love me," I said much louder than I intended to. But by now, I was tired of holding everything in, and I didn't really care who heard us. "You want me to sneak around with you, I'm not allowed to call you or send you any e-mails, and my best friends are supposed to act like we broke up just so your parents don't find out you're seeing me. That is not a boyfriend, Josh. That is just a screwed-up relationship."

"Jamie, just come with me out into the hall—"

"No," I said, shaking his hand off my arm. "Either you say you love me loud enough for everyone to hear it, you tell Derrick the roses are from you, and you kiss me right now in front of all these people who clearly can't concentrate on their lunch anymore, or that's it. We're over."

He took a step toward me, and I thought he actually was going to kiss me, but then we both saw Derrick come into the cafeteria. Josh ran his hand over his hair, and I swear his eyes looked damp, like he was fighting tears. I almost took him in my arms and told him it was okay. I'd keep his secret, and his scholarship was safe with me, but then Derrick walked up.

"What's up, bro?" he asked.

"Nothing. Not a thing," Josh said. "Let's get something to eat." And the two of them took off together without looking back.

All around us, everyone collectively let out their breaths.

I wanted to run to the theater and hide, but instantly Liz and Krista were at my side, their arms around me, leading me out of the caf toward the girls' bathroom.

"You did good, chickie," Krista said. "I'm proud of you."

Liz hugged me. "It hurts now, but you'll be okay. We love you."

I wiped at a single tear with my sleeve. I actually felt kind of . . . well, not good, but strong. And like I'd taken back a part of my life.

"I know I did the right thing," I said. "It just, it just—" I let out a shuddering sigh. "It just kind of . . . sucks."

"It does," Krista agreed. "It totally does. But that's why they make chocolate."

WHEN THE FIRE DOOR TO THE STAIRS THUDDED SHUT around eight o'clock on Wednesday night and I heard someone swear, I laid the score to *West Side Story* down. It had sounded like LaVon, but he was working. Then I heard the distinct *click-click-click* of his bicycle as he wheeled it down the hallway. I got up and opened my door a crack.

"Hey, LaVon." He stood in front of his room, balancing his bike against his hip while he dug through his pockets. "How come you're home so early?" I asked.

He shoved the bike against the wall, swore under his breath, and set a brown paper bag on the floor so he had both hands free.

"What's wrong?"

"Nothin'," he said, finally finding his key. He grabbed the bag and the bike and barreled into his room, slamming the door behind him.

I'd already gone back to learning my music when recognition hit me. A familiar sinking feeling whammed me right in the gut. On the side of the paper bag had been the Oregon liquor warning. I ran down the hall to LaVon's room. He hardly ever locked his door when he was home, I guess because he figured no one would mess with him, and I threw it open without knocking. He sat on the bed with the bottle of Jack Daniels between his knees and an empty glass in his hand. I didn't think he'd opened it yet, but I couldn't be sure.

"Get out," he growled.

"You don't want to do that, LaVon," I said, trying to keep my voice steady.

"I said get out."

"What happened?" I asked.

He didn't answer, just fiddled with the bottle. I knew if I could keep him from taking that first drink, he could get through this.

"La—"

"This doesn't concern you."

I stepped all the way into the room and shut the door. "Something happen at work?"

"What part of 'get the hell out' don't you understand?"

"Fine," I said. "I'll go if you give me the bottle." He glared at me, but I held out my hand anyway. "You don't really want it."

"Like hell I don't."

"Tonight, maybe," I said. "But what about tomorrow?"

He didn't answer, and I waited. I made my face as blank as I could, but horrible memories of the times I'd had this same conversation with my dad almost overwhelmed me, making me nauseated with fear. I'd kept him from drinking every time, though, and I could help LaVon if he let me.

"What happened?" I asked again.

He caressed the bottle. "This dickhead at work . . . he just . . . he provoked me, so I punched him."

"A customer?" I asked. I couldn't keep the shock out of my voice.

"No. Another beer guy."

"Did you get fired?"

"Nope. Lucky for both of us, he ducked, and I hit the wall. Left a hole, though, so I got suspended. Three games."

Crap. That meant a lot of lost income for LaVon. He only got minimum wage, but he earned a commission on every beer he sold, plus tips, and made a ton of money that way.

"That sucks," I said.

"No shit."

I had to get that bottle from him. I held out my hand again. "How about if I just hold it for a while?"

"How about if you don't?" he said. "You'll just pour it down the toilet."

I shook my head. "No way. I promise."

For a second I thought he was going to hand it over, but then he unscrewed the top instead. I wanted to remind him about his grand-baby, but I knew it would be a false move. He didn't need the guilt. He needed time to cool off.

"I swear," I said. "I'll just keep it in my room for a while. Then if you want it back, you can come get it." He looked up at me. I knew he didn't want to drink it. We both did. But we also understood the hold it had on him. "LaVon," I said, "I may suck at cleaning, and I can't drive worth a shit, but if there's one thing I know a lot about, it's addiction. Give it to me now, and if you still want it in an hour, it's yours."

He sat there, me staring at him, him glaring at the bottle. His clock radio ticked off five silent, dreadful minutes. Finally, he put the cap back on and handed me the booze. I clutched it to my chest and practically ran for the door.

"Call your sponsor," I suggested on my way out.

"She's in fuckin' Mexico drinking virgin daiquiris with fancy umbrellas."

"Call her anyway."

I didn't wait for his answer.

In my room, I held the bottle in my lap the way LaVon had. I considered having a drink myself, but I knew I wouldn't. Except for that one time, freshman year, when Krista and I had split a bottle of Boones Ferry wine with the college guy who lived up the street from her, I never drank. That night, it had seemed fun at first, but then I couldn't get my words out right, and it scared me.

Everyone I knew got wasted at least once in a while, but I always volunteered to be the designated driver. Driving was just easier than turning it down. My friends all thought of me as responsible instead of scared to death of becoming a drunk. The way I saw it, as a daughter of two alcoholics, I didn't have a fighting chance against the bottle.

I watched the second hand move around on a watch I'd snagged from the lost and found at work. I thought I heard LaVon's voice through the thin wall, hopefully talking to his sponsor, but no matter how much I strained my ears, I couldn't be sure.

Exactly one hour later, his door opened. I thought about not answering mine when he knocked, but I'd promised. I unlocked the deadbolt and handed him the bottle. He walked past me into the bathroom. I heard the glug, glug, glug of the whiskey going down the drain. When he came out, he handed me the empty bottle and went back to his room.

I sank onto my bed, relief flooding me. I knew some people would think I'd taken a chance, that I should've gotten rid of it, but I'd been to enough Alateen meetings to know that you can't stop an addict from drinking. Even if I'd ditched the whiskey, if

171

LaVon wanted to get drunk, he would've gone out and gotten more. I couldn't have stopped him any more than I could stop my dad from joining a cult. People do what they want, especially ones with addictive personalities.

I didn't want LaVon to start drinking again for himself, but in all honesty, I had my own selfish reasons too. In the meetings my grandpa had taken me to, they'd drummed into our heads that as the children of alcoholics, we would be drawn to others with addictions. We'd try to help them because we couldn't help our parents. I'd promised myself back then to never hang out with anyone who had an unchecked addiction problem. If LaVon had had that drink tonight, I would've ended our friendship for my own self-preservation. And missed the only adult in my life a lot, too.

While I was thinking this, I found myself walking up and down my tiny room, swinging the empty bottle ... pacing ... contemplating ... remembering what they'd told us. Was my need to help my dad get away from the Right & the Real any different from my intrinsic need to help addicts? Dad had made his choice. I'd weighed in with my opinions, and he'd ignored them. I was on my own, just as if he'd started drinking again.

And he didn't want my help. That much was clear. The church had taken him from me, but I'd allowed them to take my life too, and suddenly I was really mad at myself about it. I should've been happy and excited to get into drama school, but I couldn't enjoy it because I didn't have a plan to get the deposit. That wasn't like me. I'd always been a fighter, but lately I'd spent so much time feeling sorry for myself I'd forgotten who I was.

I looked around for a Sharpie. I needed a plan. A big plan. One that would get me to New York. I found a red pen in my backpack, but I didn't have a sheet of paper large enough for what I wanted to do, so I wrote right on the wall. Stub could fine me, I didn't care.

It's My Life!!!!!! A Plan for My Future!

The fat red letters looked so satisfying on the wall like that.

"Hmmm . . . let's see," I said aloud. "First things first."

Let my dad live his life.

I'd done everything I could. I'd tried talking to him, calling his therapist, mailing him information, being there for him. If he didn't want my help, well, I just had to get on with my own plans.

Quit West Side Story.

It was drastic, but it had to be done. It was already the middle of February, and I had less than three weeks before my deposit was due. I needed to work as much as I could. I would sacrifice one role in a high school play to make the rest of my career happen. And after that, I needed to save a lot more money for the move to New York, but that was another plan entirely.

Turn down the counselor job at theater camp.

When I'd met the camp director last fall at a theater conference and he'd offered me room and board plus fifty bucks a week to be a counselor this summer, it had sounded great because I knew it would be a blast. But it wasn't a luxury I could afford anymore. I needed to earn a lot more than that. Besides, once basketball was over, LaVon would work at the soccer stadium, and he'd told me he could probably get me a job there, where I could make a bundle selling hot dogs in the stands. Also, they paid people to sing the national anthem, and I intended to try out when they held the auditions. I could rock our country's toughest song.

Don't even think about Josh.

For my own sanity. Sometimes I missed him so much I ached, but it was better this way.

Tell my friends the truth about my dad.

That would have to wait a couple of months. On April 20, I'd be eighteen. I could tell my friends everything then, and no one could do a thing to me. Everyone always says once you turn eighteen, you're an adult, but it had never meant that much to me until now. Once I had my birthday, no one could send me to live with my mom. Also, I would go see my dad's lawyer. He was the trustee for the estate, and I was pretty sure he'd be interested in knowing what my dad was doing with Grandpa's money.

"You know," I said aloud, "I live here now. As awful as this motel is, it's the only home I've got. I might as well unpack." I pulled all my clothes out of the boxes I'd been keeping them in and put them in the crappy dresser. The drawers were hard to open, but so what?

Then I lined up my shoes under the bed, put my makeup in the bathroom cabinet, and opened the box Dad had marked *Stuff Hanging on Your Walls.* I wanted some photos of my friends and the map of Manhattan I'd bought in New York. In the very bottom of the box, under all the loose clippings from the school newspaper about the plays I'd been in, I found the large framed print of Laurence Olivier. It not only had the signed photo, but included a letter of authenticity. And on the back, Grandpa had taped the receipt, in case I had to have extra proof of its worth for any reason.

I took it over to the bed and sat down with it in my lap. Could I do what I had to do? I ran my hand around the edge of the frame, wiping off the dust from years of hanging on my wall. I smiled. . . .

LaVon was right, I was no housekeeper. Grandpa would understand. He'd want me to go to drama school.

I laid it carefully on my bed and added to my list on the wall.

Auction Sir Laurence on eBay.

Once I'd written it down, I knew it was going to be okay. Someday I'd be rich and famous, and I'd hunt it down and buy it back. I thought about opening the carton with my plays and scripts in it, just to thumb through them, but decided against it. My plan had been to wait until I was either at home, which wasn't going to happen, or in New York. For now, I'd leave them sealed up. It would be like a reward when I finally got there.

I had settled onto my bed to admire my list when I thought of one last thing.

Get rid of the Beast somehow.

There *had* to be a way to order a replacement title. Unloading it would solve almost all my problems at once. I should've been a little more careful about how I worded that last item on the list, though.

21

I SAT IN THE PASSENGER SEAT OF THE BEAST, SIPPING
my third mocha of the morning while Krista drove us to school. I'd
told her a story about a cute guy at the Coffee Klatch giving me free
coffee to explain why I'd been getting it there for the last two weeks
instead of stopping at our usual place. Krista always paid me back for
hers, which was good because only mine was free. My hands shook a
little, and I couldn't tell if it was because of the caffeine or because I
was nervous about telling her my plans. Probably both.

You'd think since Krista was the costume designer and not actually in the musical, she wouldn't care if I quit, but I knew she'd lose it
when I told her. If you're not into theater, or you only do it for a laugh,
then it's no big deal to miss a production here or there, but if you're
serious about it, your senior year, the musical is like . . . like what
prom is to all the popular girls. It's what the whole four years have
been building up to. And just because Krista worked in the costume
shop did not mean she'd be okay with me giving up *West Side*.

"Are you all right?" she asked.

"Yeah. Why?"

"Because you're acting kind of weird. You're smiling, but it doesn't seem real. You look like you're going to throw up."

That was exactly how I felt too.

"Well . . . I have some good news and some bad news," I said.

"Do tell." The Beast swerved a little into the next lane when she glanced over at me.

"Watch out," I said. She looked over at me again, making a face, and a car honked at her because she'd almost clipped its rear bumper. "Maybe I'll tell you when we get to school. You should concentrate."

"Just tell me now," she said. "How bad could it be?"

"Well . . . I have to get a job."

I saw her body tense up. "And?"

I spit it out fast. "I have to drop out of *West Side Story*."

"I missed the good news," she said.

"The job," I told her, trying to put a spin on it with a big smile. "Money for New York. We're moving to New York, remember?"

"Why would you want a job now, though?"

"I don't *want* a job," I explained. "I *need* one."

"Oh, yeah . . . Miss Princess *needs* a job. That's a laugh."

Tears pooled in my eyes, and I stared out the window. "I'm not happy about quitting either," I said.

"You can't drop out. It's our senior year. This is supposed to be our last big thing together. I have designed the most gorgeous dresses for Maria, and I know you'll beat Liz out for the part. Mr. Lazby practically told me that."

"Really?" I felt my resolve waver.

"He said they'd be for a petite actress. Does that sound like Liz?"

Oh, man . . . I wanted to play Maria so badly. I wished she hadn't told me.

She pointed at the dashboard. "That's weird. The fuel light just came on."

Crap. I'd been driving on fumes and prayers for days.

"Did it?" I said.

We came up to the huge intersection closest to the school, which is always dangerous in the morning because kids are usually racing to get to class. Instead of paying extra attention, Krista was tapping the gas gauge with her green fingernail as if that would somehow miraculously make it work.

"Oh! My! God! Krista!" I grabbed the dash as she barreled through a red light. Two cars honked at us, one from each side in stereo. A blue compact swerved, missing the passenger door by inches. "Ohmygod, ohmygod, ohmygod!"

My whole world slowed down, and it really was like they say, going into a tunnel. Everything around me closed in, instantly giving the feeling of claustrophobia. Somehow we made it across the frantic intersection without being killed, though, and everything sped up instantly. I clutched my seat, my heart thudding so hard I thought it would explode. Krista's face had gone white, but she recovered faster than I did.

"It was yellow," she said.

It was so red.

Blue lights flashed next to us, and Krista pulled over into the bike lane and turned off the engine. A minute later, Officer Pepper from the Doughnut Shoppe parking lot walked up to the driver's side window, and Krista rolled it down. I turned my head away, hoping the cop wouldn't recognize me.

"Good morning," she said in a flat sort of voice. "Do you know why I pulled you over?"

"Yes," Krista said. "I'm sorry. I'm really, really sorry. I didn't mean to run it, but the gas light came on, and it distracted me for a second because I thought the tank was full, and . . . and . . ." She burst into tears.

"It's all right," the officer said. "Just take a deep breath. No one was hurt."

"I'm . . . I'm sorry," Krista said, again.

"I'm sure you're a little shaken," she said, still in that monotone voice. Somehow it sounded reassuring, and my heart finally started to beat at its normal pace again. "Everybody's okay. Take a second to calm down, and when you're ready, I need to see your license and registration."

Krista gulped back her sobs, and I was grateful she had all her purple hair tucked up inside her newsboy hat. You never knew how authority figures would react to her look, but she almost passed for normal today.

I dug the paperwork out of the glove compartment while Krista wiped her eyes with a paper napkin and got her license out of her purse. "It's not my car," she told the officer. She nodded at me. "It's Jamie's. Her dad said it's okay if I drive it."

"You two sit tight, and I'll be back in a minute," the officer said, taking the registration and insurance info.

I didn't know what Krista was doing because I couldn't make myself look at her, but I could hear her sniffling, and it made my stomach heave. She never cried.

"That's so weird about the gauge," she finally said. "Did you know it was broken?"

"I forgot to get gas," I admitted.

I could feel her looking at me, but I stared at a muddy spot on the floor mat. "How'd you forget?" she asked. "You said you were on your way to the Quikmart right after I gave you the weekly gas money."

"I know. I just . . . spaced it."

I couldn't tell Krista I'd paid part of my rent with her cash. I'd planned to use this morning's tips to fill up, but we'd had a huge rush right when it was time to go and Trent had told me to pick them up after school.

"My mom is going to kill me," she said. "This is all your fault."

"My fault? I didn't run a red light."

"Yellow!" she said.

"Right."

"If you'd gotten gas like you were supposed to, I wouldn't have been distracted."

I was practically in tears myself by then. "I'm sorry, okay?"

She took a deep breath and let it out slowly. "Okay. . . ."

Krista reached over and took my hand in hers, and my insides immediately tightened. It reminded me just a little too much of something her mom might do right before she asked me a probing question. And it turned out I had good reason to be worried.

"Jamie," she said, "don't get mad at me, but I have to ask you this. Are you on drugs?"

I yanked my hand out of hers. "Don't be stupid."

"It's not *me* being stupid."

"Uh, excuse me, but have you ever seen me do drugs?" I demanded. "Why would you even think that?"

"Because you've been acting so weird lately. You're never there for me. You don't want to hang out. You let Josh talk you into a secret relationship. You're totally broke all the time, and now you're quitting the play. You don't think that's crazy behavior for you?"

Now it was my turn to glare at her, but she met my stare, and I ended up looking away first. In my mirror, I saw Officer Salt placing a flare behind the Beast. I sat there, my arms crossed, refusing to talk to her about it. First LaVon asked me if I did drugs, now my best friend. Did I act like my mother? I don't think so. Not to mention, I'd broken up with Josh. What did she want from me?

About five more minutes passed and then Pepper was back. "Bad news, ladies. The insurance policy was canceled two weeks ago."

"Are you serious?" I asked.

She looked at me like I was crazy. Of course she was serious. She was a police officer. I was so dumb I couldn't believe it. If Dad had canceled my phone, he wouldn't keep paying for something expensive like insurance. The officer handed Krista her license and a ticket.

"What's this?" Krista asked.

"Citation for driving without insurance and running a red light."

"Why am I in trouble for not having insurance?" she asked. "It's Jamie's car."

"I understand that," Pepper said, "but you're the one driving. When you go to court, take some proof that you're personally insured, and maybe it will be dropped. I'm sorry, but because the vehicle is uninsured, I am going to have to impound it."

"But—" I said.

"Here's the information on how to get it back." She handed me a slip of paper.

"So what do we do now?" I asked her.

"Get anything you want before the tow truck comes, and then I guess you should probably phone someone for a ride."

She went back to her cruiser, and Krista said, "Call your dad. Maybe he can straighten this out before it gets here."

"I can't," I said. "He's in a meeting this morning."

"But—" Krista said.

"Let's just get our stuff and go to school. It's not that far."

Krista stood there scowling while I took everything out of the glove compartment. I dug a few library books from under the seat and then we started walking the half mile to school.

"You should've called your dad," Krista said as we walked.

"He can't answer calls today."

"Not even for an emergency? Like what if we'd had an accident?"

I sighed. "I don't know . . . I just know I can't get him on the phone." She'd probably accuse me of being a meth addict just because I couldn't reach my dad. "Can we drop it?"

"Fine. Whatever."

We walked along in silence, my dance bag cutting into one shoulder and my backpack digging into the other. We were still a few blocks from the school when it started to drizzle. Fantastic. Exactly what I needed to round out my perfect morning.

I would never have the money to get the Beast out of hock. And how was I going to get to school every day now? Could my life possibly suck any more than this?

22

"KARMA." LAVON SAID WHEN I TOLD HIM ABOUT the Beast being towed away.

"What did I ever do to deserve all the crap that's happening to me lately?" I asked.

He loaded a bowl with the linguine he'd tossed with a white, creamy sauce and handed it to me. I sat on his only chair and waited while he served himself. It was the first time I'd seen him since the whiskey incident, and neither of us mentioned it.

"Not your karma," he said. "Your dad's."

"How do you mean?"

"You're shit outta luck over the title 'cause he disappeared, right?"

"Yeah."

"And you couldn't get a new one 'cause his name's on it."

"Uh-huh."

LaVon grated some Parmesan onto my pasta and then ground fresh black pepper over it.

"And he canceled your insurance, which was not cool. But . . . who gets the bill for towing and storage?" he asked.

"Ohhh . . . I see."

"Karma."

"Yep. I guess. But how am I going to get to school?"

"Simple. Bicycle."

I glanced at the huge bike he had hanging from the ceiling.

"Not mine," he said. "We'll get you a used one."

"I don't have much money." I'd have to pay Krista back her fifty dollars gas money too.

"I know a guy," LaVon said. "Eat that food, and we'll walk over to his house."

I hoped it wouldn't be a stolen bike, but I was too afraid of offending him to ask. "Okay. Thanks."

"No prob."

LaVon's friend had a whole garage full of bikes, but they weren't stolen. They were all donations. He fixed them up to give to people at the homeless shelters so they could get around the city. The bike LaVon chose for me was pale green where it wasn't rusty, but he said not to worry about appearances because then no one would want to steal it. The chain creaked and looked like it would snap any second, and the seat leaked yellowed foam padding, but his friend had given him replacement parts.

"No offense, but this bike's a piece of crap," I said.

"You need to chill," he told me as we walked it home. "I told you. It's mostly cosmetic. I can fix it."

"By tomorrow morning?" I asked.

"Yeah, right. You'll be walking from the bus stop, so leave early."

"I doubt Trent will let me. I'll just have to miss first period."

"I'll write you a note," he said.

"Really?"

He shook his head and grinned at me. "No. Not really. You so gull-ible it's amazin' you survived this long on your own."

But we both knew I wasn't on my own.

On Friday morning, I watched Trent make a design on a cup of hot water with milk foam. His latest plan for raising money for NYU was to win ten grand in Las Vegas at one of those contests for baristas where they drew fancy pictures on cappuccinos. He practiced whenever it was slow.

Trent had been almost cold to me the first couple days after the big Valentine flower delivery, and even now that he was acting friendly again, he'd totally stopped flirting with me. I wanted to tell him I'd broken up with Josh, but I was afraid it would look like I was desperate for a boyfriend. Also, I'd flirted with him a lot when I had one. Now that he knew that about me, he might not trust me very much any-more. That made two of us. It seemed like every time I turned around, I discovered I'd lost sight of everything I thought I was.

"Maybe I should learn that too," I said. "I could use the money for New York."

He pushed his bangs out of his eyes, and I couldn't help wishing I'd done it. His hair looked so soft.

"What you should do," Trent said, "is find an agent and get some auditions. I bet you could cash in."

"Wouldn't that be cool?" I said. "A national commercial could pay for the whole program."

I'd considered trying to land a local agent before, but there wasn't a lot of work in Portland. Still, maybe I would look for one after graduation.

"I closed for Amanda last night," Trent said.

I could see the tip of his tongue sticking out between his teeth as he concentrated. Just like Krista when she sketched.

"Yeah?" I couldn't tell what the picture was yet, but it looked like a horse's head.

"That guy came in looking for you."

A little shock of alarm raced through me. "What guy?"

"The one who was here before. Blond crew cut. Looks like a linebacker."

"Josh?"

Trent shrugged and added a horn to the horse's head, turning it into a unicorn. "I guess. I don't know his name."

With my new resolve to take my life back, I'd thrown off all thoughts of Josh. Or at least I'd tried. But sometimes I still missed him. It had only been four days, after all. Still, I was curious. "What'd he want?"

"Well," Trent said, finishing his design with a flourish and then dumping it out before I could even compliment him, "I guess he wanted you. He said he was your boyfriend."

Trent looked up at me, a question in his brown eyes.

I shook my head. "He's not," I said. "I mean, he was. But he's not now."

"Good to know," he said, without a smile. And then he went into the back room, leaving me standing there to help a couple of customers who had just come in.

I was on my way to school when he called my name.

"Hey, Jamie, I almost forgot. That guy, Jon or whatever his name was, left you this." He held out a napkin with Josh's handwriting on it.

I read it aloud. "Blue Raspberry Popsicles?"

"He said you'd know what it meant."

"No clue." I tossed the napkin into the garbage.

I'd have to find Josh and ask him. Also, I wanted to remind him he was no longer my boyfriend.

Krista was at the locker when I got there right before fourth period. "Hi," I said. "Hold the door. I need my shoes."

She slammed it like she hadn't heard me, but we both knew she had.

"Oh, sorry," she said, her voice icy.

"Whatever." I spun the combination.

"Thanks for picking me up this morning," she said, the sarcasm dripping all over the floor.

"What? I don't have a car, remember?"

"You could've called."

I sighed. "You know they towed the Beast away."

"So what? I figured you'd borrow your dad's car or something. I was late to first period."

"How would my dad get to work if I took his car?" I immediately felt a pang of guilt, because this lying thing was getting way too easy. I didn't even have to try anymore.

I could feel her glare burning into me. "Oh, and even though you don't care enough to ask, my mom said I'm covered by her insurance, so I shouldn't lose my license or anything."

I slammed my math book onto the shelf. "Krista. I care, okay? And I'm sorry I didn't ask, but I just walked up, and you went off on me. Jeez. Give me a break."

"Why don't you give me one? Just tell me what the hell is going on with you?"

I dug through the junk on the bottom of the locker, looking for my jazz shoes. The ballet unit in PE was over, and we were changing to modern dance today. "Nothing is going on, okay?" I gave up looking for my shoes. I'd just go barefoot. It wasn't like it was a real class at Bright Lights, where I'd have to sit out if I didn't have my shoes. I left Krista standing there.

At lunchtime, I went to the theater to find Mr. Lazby. I'd missed English because I'd worked late and then had to take the bus and walk two miles. And we'd had a sub the day before, so I hadn't seen him yet to tell him I was dropping out of the musical. I figured he'd consider me a traitor for choosing a job over *West Side,* and I was right. I found him hunched over the sewing machine, yards of blue-checked fabric pooled around him as he sewed what looked like a nineteen-fifties poodle skirt.

"Hi, Mr. Lazby," I said.

He kept his eyes on his work. "Jamie."

The way he said my name told me he knew already. "I guess you heard."

"It's your life," he said. "I saved *West Side Story* for your senior year because I knew you'd shine, but it's not a big deal."

Okay . . . could he make me feel any worse? It wasn't like quitting was something I *wanted* to do.

"I need a job," I said. "To pay for New York."

His posture straightened a little.

"You're the one who always says high school theater is just for fun. That even if we're really good here, it doesn't mean anything in the real world," I reminded him. "I'm thinking of the big picture."

The sewing machine buzzed as the needle pierced the fabric and he pushed the material along.

"Mr. Lazby," I said, sounding a lot like I was begging, but trying not to, "what do you always tell us? *To be a professional, personal sacrifice is required.* Right?"

Finally, he shoved the material aside, and the smile that flashed across his face was the one of a young man who still had dreams of being a pro himself. "You're right," he said. "I just hate to lose my star pupil. What if I gave you a couple of days off each week so you could get a job?"

I knew how that would work. He'd say I could have Sundays, Tuesdays, and Thursdays off, or something like that, and then after a week or two, he'd be scheduling me those days anyway. "Thanks, but I need to be more flexible than that," I said.

"Are you sure?" he asked. "Because I was counting on you to play Maria."

An arrow plunged into my heart. To hear him actually say it almost killed me. My mind whizzed around like a rat trying different avenues of escape from the maze. There had to be some way I could play the lead after all. I shook off the thought, reminding myself I'd be a pro someday. There'd be other chances for fantastic parts.

By now, I was sure Krista had told Liz I was quitting the musical, and she was probably already learning Maria's lines. "You've got Liz Rafferty," I said, trying not to choke on the big lump in my throat.

He shrugged. "True." That was so not what I wanted to hear. "But no one sings quite like you," Mr. Lazby said, making me feel a little better. "Still, if you need a job, you need a job. That's life."

I made myself smile. "Yeah. . . ."

Acting was a weird profession. I'd always felt that . . . well, because I was probably the most talented in our school, I sort of ruled the drama department. At least as far as the girls were concerned. But

Mr. Lazby had inadvertently given me my first lesson. Everyone can be recast, because there's always someone just as good waiting in the wings.

I wanted to avoid Krista, and there were only four minutes of lunch left by the time I finished talking with Mr. Lazby, so I jogged through the halls, hoping I wouldn't get stopped by a teacher. I could see something bright yellow sticking out of one of the vents of a locker, and when I got up close, I saw it was ours.

I yanked out a piece of folded-up cardboard and smoothed it flat. A Popsicle box? Okay, that was too weird to be a coincidence. First the note at work and now this. What was Josh up to? He obviously had something to tell me, but ever since the scene in the caf on Monday, he hadn't come near me. This was just stupid.

I peered around every corner looking for him on my way to class, but didn't have any luck. A weird thing did happen, though. I got a flash of a memory from when I was little, before Mom had started drinking her breakfast and my parents' marriage had fallen apart. I was sitting on concrete steps eating a blue Popsicle. I must've been about three. Both my mom and dad were in the yard eating them with me, and we were laughing at Mom because she'd used her cherry one like lipstick and painted her mouth clown red. Dad had the same flavor as me, and he waggled a blue tongue at us. I stuck mine out at him, grinning.

But what could that have to do with Josh? Nothing, as far as I could figure out. The warning bell rang, and I shook off the vision as the halls flooded with noisy kids. Something more than that memory did nag at me, though. What the hell was he trying to tell me?

I'D FOUND A NOTE DURING MY MORNING SHIFT FROM Amanda asking me to fill in for Jezziray that night, so after school, I went back to the motel to drop off my bag and change before heading over to the Coffee Klatch. I wanted to say no to an extra shift because I was so tired that the stairs felt like Mount Everest, but I needed the money. Plus it was Friday night, and the motel would be crazy with partiers.

I'd just set my bag down when I heard LaVon rap on the wall between us—one loud thump followed by three, sharp raps meant he wanted to see me. After triple-checking my door was locked behind me, I dropped by.

"What's up?" I said.

"Whaddaya think?" he asked.

He'd polished the bike within an inch of its life. The chain glistened black and oily, there was a shiny new seat, and he'd even cleaned the tires. He'd added a rack to the back and stuck a secondhand blue helmet in a wire basket attached to the handlebars.

"Wow. It looks fantastic."

"Wanna try it out?" he asked.

"Yeah . . . oh, no . . . I can't. I have to work, but tomorrow, okay?"

"That's cool," he said. "I got group tonight anyway." I was glad to hear he was going to AA. "What time you done?" he asked.

"About twelve thirty."

"I'll be there. Don't be walking home alone."

"I won't. Thanks."

I started to leave without the bike. "Take your ride. This ain't no storage warehouse."

"Oh, right. Sorry." As I wheeled it out the door, it occurred to me that LaVon must've put a bunch of time into fixing it up. "Ummm . . . LaVon? Can I give you some money?"

"For what?"

"Your labor."

"Nah," he said. "It was fun."

"But—"

"Seriously, we're cool. The way I see it, one less SUV out there messin' up the planet."

I grinned. "That's true. Thanks."

"Later."

The Coffee Klatch didn't open until eight o'clock on Sundays, and Trent offered me a few hours doing the weekly inventory and supply order with him before the morning staff arrived, so I jumped at it for more reason than one, but I told myself it was only for the money, and not his company. Because it was pitch-black at five thirty in the morning, I always ran with my pepper spray in one hand. When I got there, the café was still dark, but a car came around the corner, its headlights cutting through the night. Trent's engine shuddered to a stop. He climbed out, rumpled and unshaven.

"Whose stupid idea was it to come in on a Sunday?" he asked me.

"Yours," I said.

"Right. What was I thinking?"

That we could be alone? Instead I said, "That we could get the inventory done without interruption?"

He dug around in his pocket for the front door keys and then realized he was already holding them in his other hand. "Coffee," he mumbled. "I need coffee."

We crossed the room without turning on the main lights. "I don't know why you're so tired," I said. "You get up this early every day."

"To say I got up implies I went to bed," he said.

"You've been awake all night?"

"I think so. I'm too tired to remember for sure."

"What were you doing?" I asked, hoping he wasn't out on a date.

"Video game marathon with my roommate."

Geeky, but still . . . it made me happy.

He flipped on the lights behind the counter and turned on the espresso maker. Within minutes, we were each holding steaming cups. I licked the whipped cream off the top of my mocha, waiting for it to cool a bit, and eyed Trent, who was already downing a triple shot of espresso, scalding hot and black.

For the first half hour or so, we worked mostly in sleepy silence, moving bags of coffee and boxes of tea around in the storage room, Trent counting, me noting it down. And then the caffeine kicked in.

"Sleep is for pussies," Trent said, pumping his fist in the air.

"Totally overrated," I agreed.

He jumped up and down on the balls of his feet like a fighter. "I feel great."

"Must be your second wind."

"My second wind was around midnight. This is at least my third or fourth wind." He put his arm around me like we were a couple of football players in a huddle. "What's next?" he asked.

All I could think about was that he was touching me for the first time in almost a week.

"Yo? Earth to Jamie. What's next?" he asked again.

I looked at my clipboard. "Uh . . . chocolate coffee beans."

"Watch this." He took a handful of beans out of an open bag and tossed one in the air, catching it in his mouth. "Bet you can't do that."

"Oh, you're on," I said. "I'm awesome at this game." I threw a bean in the air and caught it easily, crunching it between my teeth, the sweet chocolate and bitter coffee giving me a little jolt of pleasure.

"You're good," he said. "Still, bet I can catch more in a row."

"What's the bet?" I asked.

"I win," he said, "you tell me a secret."

"And if I kick your ass, which is definitely going to happen?"

"I'll clean the bathrooms for a week."

"Deal." He knew I hated that job more than anything else. Plus, there was no way I was telling him any of my secrets.

We played rock, paper, scissors to see who had to go first. Trent lost, and I counted aloud as he threw bean after bean into the air, his mouth opening like a gasping fish. He got to seven before he took his eye off the ball and the bean bounced against his chin and skittered across the floor.

"Seven?" I said. "That's all you've got?"

"Put your money where your mouth is," he said, handing me the bag of beans.

I had an unfair advantage over Trent in that this was a game we played in the wings of the theater all the time. We didn't use coffee beans, but Hot Tamales were almost the same size. When I caught number eight, I offered Trent double-or-nothing odds.

"You're on," he said.

I flipped a bean into the air, but before I could catch it, a hand reached out and snagged it. "Hey," I said, grabbing at him. "Cheater!" I tried to wrestle it away from him, but he held his arm way up over my head. I pulled at his shoulder, but Trent was solid. Through his shirt, I felt his muscles flexing against my fingers.

"I can't let you win," he said, laughing. "How would it look if the boss was scrubbing toilets?"

"You totally cheated." I yanked on his arm, and when he lowered his hand, I thought he was giving in, but he popped the bean into his mouth and put his other arm around my waist.

"Since you lost," he said, "you have to tell me a secret."

It was stupid, because we were just flirting and messing around, but I panicked. All the fun drained out of me like someone had yanked the stopper out of the sink. Maybe I was just tired, but I couldn't think of a single innocent secret to tell him. Nothing.

All I could come up with was the truth—My mom was a druggie in Hollywood doing God knew what, my dad had disowned me and joined a cult, I lived alone in a skanky motel, my best friend was still mad I'd dropped out of *West Side.* . . . Those were not the kinds of secrets Trent had in mind, and yet they were all I could think of. I pulled away, putting the width of the small storage room between us.

"What's next on the list?" I asked, picking up my clipboard.

He took a step toward me and I took one away. "What'd I do?" he asked, baffled.

I felt kind of bewildered by my reaction too, but I guess when I was dating Josh, all the flirting with Trent seemed totally harmless, and now it was maybe a little too intense for me to deal with. I had a lot on my plate these days.

"You didn't do anything," I said. I tried to laugh and keep my voice light. "I just don't really do secrets. Besides. I totally won, and you're a cheater."

He rubbed the back of his neck, looking confused. I really wanted to pull him close to me and tell him my *real* secrets, but how could I? It was funny, but a few weeks ago, I might've confided in Trent. Now I liked him too much. Now I didn't want him to know how screwed up my family was, how I'd let my boyfriend keep me a secret, and how afraid I was every night when I locked my door and climbed under my comforter.

"Anyway," I said, "it looks like we need to check on the filters next."

"Jamie, I didn't mean some deep dark secret. I was thinking more like when your birthday is or your favorite flower or something lame like that."

I fumbled with some boxes. "Yeah, I know. Ignore me. I just hate losing." I nudged him with my elbow. "Especially to a cheater. And you still have to clean the toilets all week too. I am soooo not letting you out of that one."

He smiled, but I could tell his heart wasn't in it anymore. By the time the morning crew showed up, all the inventory was recorded and we'd placed the supply order online. We were both so buzzed on caffeine that we'd slid back into our normal give-and-take joking-around mode, but again, he didn't try to touch me, and I'd kept distance between us too.

Trent was getting in his car as I came out. "See you tomorrow," he said, slamming the door.

"Yeah, okay." I rapped on his window and he rolled it down. "April twentieth," I said. "Daffodils."

"What?" he asked.

I smiled and walked off.

I kept meaning to list my Olivier picture on eBay, but Saturday was really busy with dance class and rehearsal, and then there was the inventory on Sunday. I could've made the time, but I guess I still felt bad about doing it at all.

After I clocked out on Monday morning, I made myself sign onto one of the computers and set up my auction. I debated over how long to make it last, and decided to go with five days because I still had two weeks before the deposit was due. I set it up to end on Saturday the twenty-sixth of February, with a minimum bid of three hundred dollars. Grandpa had paid six hundred almost four years ago, but I had to get what I could for it. I hoped the low price would interest more bidders.

The bike had seemed like a great idea when I rode it around the block on Saturday, but plowing through a driving rain that morning, I changed my mind. I arrived at school soaking wet, frozen, and exhausted. "This really sucks," I told my bike as I snapped the bar lock into place with bright red fingers.

Krista had barely spoken to me since the Beast got towed away, so when I got inside and she ran up to me and gave me a big hug, I dropped my bike helmet in surprise.

"Oh, my God!" she said. "You're soaked."

"I know, sorry." The front of her faux-fur leopard-print sweater was damp from my wet jacket. "I rode my bike."

"When are you getting the Beast back?" Krista asked.

Unless the Olivier picture sold for a small fortune, I'd never be able to get it from the towing company or buy insurance, so it was probably just going to rot there. "I'm not. Dad's going to . . . he wants to sell it."

I expected her to freak out, but instead she gave me a very compassionate look and said, "Oh . . . right . . . makes sense."

I didn't know why Dad selling the Beast made sense to her, but before I could ask, Liz showed up. She gave me a quick hello hug. "Ooohh . . . you're all wet."

"She rode her bike," Krista said, giving Liz a look I didn't understand. "Her dad's selling the Beast."

"Ohhh, right," she said, nodding.

What was up with them? The warning bell rang, and we headed to class.

"Oh, Krista," I said, "I almost forgot. Your gas money." It killed me to hand it over, but it wasn't like I could keep it.

"Oh, don't worry about it," she said, pushing my hand away.

I stopped walking. "I'm not going to be driving you anymore."

"I know, but it's all right. My dad gave it to me. He has no idea how I get to school."

"Well, you keep it, then," I said.

"Forget about it. No biggie." She turned to Liz. "Did you do the calculus homework?"

Okay. Something was definitely going on here because we were talking fifty bucks, not fifty cents. Krista sold her designer clothes on her website for what I thought of as a lot of money, but she definitely wasn't rich. She needed to save for New York too. We were at my classroom by then, so I put the cash in my pocket to deal with later.

On Tuesday, the late February rains had given way to clear blue skies, and it made me think that maybe spring would come early this year. My auction was up to five hundred eighteen dollars too, so at least I knew I could make my deposit, which was a huge relief. I didn't have much time to celebrate it, though, because I was behind with all my homework, and three of my teachers kept me after class to give me the lecture about how they understood senioritis but it didn't give me permission to slack off.

And then, right after sixth period, I found another yellow Popsicle box shoved through the locker vent. This time, when I smoothed it out, I saw Josh had circled *Blue Raspberry* with a black Sharpie. This was getting ridiculous. What was his problem? If he had something to say, why did he keep avoiding me?

On the bike ride home, I decided if I couldn't find Josh to ask him directly, then I'd just have to try and figure out what he wanted me to know. Blue Raspberry *did* mean something to me, but I couldn't remember what. My concentration was split between avoiding getting run over by traffic and trying to dig up a memory that made sense. But even though I was preoccupied, I still noticed I was being followed.

LAVON STEPPED OUT FOR A SMOKE JUST AS I RODE UP.
I could've thrown my arms around him, I was so relieved.

"Someone's following me," I said.

He turned his head almost imperceptibly, but I knew under his
shades he was scanning the area.

"It's that red station wagon in the McDonald's parking lot."

"I'll take care of it."

"Wait," I said, doubting myself. "Maybe I'm imagining it."

"Well?" he asked.

"I don't know." I leaned my bike against the dead shrubs. "I got
this eerie feeling I was being followed. I guess because that car was
going really slowly, just sort of creeping along."

He pulled a half-crumpled cigarette out of his pocket and lit it
with a match, sucking in the smoke. LaVon didn't believe in lighters,
because they ended up in landfills. "Maybe it's just some old lady."

"Maybe, but then I stopped at the dollar store for peanut butter," I
said. "And the station wagon was parked in the lot when I came out.
Now it's across the street."

He positioned his hand down by his side so the smoke wouldn't blow in my face and gave me his slow grin. "Who would tail you, anyways? Trent?"

"Very funny," I said. "I don't know. Someone from the church, maybe?"

That idea seemed to get his attention. "All right," he said. He flicked the cherry off the end of his cigarette and tapped it against the building to make sure it was out. Then he put what was left of it back in the pack. "You take your bike upstairs, and I'll wait in the lobby and see what they do."

"Okay. Thanks, LaVon."

"No prob."

I half dragged, half carried my bike upstairs. As soon as I had dumped it inside my room, I went back out to the stairwell to see if I could hear anything. A few minutes passed, but nothing happened. And then a girl let out a little scream; this was followed by LaVon's rumbly voice. The door at the bottom of the stairs opened, and I heard footsteps.

"Walk," LaVon said.

"Where are you taking us? Where's Jamie?" asked a high-pitched voice.

"You better let us go, or I'm calling the police!" said another girl's voice. This one I recognized.

LaVon came around the landing, herding Krista and Liz in front of him. They both had wrapped their heads in black scarves and sported huge, dark sunglasses.

"Friends of yours?" he asked me.

"Well, it's so hard to tell," I said, "what with their excellent disguises."

"What's going on?" Krista asked.

201

"I could ask you the same thing," I said.

LaVon shook his head. "I'll leave you ladies to it."

We left the "mysterious red station wagon," which turned out to belong to Liz's aunt, in the parking lot, and walked over to the Coffee Klatch to talk. A few minutes later, the three of us settled onto a couple of couches with our drinks. Krista and I were slumped into our seats, but not Liz. Her back was so straight she looked like a puppet on a taut string.

Krista scanned the little café. "So where's the cute guy who gives you free coffee?"

"He works the morning shift . . . with me. He's my boss. I work here." Eighties music blasted over the sound system, making it hard for me to think. "Look, I'm sorry," I said.

"Are you going to tell us what for?" Liz asked.

"Yeah . . . I guess," I said.

"Jamie," Krista said, "we know your dad lost his job and he has to sell his house. It's not a crime to be poor."

"Lots of people are losing their homes," Liz said.

Krista wrapped her arm around my shoulder and squeezed. "We're here for you."

"What do you mean?" I asked. "About my dad and his job?"

"We went to your house last weekend to take you out for some fun. We saw the house was for sale," she explained. "On Monday morning, I called your dad at the newspaper to ask him if he thought you were okay, but they told us he hadn't worked there for several months."

I'd never bothered to tell Krista he'd quit because I was embarrassed he was writing propaganda for the church instead of working at a real job.

"So we put one and one together," Liz said.

"Anyway, we figured out he lost his job and the house, and that's why you've been acting so weird lately," Krista said.

I have to admit, I contemplated letting their deductions stand. What would it hurt if they thought Dad, Mira, and I lived in the motel while he looked for work? The thing was, I'd never lied to either of them before all this, and the guilt had gnawed at my insides like slow-working acid for weeks now. I knew if I set them straight, I'd feel better, but I didn't know if they'd forgive me for lying all this time.

I sighed. "That's not exactly what happened," I said. "Do you guys promise not to tell anyone?"

They nodded.

"Pinky swear." Krista held out her hand.

"It's more important than that," I said. "Krista, you have to promise not to tell your mom."

She'd lined her eyes with what looked like a purple crayon, and they bugged out at me. "You're pregnant," she said.

"No. Don't be stupid." I took a deep breath and let it out slowly. "Okay. . . ."

And then, like they say in court, I told them the whole truth, and nothing but the truth.

"Ohhh, Jamie," Krista said, when I was finished, "I wish you'd said something before." She pulled me up off the couch and wrapped her arms around me. Liz joined in, encircling both of us. At that point, I burst into tears because I was so relieved they knew.

We stood there, all of us crying, until a familiar voice said, "Can I get in on this hug too?"

We pulled apart. Trent grinned at us.

"Do we know you?" Krista asked.

He put his arm around my shoulder and squeezed. "I'm the cute guy who gives Jamie free coffee every morning."

"You heard that?" I asked. *Oh, God. How embarrassing.*

"I hear everything that happens in the Coffee Klatch," he said in a silly deep voice. "Bwahahahaah." I guess he realized the look I gave him was not admiration for his eavesdropping skills because he added, "That's all I heard. Really. I was just walking by at the right moment."

"So you're the boss?" Krista asked.

"That's him," I said. "Trent, meet Krista and Liz."

"Hey," he said. "Jamie's told me all about you."

"She has?" Krista asked.

"Not really, but that's what you're supposed to say, right?" He still had his arm draped over my shoulder, and the heat of it was burning into me, making me feel a bit . . . well, fluttery.

"How come you're here now?" I asked, trying to think about something besides how close he was standing to me.

"Upgrading the computers," he said. "So do you want to tell Dr. Trent why you were all hugging and crying in the middle of the café?"

"Not really," I said.

Trent's grin was contagious, though, and I started to giggle at the absurdity of it all . . . us sobbing in the Coffee Klatch, me keeping all this from my friends, and Trent . . . cute Trent with the coffee-colored eyes and movie camera tattoo. Krista began to laugh too, and before we knew it, we were all cracking up.

"I feel so much better," I said, wiping at the tears.

"Me too," Trent said.

I shoved him down onto the couch, and he pulled me next to him. My friends sat across from us smiling like they'd never seen anything so adorable. Sheesh. All I'd said was he was cute. We weren't a couple or anything.

"So what do we do now?" I asked.

"Let's go bowling," Trent suggested.

"Bowling?" the rest of us said together.

"That's kind of random," Krista added.

"I'm a random kind of guy," Trent said. "No, seriously, it'll be cool. You get to wear those funky shoes and throw things. It's a great stress reliever. And you guys all look really tense."

"And they have those goopy fake-cheese nachos," Liz added.

"Exactly," Trent said. "Let's go."

Krista rode to Twenty-One Lanes with Liz, and I went with Trent. I sank into the front seat of his car and for the first time in forever, I felt so relaxed.

"Has LaVon told you anything about my circumstances?" I asked.

"Well . . . ," he said. I could tell he didn't want to rat out LaVon.

"It's okay."

"All he really said was you're on your own and you rent the room next to him."

"Yeah. . . . So do you even *want* to know my story, or would that be too much information?"

We'd stopped at a red light. "If you're ready to tell me," he said.

"Are you as good of a guy as you appear to be?"

"Definitely not." I could hear the laughter behind his serious tone.

I didn't believe it. He *was* one of the good ones. At least, I hoped so. The light changed, and someone honked behind us.

"Well," I said, "that guy, Josh . . . he was my boyfriend, but he belonged to this crazy church."

I was still talking when we got to the bowling alley. I told Trent

205

everything. Even about Mom's drug problems and how afraid I was that if anyone found out I was on my own, they'd send me to live with her. He didn't say much, but I knew he was listening. After a while, it occurred to me that I'd had this potentially great support network around me all this time and I'd been afraid to use it because I thought I had to be strong and take care of myself just to prove I wasn't like my mother. When I ran out of things to say, we sat there, but it wasn't awkward. Peaceful, actually. Liz and Krista got out of their car and waved at us, pointing at the bowling alley, indicating they'd be inside, and we waved back.

"So this Josh guy," Trent finally said, "he's out of the picture?"

"Completely," I said.

Except for the stupid Popsicle thing. I still had to track him down and find out what that was all about.

Trent nodded his head. "Cool."

"But I owe you an apology," I said.

"For what?"

Oh, God. This was going to be the hardest part of all. "I . . . I was still going out with Josh when you and I met. And I shouldn't have flirted with you like that. It wasn't right."

He shifted in his seat, gazing out the window. "It wasn't your smartest move ever," he said. "It kind of made me mad when I found out."

"You should've been really pissed."

"Mostly I was just bummed," he said. "That you had a boyfriend, not about the flirting. I kind of liked that because, you know, and I mean this in the best possible way, but aside from being really hot, you're also really goofy."

"Me?" I said, laughing. "Everything goofy I know I learned from you!"

"Yeah, probably."

"But there's one more thing," I said.

"Why do I think I'm not going to like this part?" he asked, his face serious for once.

"The thing is," I said, "my life is really screwed up right now. I like you, but . . ."

He sighed. "But you're not ready for a new relationship, right? Story of my life. Okay. That's fine. We can just be friends."

"Really?"

"Sure," he said. "Why not? But I won't wait for you forever, you know? No more than twenty years, tops. Or possibly twenty-five. Maybe thirty, but only if you keep wearing those low-cut sweaters I like so much. And that's my final offer too."

"You're making it really hard for me not to throw myself at you and kiss you all over," I said.

His expression perked up. "Really?"

"Really." I leaned in, but then Krista pounded on my window, making us jump.

"Well, that romantic moment's kind of shot," Trent said, and I laughed.

"I thought we were bowling," Krista yelled through the glass.

"We are!" Trent said. He leapt out of the car, ran around, opened my door, and bellowed, "Are you ready to boooooooowwwwwwwlllllll?"

There'd be time for running my fingers through Trent's hair later.

"I am sooooooo ready to bowl!" I yelled back.

"Race you," he said, tearing off across the parking lot, and I ran after him, my lungs filling with fresh air and my conscience light.

The next day, at my locker, I spun the combination, pulled the door open, and that stupid empty Popsicle box I'd held on to fell off the shelf and hit me in the forehead. In a blinding flash of memory, I made the connection.

chapter 25

BY THE TIME KRISTA FOUND ME HUDDLED AGAINST the locker, my entire body shook as if I'd been dipped in ice water.

"You've got to help me!" I said, grabbing at her.

"Jamie. You look horrible. What's wrong?"

"He needs help. It's a message. He's trying to tell me he needs help."

"What are you talking about?" Krista asked. Her words reached me slowly, as if from a long way away. "Are you sick?"

"Why did it take me so long to remember?" I demanded. "Josh brought me a note to work almost a week ago! I'm a terrible daughter."

"Jamie, you're not making sense. Tell me what is going on."

"I don't know what to do," I said.

Krista laid a cool hand on my forehead like she thought I had a fever.

"What's wrong with her?" I heard someone ask.

"I think she's delirious. She just keeps babbling," Krista said. "And she's shaking."

"Maybe we should take her to the nurse."

Through my haze, I looked up and saw Liz hovering over me, her hair neatly tucked up into its bun.

"No! Not the nurse. I need to talk to Josh," I said.

"Why?" Krista asked.

"The Popsicle box. It's a message from my dad."

"What?" they both asked.

"My dad, he needs help," I tried to explain. "When I was little, when my mom . . . when . . ."

"What about your mom?" Krista asked gently.

"When . . . she did drugs . . . and she had boyfriends . . . and . . . and . . ."

The warning bell ripped through the hallway.

"Come on," Krista said, getting me up on my feet. "Mr. Lazby teaches English first period in his classroom. No one will be in the drama room."

Liz and Krista surrounded me like a protective wall and led me downstairs. Krista turned on Mr. Lazby's desk lamp, and we sank onto the piles of cushions he kept for us, since there weren't any chairs.

"Now," Krista said, "start at the beginning."

I took a bunch of slow, deep breaths. "When I lived with my mom . . ." They nodded encouragingly at me, and the familiar smell of the room's fresh paint and musty pillows calmed my nerves. "And . . . she . . . well, as you know, she did drugs," I continued.

They waited.

"My dad and I had a code. It was a sort of cry-for-help thing. I could call him anytime, just to hear his voice, but if I was ever in real trouble, I was supposed to give him the code."

Krista squeezed my hand. "And?" she asked.

"It was Blue Raspberry Popsicle. And that's why Josh keeps leaving me notes about Popsicles."

They stared at me like maybe I'd lost it. "Don't you see?" I said. "Dad told Josh our secret code because he needs my help."

The rest of the day, I stayed on the lookout for Josh, but of course, he never let me near him. He'd said his dad and the Teacher read his e-mails and text messages, so I couldn't risk contacting him that way either, unless I wanted to get him in trouble. And I still cared about what happened to him. In fact, I missed him, but I never mentioned that to my friends because Krista and Liz couldn't understand what I saw in him when he'd treated me so badly.

"You should just ride your ass over to the church and say you wanna see your dad," LaVon told me that night.

He had practically forced my dinner on me, handing me one egg roll after another, reminding me to bite and chew when I sat there too long not eating.

"I guess I have to," I said. "I'm thinking if he sent a message instead of calling the school, then he must be in real trouble, though. Maybe they've got him locked up or something."

"Could be."

"Will you go with me?"

"Not my scene."

"Please?"

"No way. Them church people'll call the cops. I'm only two months and three days away from being clean and sober for one year. I get picked up for anything now, my daughter'll be all over me." He did a falsetto voice that I guess was supposed to be his daughter. "*I knew I*

couldn't trust you. You say you goin' straight, but are you? I don't think so!"
In his regular voice he said, "I ain't takin' no chances."

"Why would they call the police?" I asked.

"Trust me," he said. "They'd take one look at my beautiful face and find a reason."

On Thursday morning, as I rode my bicycle to school, I couldn't help feeling that same athletic rush I get when I dance. It would be March in a few days, and the air was still sharp, but you could tell spring was coming. It felt good in my lungs. I should've been happy with weather like this, but the worry over my dad was too strong. I was locking my bike to the rack when Krista and Liz came running up to me.

"Have you talked to Josh?" Krista asked.

"I just got here."

"I meant last night," she said.

I shook my head. I'd felt so desperate after talking it over with LaVon, I'd almost phoned Derrick, since Josh wouldn't answer my calls, but in the end I thought it might make matters worse for my dad.

Krista took my arm and led me into the school. "It doesn't matter anyway because we have a plan."

Because Mr. Lazby spent all his time in the costume shop, it was super easy to lift a couple of hall passes out of his desk. We filled in one excusing me from fifth period study hall, saying I was needed at the theater, and one for Josh, which we had Liz's little sister, Megan, deliver to his gym teacher at the beginning of the period while the class was still in the locker room changing. The pass said Josh was wanted in the office, and because the intercom in the gym was dicey at best, and Megan looks so innocent, Coach didn't get suspicious at all.

I hid inside the bathroom door, waiting for Josh to walk by. When I heard the squeak of athletic shoes on the polished linoleum in the hallway, I peeked around and saw him coming. As he passed, I leapt out, grabbed his arm, and put all my weight into dragging him into the bathroom. Josh was almost a foot taller than me, but the element of surprise and my strong dancer legs had given me the advantage. Unfortunately, I'd forgotten he was a "hit first, ask questions later" type of guy. He swung his arm around, his rock-hard fist clipping the very edge of my jaw, sending me reeling.

"What the hell's going on?" he demanded. And then he saw it was me. I clutched at my face, my skin burning like I'd touched it with a hot curling iron, tears already filling my eyes.

"Oh, my God!" I mumbled. "I think you broke my jaw."

He squatted down next to me and pried my hand away from my face. "Jeez, Jamie, are you okay? You scared the crap outta me. Let me see." Gently he touched the side of my face with his fingertips, running his hand up and down my jawbone. "Open your mouth . . . okay, good . . . close it . . . I don't think it's broken, but maybe you should go to the nurse."

I struggled to my feet. "I'm fine. Just . . ." Stars floated in front of my eyes, and Josh reached out to steady me.

"Sit," he said, guiding me to the floor. "Wait here."

"No! Josh, no. I need to talk to you."

"Shhh . . . we're gonna get busted for being out of class. Wait here. I'll be right back. I promise."

I leaned my head against the cool tile wall. This was not how it was supposed to go. I hadn't even gotten a chance to ask him about my dad, and now he was gone. I held my hand to my aching jaw, and tears slid over my fingers, dropping onto the concrete. Oh, gross. I was on the bathroom floor. I had to get up. I reached for the sink to give myself something to hold on to, but before I was on my feet, Josh was back.

"You need to sit down," he said. He shook a cold pack to activate it and handed it to me. "I had one in my locker left over from football season."

I pressed it to my throbbing face, instantly feeling a little relief. "Thanks."

Josh squatted down next to me. "Why'd you drag me in here?"

"Because you left me a note at work that said 'Blue Raspberry Popsicles,' and I've been trying to find you to ask you about it ever since, but you won't let me get within half a mile of you."

"Oh, right." He sat down next to me. "I don't know what that means. Do you?"

"Let me get this straight," I said. "You've been leaving me messages, and you don't know why?"

"Well, yeah. Your dad seemed so stressed about it. Like telling you he said 'Blue Raspberry Popsicles' was the most important thing in the world. I felt bad for him, so I said I'd get you the message. I figured it was something from your childhood. . . . You know, like he wanted you to know he was sorry or he's all right or something."

I stared at Josh. How could he be so dense? "Josh, they *are* a message . . . code for he's in big trouble and needs help. Why didn't you just tell me in person?"

"I tried," he said. "I went to your work, but you weren't there."

"And you couldn't have written a better note than that?" I asked.

"I should've, but that guy . . . well, he wasn't very friendly and I didn't know if he'd give it to you or not. He wouldn't tell me what motel you were staying in."

I wanted to smile, thinking of Trent protecting me, but my face hurt too much.

"I got the note," I said, "but it didn't mean much without an explanation."

Josh reached out and cupped my chin. "Your face," he said. "I'm so sorry about your beautiful face." He kissed me on the forehead, and I almost raised my mouth to meet his, but I shoved him away instead.

"Stop it! All I want to know is what's going on with my dad. Why is he sending me messages? Why doesn't he just leave?"

"They won't let him," Josh said. "Because of the inheritance."

"They must know the money is all tied up. The most he can give them is his monthly allowance. My grandpa knew better than to trust him with it all at once."

"They'll take it however they can get it. Besides, they've made him a disciple. He knows too much about the inner workings of the church for them to let him go without a fight now."

The pain in my jaw had moved up to my cheek, and my entire head hurt. What was Josh talking about . . . the inner workings of the church? The ache in my face made it hard to follow the conversation.

"Are they keeping him there by force, Josh? Is that why he's sending me messages?"

"Well . . ."

Panic surged through me. "They haven't beaten him up, have they?"

"I don't think so," Josh said. "But now that he's a disciple, it's serious business to them. Mira's getting really fanatical now too. She'll do anything the Teacher asks her to. Even spy on your dad. They're all working on his mind, telling him they're the only ones who care about him."

"But he's asking for help," I said. "Maybe the brainwashing isn't working."

Josh shrugged. "I don't know. . . . The message might not be what you think. Maybe he's trying to say he's sorry."

I pulled myself up, shrugging off Josh when a wave of dizziness came over me and grabbing the windowsill for support instead. Josh might be right. My memories could be mixed up somehow.

"I have to find out what he wants," I said. "How can I get inside?"

"I don't see how," he said.

"Maybe Krista could go to a Friday Mixer with you," I said.

"With purple hair and those clothes?"

I took the cold pack off my face so he could see the angry, red welt. "Come on, Josh . . . please . . . It's the least you could do."

"Dammit, Jamie. Don't look at me like that."

He crossed his arms like I'd seen him do so many times when Derrick wanted him to do something he didn't want to, like go to an extra church meeting. He always gave in to his brother, so I waited, not taking my eyes off of him.

Finally he said, "Oh, all right. But not Krista. I could maybe take Megan to a dance."

"Rafferty?" I asked.

"She's in drama with you, right?" he said. "And isn't she your friend Liz's little sister?"

"Well, yeah, but do you even know her?"

Not too many seniors were aware of the freshman girls unless they were super hot. Megan looked pretty much like Liz; tall, skinny, flat-chested, and always wore her hair in a bun.

"She's in my chemistry class," he explained. "And Derrick won't connect her to you."

"That would be great, Josh," I said. "Liz can go along as the chaperone."

The church loved old-fashioned ideas like a sibling as a chaper-one, and even though Liz was one of my best friends, Derrick would probably buy the idea.

"This is strictly to find out what your dad wanted to tell you," Josh said. "No heroic rescues that get me kicked out, because my father will never let me see Mom or Derrick again, and they need me."

This time, I was the one who reached out and touched him. But it was just my hand on his arm . . . like a friend, not a girlfriend. "You can trust Megan and Liz," I said. "I promise."

DAD HAD NEVER LET ME STAY OVERNIGHT WITH FRIENDS on school nights, but since I was in charge of my own life, Krista and I went home with Liz. We needed to figure out what she and Megan would wear to the Mixer.

Liz waved away the matching yellow bridesmaid dresses Krista had chosen for them. "I'm not wearing that rag," she said for the third time.

"I will," Megan said.

"Suck-up," Liz said. "Don't you remember, they're super itchy and they gave us both rashes during Lydia's wedding reception?"

"It's one night," Megan said. "If that's what Krista thinks we should wear, then we should. She's the expert."

We'd pitched the whole idea of the dance to Megan like it was an acting gig, and she'd jumped all over it. We gave her a role to play—the demure, innocent date. We couldn't figure out any way to keep the reason she was going along a secret, so we had told her pretty much everything about my dad, Josh, and the church, but we knew we could trust her. For the most part, she was just Liz's little sister, but I had known her since she was five years old, and we'd danced the *Nutcracker* together every year since then, so we did have a bond.

"Those are perfect for the R&R," I said, agreeing with Krista. "I swear, all the girls there will be dressed the same way."

"Like extras on *Little House on the Prairie*?" Liz demanded.

"Yeah," I said. "With pantyhose and flat shoes too."

"No way."

I nodded. "Trust me. They're fashion-challenged."

Krista took one of the offending dresses and examined it. "I can remove the lace so they're not so scratchy, and I'll sew a cell phone pocket into Liz's in the seam below the sash."

Liz collapsed onto her bed in defeat. "But when are you going to do that? We need them tomorrow."

"I'll help," I said.

Krista rolled her eyes at me. "You can rip out the seams." We both knew that unless she hemmed my jeans for me, I was perfectly happy to do it with duct tape.

After school on Friday, I locked my bike up outside the motel and climbed the stairs. I was digging for my keys in the hallway, when with a big whoosh, someone flung my door open from the inside, and a voice bellowed, "Where the hell you been?"

I staggered into the room and collapsed onto my bed, clutching my chest dramatically, but my heart actually thumped hard, even though I was goofing around. "LaVon!" I said. "You seriously almost scared me to death. How'd you get in my room, anyway?"

"Stub let me in. James, you've been gone for—" I flinched as he reached out with a huge hand, but he simply lifted my chin to see my face better. "Who did this to you?" he growled.

"Josh, but it was an accident. I'm all right."

LaVon let go of me. "Where you been? I go to the Klatch last

219

night to get you, and you're not there. Then you don't come home. So I'm thinking you're dead somewhere."

"You couldn't have been that worried," I said, laughing at his mother-hen tone. "I was at work this morning. Why didn't you come in to see me then?"

He glared at me for not taking him seriously. "I had a meeting with my parole officer," he said. "Besides, I don't have all day to check up on you, ya know? You coulda called my cell."

I sobered up quickly. "I'm sorry. I stayed at Liz's last night."

He shrugged like the matter was settled. "You hungry?"

"Sure." Krista and I had planned to order a pizza, but to make him feel better, I let LaVon take me to his room and give me a huge bowl of vegetable soup and a hunk of fresh bread with cheddar cheese.

"Nice wallpaper," he said.

"What?" I asked, not following.

"Your list," he said. "I saw the stuff you wrote on your wall."

"Oh, that. Yeah, Stub'll probably be mad. But guess what? The Olivier picture is up to eight hundred and eleven dollars and seventy-eight cents on eBay. And it doesn't end until tomorrow."

"You're shittin' me," he said.

"I'm not. I kind of hate having it in my room now that I know someone will pay that much for it."

LaVon shook his head in disbelief, and honestly, I kind of felt the same way. Before, when cash wasn't an issue, it hadn't bothered me at all that Grandpa had spent a ridiculous amount on a photo just because he knew I'd like it. But now . . . well . . . on my way home, I'd seen Vanessa and Ruby parked around the corner, and it looked like they were living in their car. Somehow, owning such an expensive photo seemed obscene when I knew a pregnant teen who had to live on the street with a toddler. I didn't tell LaVon I'd seen her, though, because I felt embarrassed for her. Knowing him, he already knew all about it and took them regular meals anyway.

"I won't be home tonight either," I said, my mouth full of the yummy bread.

"Not my business anyway," LaVon said.

"It *is* your business," I argued. "You've been great to me, and I should've called."

Over second bowls of soup, I updated LaVon about Josh and our plan for the dance.

"Be careful," he said when I got up to leave.

"I will."

"Keep me informed, 'kay?"

"Yeah," I said. "I'll check in tomorrow if I'm not going to be back this weekend."

LaVon took my empty dishes from me. "Stay with your friends. You're safer there."

"LaVon, I really am sorry."

"We're cool," he said, coming out of the bathroom with the dishes he'd washed. His face was back to that unreadable masked look he usually had. "No big deal."

"Thanks for the soup. Thanks for everyth—"

"I gotta get to work."

"Yeah, okay. See you."

LaVon was a caretaker by nature, but he never was big on the thanks that goes with it. I hoped he knew how much I appreciated him, though. I rode my bike double-time all the way to Krista's, where we were meeting to help Megan and Liz get ready for the dance. When I got there, Krista was in her room alone with her cell phone in her lap.

"What's up?" I asked.

"Shhh," she said. "We're testing the phones."

Liz's voice came through the cell. "Are you there?"

"Yeah," Krista said. "Where are you?"

"We walked around the block," she said. "I'm putting the phone in my pocket now. See if you can hear us talking."

"Okay."

Krista held her cell up between us.

"Hi, Megan," Liz said.

"Nice dress," Megan replied.

"Bite me," Liz told her.

"That's hardly church language, young lady," Megan reprimanded in a fake-snooty voice.

There was a bit of static as Liz pulled the phone out of her pocket. "Could you hear us?"

"Yeah, pretty good," I said.

"Okay. We're on our way back to your house. We should leave soon so we're not late."

Liz's mom had to work and her aunt had plans, so she couldn't get a car. Krista could've given them a ride, but Josh said he wanted an adult to drop them off, in case anyone from the R&R was watching. Luckily, we were able to bribe Krista's stepfather, George, with pizza and Ding Dongs. When Megan and Liz got back from their walk, we all stood around the dining room, waiting for him to finish eating.

"Why aren't you and Jamie going too?" he asked us.

"Nothing to wear," Krista joked.

"Shut up," Liz said. She tugged at the collar.

"You've got to be kidding me," George said. "Krista's got a whole closet full of clothes."

"Pizza for the road?" I asked, holding the box out to him.

"Sure." He grabbed the last slice, and the three of them took off.

Upstairs, in Krista's room, the two of us sat on the purple beanbag chairs, her laptop positioned between us, already signed into her e-mail. I held her cell in my sweaty palm, waiting. When it finally rang, I put it on speaker.

"We're at the church now," Liz said. "I'm putting the phone in my pocket. Thanks for the ride, George."

"There's Josh," we heard Megan say. "Hey, Josh. Over here!"

"Thanks for coming," he said, formally.

The sound of him being so polite reminded me of how nice he was when we first dated. I actually surprised myself by feeling a tiny bit jealous when Megan said something I didn't quite catch, and it sounded flirtatious. I made myself think of Trent's crooked-tooth smile, which wasn't hard to do.

Any minute, Liz and Megan would see my dad. It'd been five weeks since the wedding. How would he look? Part of me could hardly wait to find out, and the other part was really scared he'd look like one of the disciples.

"Let's go," Josh said.

As they went inside, their chatter was replaced with orchestral music, which drowned out almost everything. It was funny, but as stuffy and old-fashioned as the mixers were, Josh and I had kind of enjoyed them. One time, I'd taught Josh to waltz. He spun me around the floor, weaving in and out of the other couples. "One, two, three, one, two, three," I'd coached him. "You're pretty good."

"Football," he said. "We do lots of footwork drills."

"Oh, right."

223

The music coming through the phone swelled, and the babble of voices mixed together.

"I can't hear anything," I said.

Krista squeezed my shoulder. "Don't worry. The plan will work anyway."

"What plan?" I asked. "They're just supposed to see my dad and find out if he needs my help."

"Yeah, I know," Krista said. "That's what I meant." But she started braiding a gold ribbon into her long hair and wouldn't look at me.

"I promised Josh," I reminded her. "Remember?"

"We know . . . we know. Don't worry."

"They're not going to do anything stupid, right?"

"Relax and enjoy the music," she said.

I laughed in spite of myself. An old song I recognized called "As Time Goes By" poured through the tinny speaker. "Over the phone, it sounds like that crap you hear in an elevator," I told Krista. "But it's a live band, and it's actually really great."

"Whatever," she said. "How long do we have to suffer through it?"

I didn't answer because she knew. We'd arranged for George to pick up Megan and Liz at ten o'clock. We sat through twenty more minutes of music and could hear murmurings, but no real conversations. Then a door opened and closed and the music faded.

Megan announced clearly, "Josh said the bathroom was out here somewhere in the lobby."

"Did you see anyone you knew in there?" Liz asked loudly, so we could hear her.

"*Just Mr. Cross.*" Megan overenunciated. "*You know, Jamie Lexington-Cross's dad?*"

My heart jumped, and I squeezed Krista's hand. We both stared at her cell as if my father would magically climb right out of it. My hands trembled so badly Krista took the phone from me and laid it on the floor in front of us.

"Oh, right. *Mr. Cross*," Liz said. "I haven't seen him in ages. He looks *okay*, though, doesn't he?"

"Definitely. He looked *fine*," Megan said.

I knew they were trying to reassure me, and I would hug them for it later.

Hollow giggles filtered through the phone as Megan and Liz entered the bathroom. We heard them greet some other girls, and one asked if they were there with Josh.

"I am," Megan said. "We go to school together."

"He's sooooo cute," said a high-pitched, whiny voice. "You're sooooo lucky."

"Yeah," Megan agreed.

A door banged and then silence.

"Anyone else in here?" Megan asked.

"Nope," Liz said. "I checked under the stalls."

We'd decided they shouldn't take any chances and talk to us anywhere inside the church, so even though the bathroom was empty, Liz didn't take out her phone. We didn't know what kind of surveillance they might have.

"It's really loud in the dance, so it's hard to hear," Megan said, "but I think tonight will be a *big* success."

"Yep," Liz said. "Oh, yeah, Josh told me the Teacher said it's okay if I take a picture of the two of you for Mom and Dad, so I'll do that when we go back out there. Maybe we can get a *chaperone* in it too."

"She's going to get a picture of my dad," I said to Krista.

"But first I have to pee," Liz told Megan.

"Oh, God, no," Krista said.

"Please don't," I pleaded. "I so don't want to hear it."

But no matter how we begged, Liz couldn't hear us, and pretty soon there was a light tinkling sound. Krista and I grimaced at each other. Then it got stronger and louder until it sounded like rushing water.

Over the noise, we could hear Megan and Liz practically cackling with glee.

"That's the faucet," Krista said, cracking up, and I laughed too.

"Gotcha," Liz said. "Just a little comic relief."

"Don't admit we were so gullible," I told Krista.

"Never," she agreed.

For a long time we couldn't hear much more than the music. I sat there, my posture as good as Liz's always was. I must've checked the battery on the cell a dozen times, but Krista's phone was new, and it was still going strong. Liz said hers usually lasted about four hours, and they had Megan's for backup, so we would make it through the dance.

Krista unwrapped the foil on a Ding Dong and offered me half, but after all of LaVon's chocolate lectures, I turned it down. Finally the music stopped.

"Time for a band break," I said.

"Thank God for small favors."

Voices bubbled through the phone's speaker, and we caught bits and pieces of the conversation.

"Take a picture of me and Josh. Over here. . . ."

"Stand by that mural of the baby Jesus. . . ."

226

"Here?"

Laughter. Mumbled voices.

"Not there . . . next to those chaperones. . . . Smile!"

". . . something to drink . . ."

". . . wait here . . ."

"I can't find my lip gloss," Megan said very clearly.

"Use mine," Liz offered, loudly.

"No way. It'll make my lips blue."

"My lip gloss is not blue," Liz said. "That's just the flavor. *Blue Raspberry.*"

"Oh, *Blue Raspberry* like the *Popsicle?*" Megan asked.

They'd planned to mention blue raspberry so my dad would know why they were there and to give him a chance to say something, but if he answered, I didn't hear it because Krista shouted, "Look!" She pointed at the computer.

An e-mail had popped into the inbox. She clicked on it. In the picture, Megan held on to Josh's arm like they were at prom together. He stared directly into the camera, not bothering to smile. Megan was as poised and ready as any actress could be, her smile demure, eyes sparkling. Standing next to her was a thin, pale man. It took me a full beat to realize it was my dad.

"Krista! He looks awful."

"Be quiet, I want to hear what they're saying," she said, waving cell at me.

"Look how skinny he is! And he's got a beard like the Teacher!"

"Shhh. . . ."

". . . blue raspberry?" whispered a voice, a man's voice. My dad's voice.

"Thanks, Mr. Cross," Liz said cheerfully and loudly. And then, even though she whispered it, I clearly heard her say, "Look in your jacket pocket."

Before anyone could say anything else, the music started up again.

"What happened?" I asked Krista. "I didn't hear. Why did she say that about his pocket?"

"Mission accomplished," said Liz's voice directly into the phone.

"What is she talking about?" I asked Krista again.

"Relax, Jamie. It'll be fine."

"But what's going on?"

"Well, we know *you* promised Josh tonight was only a chance for Megan and Liz to check in with your dad about the message, but . . ." She paused for dramatic effect.

"What? You guys did something, didn't you?"

"But *we* never promised Josh," she said. "Liz dropped her lip gloss at your dad's feet and when he bent over to pick it up for her, she slipped him a note."

"What did it say?" I asked.

"It said . . . " Krista paused again, not realizing how close I was to grabbing her and shaking her until all her little sparkly hair clips flew across the room. "It said *You'll have to leave everything behind. At the end of the dance, walk me to my car and get in.*"

"Krista! You didn't."

"Yeah! We did! We're gonna bust him out."

"But what's George going to say when my dad gets in the car?"

"Nothing. George isn't picking them up," she said. "We are."

KRISTA HAD BORROWED A WHOLE GETUP FROM THE costume shop. Blond wig, big glasses (with no glass in them), and a moth-eaten fur coat. "I'll be Liz and Megan's mom, and you will hide in the backseat of the minivan," she told me as she applied bright red lipstick.

It seemed a little excessive to me, and I thought Krista was just exercising her flair for the dramatic. "This is never going to work," I said. "Mira will be there. She'll stop him."

"That's why you're lying low." She smacked her lips together and blotted them on a tissue. "But if he hesitates, all he has to do is look inside the van. He'll see you and remember why he wants to get away."

"*If* he wants to leave," I reminded her. "We still don't know. That's what they were supposed to find out."

"Well, I'd say if he walks them to the van, he wants out of there, wouldn't you?"

She had a point. But the Teacher had beaten me before, and I wouldn't put it past him to use Mira to get what he wanted. Plus, all the church disciples would be there too. All she'd have to do is call out to them, and they'd come running to remind Dad I was a sinner and they could save him. And who knew what punishment they'd give him for having doubts.

Krista handed me a black hoodie. "Here, put this on."

Dance music still blared from the cell phone as we drove to the Right & the Real, but when we were about a quarter mile away, it stopped and people clapped. There were a few minutes of mumbling, and then everything got louder. It sounded like Liz had walked in on an argument. The longer it went on, the shriller and angrier the voices got too.

"What's going on?" I asked Krista from the backseat. She had the phone in the hands-free holder up on the dash.

"I'm not sure," she said. "It sounds like some kind of fight."

We were in the parking lot now, and I couldn't risk being seen, so I crouched in the back, trying to decipher what everyone was saying. Krista pulled up under the covered driveway by the big front doors, and light filled the van. Instinctively, I shrank farther into the corner, although no one could possibly see me through the tinted windows. Seeing the church again made my stomach tighten up. I got a flash of a mind-video of the Teacher with those girls touching his naked body, and I had to swallow hard to keep down that sour taste you get right before you throw up.

The noise coming through the phone sounded like all-out shouting now. Two men's voices drowned out a woman's high-pitched yell. Then the noise faded, replaced by running footsteps. Through the phone's speaker we heard Megan say, "God, I hope they're out there waiting for us. Please be there, Krista!"

"We're here," Krista shouted as loud as she could, thinking maybe they'd hear her from inside the pocket.

Megan yanked so hard on the passenger door it bounced back, hitting her arm as they tumbled into the van, practically on top of each other.

"Abort plan! Abort plan!" shouted Liz. She slammed the door, and Krista peeled out of the lot.

I clambered over the seats and met Liz in the middle of the van. "What happened?"

"Wait!" Krista said. "Don't tell yet. I'm trying to drive, and I want to hear."

"Pull over, then," I told her.

Krista turned into the Save-A-Bunch parking lot, found a spot, and killed the engine. "Okay," she said. "Talk."

The streetlight shone in through the windshield, and for a second, Megan and Liz looked at each other, not speaking, and then they did that sister thing and said at the same time, "Oh, my God. It was so awful."

"So you know I slipped him a note, right?" Liz asked.

I nodded.

"Well, Mira found it before he did."

"What?" Krista and I both yelled.

"Did she see you put it in his pocket?" I asked.

"I don't think so," Liz said. "What happened was, you know when I dropped my lip gloss and your dad bent over to pick it up for me? Well, I think your dad was so focused on the fact that I'd said blue raspberry, he missed the part where I told him about the note."

"We tried to watch him the rest of the night," Megan said, taking up the story. "And neither of us saw him get anything out of his pocket, but Mira was always next to him, so we figured he was waiting for the right moment."

231

"Except he never tried to get away from her," Liz said. "So we started to worry."

"When the dance was over," Megan told us, "I asked him if he would walk me out to wait for my mom, and he said yes, but then Mira came along too."

"And Josh," added Liz.

"Anyway, we were all standing in the lobby, and Mira told your dad she needed a mint and reached into his jacket pocket to get it, and she ended up with the note instead," Megan said.

My head started to spin, and I realized I'd been holding my breath during their whole story. I inhaled deeply and let it out slowly. Josh was going to kill me. I'd promised not to do anything stupid, and now Liz and Megan had gotten caught. Plus, if the church really was holding Dad hostage, they'd ruined any chance we had of getting him out of there.

"What happened?" Krista prodded them.

"Well, Mira read the note and she turned on Mr. Cross and demanded to know what it meant. He looked totally confused. He obviously didn't have a clue."

"So your dad goes, 'What is it?' and then Mira freaked out!"

"She totally yelled so everyone could hear," Megan said. "She shouted at him that he was having an affair. And get this, she actually told your dad that he's not allowed to take a second wife in the first year of marriage. How weird is that?"

"Your dad's face went all white, and he was all 'I am not having an affair,' but she wouldn't listen. And then some of the disciples came over and tried to calm her down, and so she read the note out loud," Liz said.

"She was all, 'Listen to this: *You'll have to leave everything behind. At the end of the dance, walk me to my car and get in.*'"

"And then that disciple guy," Liz said, "the one with the brown beard—"

"Not a disciple," Megan said. "The Teacher."

"Whatever." Liz gave her a look for interrupting. "Anyway, he asked your dad who gave him that note. I wasn't sure what to do. If we ran out of there, then they might get suspicious, and so far no one seemed to know it was us, so—"

"And we didn't know if you were out there yet either," Megan said.

My breathing was totally calm, like right before I go on stage, but my heart thumped hard in my chest, and I still felt light-headed trying to process the whole scene. The sound of fabric tearing filled the van as Liz tugged at the front of her dress and the material gave way.

"Oh, thank God. I've been choking all night," she said.

"Me too," Megan said. "Help me rip mine."

"You guys!" I said. "We're waiting for the rest of the story here."

"Oh, sorry," Megan said. "Okay, so the Teacher was demanding your father admit who the note was from, but your dad didn't know. So I said really loudly to Liz, 'Do you still have that *Blue Raspberry* lip gloss, because my lips are really chapped.' And Liz said, '*Blue Raspberry lip gloss is the best. It really, really helps when you need it.*'"

"Then your dad started to cough really hard," Liz said, "and his eyes bugged out, and everyone patted him on the back. We knew he totally got it then, but we didn't think he'd be able to get away. So I said I planned to buy some more Blue Raspberry lip gloss *tomorrow afternoon*, thinking we could break him out then."

"But then Josh got mad and ordered us to shut up about lip gloss,"

233

Megan said, "because he totally knew what we were up to, but he'd helped us, so he was kind of screwed if we got caught, and then that Teacher guy got really red in the face and told your dad they'd have to go talk privately about his doubts in God." She'd been talking so fast she had to gasp for a breath and Liz took over.

"Just when we thought we would get away with it, Josh's mom, Mrs. Peterson, says—"

"'The note was from me!'" Megan said.

"Josh's mom said it was from her?" I asked, confused.

"Yeah, I know. Weird, right?" Megan agreed.

"Wait a minute," Krista said. "You lost me. Why would she say that?"

"We have no idea," Liz said. "But that's when things got totally crazy."

"Josh's dad was there, and he completely lost it. He yelled about fire and brimstone and hell and harlots and called her names until she cried. Some of the other chaperones tried to get the rest of the kids back into the main room or outside, but everyone crowded around listening."

"Josh's dad banished Mrs. Peterson from their house," Liz added. "He told her she wouldn't get a cent from him, and he'd never let her see her sons again."

"What did Josh do?" I asked.

"At first he was too stunned to do anything, but then he tried to tell her she shouldn't lie, and he knew she didn't give your dad that note, but she stood there, her face hard, like stone. She's really tiny, you know, but she looked big and strong, even though black mascara tears ran down her cheeks. She didn't move. She faced them all and said they were *not* having an affair, but they both wanted to leave, and she had offered to help your dad by driving him in her car, and that's why she put the note in his pocket!"

"What did my dad do?" I asked.

"Well . . . ," Megan said.

"He looked like he wanted to go with her, but also like he was scared to stand up to them," Liz said.

"And?"

"And so Josh's mom said, 'Are you coming with me or not?'" Megan said.

"But before your dad could answer," Liz said, "the disciples whisked him away."

"Oh, my God," Krista said.

"And then we ran outside, and you guys were waiting for us."

We sat there in silence, thinking for I don't know how long, trying to make sense of it all. When Megan's phone beeped, we jumped. She pulled it out of her purse. "It's a text message from Josh."

"What does it say?"

In a quivering voice, Megan read it aloud. "Mom kicked out. J's dad in lockdown."

"I KNOW WHAT LOCKDOWN IS IN A PRISON," KRISTA said, "but what do you think it means in a church?"

"I don't know."

"I'm kind of scared, you guys," Megan said. "Maybe we should tell Mom."

"You promised to keep it a secret," I reminded her.

"No one's going to say anything," Liz said. She put her arm around her sister and whispered something into her ear, and Megan nodded.

"First, let's see what we can find out," Krista said. "We'll start with the Internet."

"I already tried that," I said.

"No offense," Krista said, "but I am a Google queen."

It was true. When I had a computer, I mostly used it for typing my papers and sending e-mail, so it wasn't that surprising I hadn't found much about the church. Krista can find anything on the web, though. If it's out there, she's your girl.

"Can we get some coffee?" Liz asked.

"Excellent idea," Krista said.

We ended up at the Coffee Klatch. Liz and Krista went straight for the computers, but Megan followed me to the counter, where Jezziray made our drinks. I got Orange Bliss tea because I was already too shaky to have caffeine.

The place was totally deserted except for a couple of guys dressed all in black playing backgammon in the corner and Trent, who was at one of the computer stations. Megan took the drinks over to Krista and Liz, and I made a bit of a circuitous route so I could go past Trent.

I hip-checked his shoulder and said, "Can't get enough of this place?" Immediately, I felt overwhelmed by guilt. I couldn't believe I'd just flirted when my dad was in so much trouble.

He gave me his big grin. "Oh, hi. Nah, I'm just here 'cause Amanda wanted to go to a party."

My face totally crumpled. The worst part was, Trent saw it.

"Oh, no . . . it's not like that," he said. "I came in to close for her so Jezz isn't here alone. Amanda left already."

He probably saw the relief too, even though I tried not to show it. "That's cool," I said.

"Are you all right?" Trent asked. "You look kind of . . . pale."

"Well, I—"

"Hey, Jamie," Krista called over her shoulder to me. She still had her blond wig on, and Trent did a double take when he looked at her. "This is what I've got. Lockdown: mostly used in prison—but Wikipedia says this too: it's an emergency protocol to prevent people or information from escaping, which usually can only be ordered by someone in command."

"Who's in lockdown?" Trent asked.

"My dad," I said. I sat in one of the plastic chairs and gave him the update in a few sentences. "I don't know what to do."

"Maybe we should call the police," Trent said. "I mean, they're holding him hostage."

"No way," I said. "They'll get my mom involved."

"We could try breaking him out," he suggested.

Trent was so sweet. "I wish we could," I said. "I don't even know where they've got him, though."

We had to figure out some sort of plan, but every part of me ached with exhaustion. Not just my body either, but my brain too. I leaned closer to Trent and looked at the computer monitor, needing a distraction. "What are you doing?"

"Oh, nothing. Just updating 'Coffee Clips.'"

"I've never seen those. Can I watch one?"

"Sure."

I shifted my chair closer to his until our thighs were pressed up against each other. "Hey!" I said. "That's me. Who said you could video me?"

"Uh, maybe you should watch a different one," he said.

I looked at him. Color crept up his neck.

"Why?"

"No reason." He tried to grab the mouse from me, but I held on and clicked the video.

The clip was about thirty seconds long, and at first, the only thing it showed was me making a drink and laughing with a customer you couldn't see. And then red text started flashing across the bottom of the screen.

Check out our HOT new Barista Babe! Check out our HOT new Barista Babe!

"Trent!" I said. But I couldn't help laughing. I knew my face must be bright pink, and when I looked at him, he stared pointedly at the computer.

Krista let out a little gasp, followed by a squeal.

"What have you got?" I asked her, jumping up.

"Yeah, what'd you find?" Trent asked, hurrying over to her station too, the back of his neck a deep red.

"Hang on," she mumbled. We watched her mouthing the words as she read.

"What is it?" we asked.

"Give me a sec." We all peered over her shoulder, but she pushed us away. "Don't crowd me."

I tried to see the URL, but it was too long to remember. I gave her another thirty seconds and then I couldn't stand it anymore. "Just tell us already."

She looked up at us. "I am soooo good. You're gonna love me for forever. Your dad might not be married to Mira after all."

"What? Really?"

"Listen to this," she said. "I found an interview with a woman who got kicked out of the church."

"Read it aloud," Megan said.

"Okay . . . *My husband kicked me out and*," Krista read, "blah, blah, blah . . . Here's the part you need to hear. . . ." We all leaned in closer. "*I went to a lawyer and when he tried to file divorce papers, we found out none of the weddings the Teacher performs are legal. They're what you call spiritual commitments. He doesn't have a license to marry people.*"

"Oh, my God! This is so great!" I said. I threw my arms around Krista, knocking her wig askew.

"It doesn't get him out of lockdown," she said, "but that's one good thing, at least."

Not hearing anything about my dad all weekend made me super edgy and tense, and I snapped at Krista every time she told me to try to chill. By Sunday I just wanted to be alone, so I went back to the motel, claiming I had homework and needed to be at work early on Monday, so it would just be easier. Both were true anyway.

When I heard LaVon come through the fire door, I jumped up and opened my door. "Hi."

"Hey, James. Nice kitty cats."

I looked down at the kittens playing with balls of yarn on my pajamas. "I'm a fashion goddess."

LaVon held up his cloth grocery bag. "Wanna fill me in on your dad while we cook?"

"Okay."

I sliced carrots (after he showed me how) and told him the whole story. LaVon's large hand moved his knife expertly through the garlic, mincing it in seconds.

"You know where he's at?" he asked.

"Not exactly. I mean, we think he's in one of the disciple trailers."

"Find out. I'll go get him."

"What?" I asked. "You can't do that!"

"Like hell I can't. I'll walk in there and drag his ass out. Who's gonna stop me?"

"The police?"

"Be long gone before they get there." He picked up a mushroom the size of my hand and chopped off the stem, then he slid his knife through it and thick slices fell away.

240

"I asked you to go to the church before, and you said no," I pointed out.

"This is different. You wanted me to talk to them. That's what my court-appointed shrink calls a *possible confrontational situation* 'cause I might get real angry, and the next thing ya know, people are yellin', and somebody gets punched, and the cops are there haulin' me off to jail. I'm supposed to avoid that crap."

"And you don't think breaking into his trailer is confrontational?" I asked.

"I don't care anymore. They got him locked up. I can't let that shit slide."

"You'll get caught," I said.

He grunted.

Why was I trying to talk LaVon out of this? If he wanted to rescue my dad, I should be thanking him. But still . . . "You're on parole," I reminded him.

LaVon slammed his knife down on the cutting board. "You think I don't know that?" he asked. "You think it slipped my mind?"

"Uh . . . no . . . no . . . I mean—"

"This is bullshit." He grabbed his knife and chopped the mushrooms so fast he practically pulverized them. "Don't you get it? I hate bullies. Those goddamned church people latched on to your dad for his money, James. They don't give a damn about his soul. It pisses me off."

"Ummm . . . okay . . . but—"

"But nothing," he growled.

I finished slicing my carrots in silence while LaVon banged pans around me until he found the wok. He plugged it into the wall and poured peanut oil into it. I stood over my carrots, not sure what to do, but kind of afraid to ask.

241

"You done?" he said.

I nodded.

"Have a seat," he said. "I forgot to buy rice at the store, so I picked it up at the Chinese place." I watched LaVon chop peppers, broccoli, and something green I didn't recognize, noting his technique for next time. "Sorry about yellin'," he said after a while. He tossed handfuls of vegetables into the hot oil, and they sizzled and jumped. "I hate it when the big guys pick on someone weaker than them, ya know?"

"Yeah."

"And you're right. I can't be breakin' the law, or my daughter will find out. I won't be seein' my grandbaby anytime soon if I screw up now."

"I know. But thanks anyway."

LaVon moved the vegetables around in the crackling wok with a wooden spoon and the odor of garlic filled the room. "You come up with some way to get in there without gettin' me arrested," he said, "and I'll go with you."

"Really?" I asked.

He handed me a plate of rice and vegetables.

"Hell, yeah," he said. He gave me a wide, almost evil, smile. "I can't be breakin' the law, but I wouldn't mind puttin' the fear of God in those people."

chapter 29

THE ONLY GOOD THING THAT HAPPENED OVER THE weekend was the Olivier picture sold to someone in Japan for twelve hundred dollars. I still had a week because the deposit wasn't due until March 7th, so as long as the buyer paid the money into my PayPal account in the next couple of days, I was golden.

Josh wasn't in school on Monday or Tuesday, and I got in trouble four times in class for not paying attention because I was imagining the worst. Krista had called the Right & the Real during morning break, asking for Mr. Cross, pretending she was the secretary from the newspaper's sales office where he used to work, but she'd spoken to a woman who said he wasn't available and would call her back. He never did.

Finally, on Wednesday, I saw Josh, but every time we passed each other in the hallway, he turned away, not looking at me. Above his left cheekbone was the faint greenish tinge of a black eye. When Megan tried to talk to him at lunch, he stonewalled her.

"He acted like I wasn't there," she said. "Derrick too."

During last period, I sat with Liz and Krista on pillows in the drama room. While they gossiped, I sorted through my overdue French homework. This was probably the first time I'd ever tried to do an assignment during drama class, and it was impossible because of all the noise.

"I'm going to get a drink," I said, heading for the fountain in the hall. I was slurping the tepid water when Josh came down the stairs, presumably looking for me. Thirty seconds later, we were sitting on the couch in the back of the scene shop. The single bulb over the prop shelves cast an ugly shadow over the green bruise on his face.

"Is my dad okay?" I asked. "Is he still living in disciple housing? Do you—"

"They've got him in lockdown in the first trailer, right next to the guard station."

Crap. Figures they'd keep a close eye on him. "What about your mom?" I asked.

"Listen, I don't have very much time," he said. He ran his hands over his cropped hair, reminding me how much I loved to do that. It was prickly and soft at the same time. I shook my head to wipe away that thought.

"Your dad needs help," he continued, "but I can't do anything else. I can't risk getting kicked out."

"You could live with your mom."

"Not without Derrick, and he won't go."

"I know he's your brother, but he *likes* the church. It's not as if you could get him out of there and he'd suddenly change or something."

"He needs me."

We sat there, at an impasse. I'd needed Josh, but he hadn't seemed to care about that.

"Jamie," he said, "Derrick is . . . well, when we were little, he used to draw a lot. He's a really good artist. And he likes to read novels too. He's gay."

I couldn't help it, I laughed. "That is the stupidest thing I've ever heard. You think he's gay because he's artistic?"

Josh gave me one of those withering looks you read about in books. "No, I think he's gay because he told me he's attracted to guys. I just mentioned the art stuff so you'd understand what you see is not who he is."

"Derrick said he likes guys?" I asked.

"Yeah, a couple of years ago."

"Wow." No wonder Josh wasn't homophobic like his other jock friends.

"Unfortunately, my dad overheard us talking about it. You can guess how that went over. Derrick ended up having to go to special meetings with the Teacher to 'learn to be a man.' It's pretty much the only reason they let us go to public school. They thought sports would toughen him up and the cheerleaders would turn him on, but it made him shut down instead."

I scooted closer to Josh on the couch. "I still don't understand why you can't leave. Maybe it would set a good example for him."

"They'll keep us apart, and I don't want to lose him."

I laid my hand on his shoulder. I hated to see him looking so . . . defeated. I'd cared for Josh for a long time. I couldn't turn it off like a light switch. I slid up next to him and took his big hands in both of mine.

"I don't know what the hell to do anymore," he said.

"It'll be okay." He leaned into me, his forehead on my shoulder, and I stroked the back of his neck. As my hand touched him, a flash of a movie camera tattoo played across my mind. I'd told Trent that

Josh was history, but was he? It was like our lives were tied up together, whether I wanted them to be or not, because of the church. I forced myself to forget about Trent for the moment. "I'm sorry, Josh. . . . I'm really sorry."

His life seemed even worse than mine. His family was at odds, he had to fight to stay in school, and his dad was a total dictator. I had drama school ahead of me, my friends, my job, maybe something romantic with Trent, and LaVon to look out for me too. And Josh didn't even have anyone to confide in anymore now that I'd broken up with him.

After a few minutes, Josh pulled away. "So what are you going to do about your dad?" he asked.

"I don't know," I said. "I mean, we have to get him out, but I'm not sure how."

"You need a legitimate reason to get past the guards, but I don't know what." He stood up. "I really have to go, but if I hear any news, I'll try to let you know."

"Okay, thanks."

"Jamie?" The light glowed behind him, leaving his face in shadow so I couldn't see his expression, but his voice was soft and pleading. "Jamie, I—"

His phone beeped in his pocket and he pulled it out to look at the screen. "I gotta go," he said. "Dad's freaking. The house is a disaster since my mom left, and he's hosting the disciple supper on Saturday night. I've got to catch Derrick before he goes to wrestling and make him come home with me to help clean it up, because we won't have time later this week."

Something clicked in my brain. "Your house is a mess?" I asked.

"A dump."

"In only four days?"

"We're guys. What can I say?"

I jumped up and threw my arms around him. "I've got it!"

"What?" he asked. "I missed something."

"Housecleaners!" I said. "We'll make a flyer and use Krista's phone number, and you can give it to your dad, and he can hire us to clean for him on Saturday. It'll be short notice, so the only time we'll be able to come is in the morning while everyone's in Assembly. And once we're inside, we'll get my dad out of there somehow."

"It might work," he said.

I was so excited, I squeezed him tightly, and he hugged me back. Then, just like a cliché in a romance novel, he brushed a stray piece of hair out of my eyes, and the next thing I knew, I was being kissed. Part of me wanted to shove him away. He'd betrayed me, leaving me on my own when I needed him most. But a warm rush of comfort and reassurance flooded through me too, and I let him push me back down onto the couch.

The weight of his body, familiar and warm, pressed me into the sofa, and he cupped my face with one hand while he stroked my hair with the other. I melted under him, my hands grabbing at his back, pulling him even closer if possible. I wanted to disappear into the heat between us.

"Jamie, I've missed you," he said.

Just the way he said "I've missed you," so whiny and needy, made something snap inside me. He sounded like he thought it was me who had ruined everything, when he'd been the one who caused us so many problems with his stupid secret relationship. I shoved him off and scooted out from under him.

"You don't have any right to miss me," I said.

"I know. I know—"

"You're the one who decided I wasn't worth it," I said. I adjusted my shirt, and my breath came short and fast. I didn't know if it was from the kissing or anger. "You let me down, Josh."

"Don't you think I know that?" he asked.

"Let's just go," I said.

"Yeah . . . okay."

In the hallway, I put my hand on his arm, stopping him. "I'll slip a flyer for our cleaning company into your locker."

"I'll do what I can," he promised.

He went up the stairs, and I tried to shake off what had just happened. It didn't mean anything, and I would not let him get that close to me again. There was a certain someone with silky brown hair who needed to know he could trust me too.

I took a deep breath and then flopped over at the waist and let it out in a big sigh, shaking my body, like we do for dance and acting warm-ups. I could feel myself finally really letting go of Josh, and it felt great. I skipped happily back to the drama room to find Liz and Krista.

"I need a phone to text Trent," I told them.

Krista handed me hers. "What for?"

"Just about a video project I have in mind," I said, smiling. "I'll tell you later. Right now, we have a lot of work to do."

chapter 30

IT WAS JUST AFTER SEVEN O'CLOCK, BUT THERE
wasn't any moon, and the weak porch light barely lit up the yard. All
I could see of LaVon was the glow of his cigarette, even though he
wasn't more than four feet away. Behind me, Krista shuffled through
the grass, holding on to the back of my black hoodie. A guy LaVon
knew called Gyp led the way, and he stuck to the shadows so well I
couldn't see him at all. When we got to the backyard, he stopped by
the kitchen door, and Krista and I crashed into LaVon.

"Always check the back entrance," Gyp said, speaking so softly we
all had to lean in. He was as tiny as LaVon was huge. Almost as small
as me, actually. "No point in breaking a window if some fool's left the
door unlocked." He tried it with no luck. "What you need to do," he
said, taking us around to the side yard, "is check out the whole building first and find the easiest window to target." After we'd made a
complete circle around the house, he said to me and Krista, "So what
window would you choose?"

"Ummm . . . the kitchen?" Krista said.

"No way." He adjusted his black hood so even more of his face was
hidden. "Look how high it is off the ground."

"But it's in the backyard," she argued. "No one would see me."

"You'll break your neck trying to get out fast if there's someone inside." He leaned in toward me, and I almost gagged on the smell of stale cigarettes on his breath. "Well?"

"The bedroom?" I guessed.

He shook his head. "Nah. Someone might be sleeping in there."

"I ain't got all night," LaVon said. "Just tell 'em, man."

"I thought you was payin' me for my expertise," Gyp said.

"I ain't gonna pay you nothin' if you don't get us inside the house in the next three minutes."

Gyp glared up at him, which I thought was pretty brave, since LaVon could probably squash him flat with his thumb. "Hey, man, I don't hafta help you. I got other places I could be, ya know?"

LaVon growled at him. An actual growl. It was pretty effective too, because Gyp turned to us immediately. "This way, ladies," he said. On the side of the house he pointed at a large sliding window. "This is the weak spot."

"But it's got a wood dowel in the track inside so you can't get it open," Krista said.

"Don't mean shit," Gyp said. He pulled a screwdriver out of his pocket, slid it under the edge of the screen's frame, and popped it off. Then he palmed the window and pushed up, jiggling it. The piece of doweling rolled right out of the track and off the sill into the living room. Half a second later, the window stood wide open.

"Who's first?" he asked.

"Me," I said.

LaVon gave me a boost, and before I was all the way through, Krista grabbed my legs and shoved me inside. I fell onto the living room floor in a heap, and she landed on top of me. A man bolted from a reclining chair, and Krista screamed.

"What the hell?" we heard LaVon shout.

"Later, dude!" Gyp yelled.

George flicked on a floor lamp. "Jeez. You two almost gave me a heart attack," he said, clutching his hands to his chest.

"Sorry," Krista apologized. "We . . . uh, I forgot my key. I didn't think you were here."

"Maybe knock next time," he suggested.

As he said it, there was a loud thumping noise.

"Oh," I said. "We forgot about LaVon."

I opened the front door, and he stepped into the living room. George took one look at LaVon's hulking figure and jumped up from the chair he'd just settled back into. "Who are you?" he asked.

"George, this is LaVon," I said.

"Jamie's uncle," Krista added.

LaVon and I looked at her like she was crazy.

"Your uncle?" George asked. He was still standing, and he moved so the chair was between them. I never knew he was such a chicken! Maybe it was because he was still half asleep.

"By marriage," I said, quickly.

"Yeah . . . by marriage," LaVon said. I could hear the smirk in his voice.

"I'm making a uniform shirt for him," Krista said. "For his new job. He couldn't get one big enough."

"I can imagine," George said.

"We'll be upstairs." Krista led us away.

"In your room?" George asked. "I don't know—"

"It's fine," Krista called back over her shoulder. "I told you, he's Jamie's uncle."

"What is wrong with you?" I asked her as we went up the stairs. "You were supposed to say LaVon's in a play and you're making his costume."

"I totally froze," she admitted.

"Uncle, my ass," LaVon muttered, laughing. It died on his lips when he saw Krista's bedroom. "You gotta be kiddin' me."

"What?" she asked.

"You live in this room?"

I was so used to the hot-pink-and-deep-purple color scheme I hardly noticed it anymore, but seeing it with LaVon's eyes made me smile. It *was* super startling after the bare rooms that he and I lived in. Plus, there were all the design sketches and pictures of eighties pop stars on the walls. It was actually kind of scary. When Krista and I got our apartment in New York, we'd have to set a few ground rules about decor.

"I love my room," Krista said. She reached out and pulled LaVon inside. "Stand here while I get my stuff."

I plopped down onto one of the beanbags. The look on LaVon's face as he surveyed the room cracked me up. It was somewhere between bemused and nauseated. Krista came out of her walk-in closet with a huge red shirt and a pin cushion.

"Usually I put whoever I'm fitting onto this stool," she said, "but I'm going to have to stand on it instead." She dragged it over to LaVon, and he slipped on the shirt. "It fits pretty good," she mumbled through a mouthful of pins.

"I'm stylin', man," LaVon said, holding out his arms.

We'd wanted to get three matching polos but we couldn't find any at the thrift store, and they were too expensive to buy new. Krista had a pattern for a simple bowling shirt and a large piece of red fabric she'd bought on sale, so she'd made us each a uniform last night. One thing about Krista, she can sew fast.

She tugged at the front. "That's what I was afraid of," she said. "I was going to mark where the buttonholes go, but I don't think you'll be able to do it up. I was kind of short on material. But you can wear a T-shirt under it instead."

"Cool. I like it loose anyway," he said.

"Well, I guess you can take it off, since I won't bother with buttons. All I have to do is finish the hem."

"Nice touch," LaVon said, fingering where she'd embroidered his name on the front. Well, not his name, because we didn't want to give anything away. Instead it said FRANK.

"I think I'll call you that from now on," I joked.

He lifted up his silver shades and eyed me in his way, shaking his head.

I laughed. "Or maybe not."

LaVon held the lobby door open for me, and I wheeled my bike inside, then stopped short, making him bump his bicycle into mine. Josh sat slumped in an orange vinyl chair in the corner, studying his chemistry book.

"Josh? Is my dad okay?"

"Oh, hey, Jamie," he said, standing and stretching. "I was about to give up and go home."

"Is he okay?" I asked again.

"He's fine."

"How'd you know where to find me?" I asked.

253

"Megan told me."

"James," LaVon said, "move outta the door so I can get inside."

"Oh, sorry." LaVon walked past us and went up the stairs. Josh gave him an inquisitive look, but I didn't explain.

"I wanted to give you this," Josh said. He handed me a silver key. "It fits the back door of your dad's place. All the trailers have the same locks so the Teacher can visit unannounced."

"How convenient. When's your dad going to call and book us to clean?"

"He told me to set it up, so you're good," Josh said. "He was actually pretty relieved by the idea. I've added you to the guards' list for Saturday at ten A.M. Don't forget, no cell phones, and they'll search the car before you go in."

"What are they looking for?"

"Mostly cameras, which is why they don't want you taking in your phones."

"But I always used to take mine into the church," I said.

"You weren't a stranger," he explained. "Whatever you do, don't lose the key. They're numbered, and that one will lead back to me."

"Okay. Thanks, Josh."

He went for a hug, but I sidestepped him, and he brushed his hair with both hands, like he hadn't reached out for me. I went up the stairs without looking back.

chapter 31

ON SATURDAY MORNING, I SKIPPED DANCE CLASS for the first time since I'd had the flu in tenth grade. Liz had borrowed the red station wagon from her aunt again and brought it over to Krista's, where we'd filled it with brooms, mops, a couple of orange buckets, a vacuum cleaner, and some rags. And one expertly hidden package of cell phones.

We made sure all the cleaning equipment was easy to see, sticking up, so we looked like an authentic maid service. Then we added a sign Krista had hand-lettered to the driver's door.

ANGEL CLEANERS
BECAUSE CLEANLINESS IS NEXT TO GODLINESS

Krista stopped at the gate. The guards wore brown servant robes, which made LaVon snicker. I was glad to see I didn't recognize either of them. Because the R&R had close to a thousand members, I hardly knew anyone, mostly only the ones who chaperoned the dances and youth Bible study.

The blond one, holding a clipboard, stepped up to Krista's window. "Bless you, sister," he said.

"Uh . . . you too." She took her fake paperwork from me and scanned it like she wasn't sure where we were supposed to be going. "We're here to clean number eight."

The guard leaned over and peered into the car. Krista had tucked her hair up in a scarf to hide the color, and she had the name KELLY embroidered on her shirt. By the time she'd gotten to mine, she'd run out of time, though, and NICOLE was handwritten in Sharpie pen above my pocket. I also wore one of Krista's fashion wigs, a long black one with bangs, and I stared out the passenger window, in case the guard recognized me after all.

"You're a cleaner, brother?" the guard asked LaVon. He sounded a bit like he wanted to laugh, but he held back.

"You got a problem with my choice of vocation, *brother*?"

"No. I most assuredly do not," the guard said soothingly. "God shows us our path, and He has chosen you to be a servant like me. Who am I to judge?"

"He moves the furniture for us," Krista said before LaVon could get huffy about being called a servant. "Where do we go?"

"First, we must check the vehicle for devices of Satan," he said. "Please, step out of the car."

We all got out, and LaVon lit a cigarette. You could tell both the guards were itching to tell him not to smoke but didn't have the nerve once they saw how big he really was.

"I am Samuel," the blond one told us, "and this is Peter."

Peter looked wiry and maybe a bit hungry. They stuck their heads inside the car, rummaged in the glove compartment, and asked Krista to open up the back so they could look through our cleaning supplies.

"It is God's will that you empty your pockets and lay everything on the hood of the car," Samuel said. "If you ladies have handbags, the Teacher respectfully requests that you allow us to see what's in them."

"We were told not to bring cell phones," Krista said, using a falsely sweet voice. "Was there anything else we're not supposed to have?"

Samuel smiled serenely at her. "What a woman carries with her tells us about her character. Only people of high moral standards are allowed through these gates."

"So, what," LaVon asked, "you're looking for condoms or drugs or somethin'?"

"We're good girls," I said, intervening and smiling at the guard, but keeping my eyes down. "Praise God."

"Indeed," he said. "Praise God."

We handed him our purses and watched while he rummaged through them. Not finding a cell phone or anything else he didn't approve of, he gave them back.

"Seems like ya'd search us on our way out," LaVon said, dumping out his keys, change, and wallet. "Not on our way in."

"But don't you see, Frank?" Peter said, reading the name off LaVon's shirt. "We're establishing a friendship now. Once we trust you enough to go into our homes, then we have no reason to search you on the way out."

We got back into the car as Peter unlocked the big metal gate and swung it open for us. "Number eight's around the bend in the road," Samuel said. "On the left. The front door's open for you. Please be finished in one hour."

"Thank you," Krista said. She gunned the motor, and we were inside. I watched in my mirror as they shut the gate, locking us in. We'd already passed my dad's single-wide trailer before I remembered to check it out.

"That was surreal," Krista said.

"I thought LaVon was going to get us in trouble," I said.

"I was just making conversation."

I rolled my eyes, but he couldn't see me.

"Back into the driveway," LaVon told Krista. "And leave the keys in the ignition."

"Yes, boss," she said.

We all got out, and Krista and I ran up to the front door. Sure enough, it was unlocked.

"What?" LaVon called after us. "You think I'm carrying all this shit in myself?" He opened the back of the station wagon and began unloading our supplies.

We ran back to help him. "Sorry."

Looking around to make sure no one was watching, I reached under the bumper and pulled out the padded envelope with the cell phones.

Inside the trailer, we all staggered to a stop. "It smells like something died in here!" Krista said, pinching her nose. Empty chip bags, pop cans, and fast-food containers covered every flat surface. Laundry—clean or dirty, we couldn't tell—was draped over the couch in piles. Papers seemed to be randomly thrown all over the living room, and my shoe was glued to something sticky in the entryway.

LaVon pulled out a huge pair of pink rubber gloves. "Don't give me any shit," he said, when we laughed. "Only color they had."

"What are your hands made of? Gold?" I teased.

"I know what's in my own toilet," he said. "I ain't stickin' my bare hands in no one else's."

"You're not really going to clean the toilet, are you?" Krista asked.

"Hell, yeah, I am. That's what the man's payin' us for." He grabbed the fifty-dollar bill off the table where Mr. Peterson had left it for us. "You two better get goin'," he said. "We got less than an hour to get outta here."

"You're not coming with us?" I asked.

"I thought we was clear," he said, looking at me like I was a dummy, "there's this little thing called parole that I'm not gonna screw with."

"You're on parole?" Krista asked, her eyes bugging out. "What for?"

"You got fifty-two minutes," LaVon said, ignoring her. "You goin', or what?"

"But why did you come along?" I asked.

"I'm your cover," he said. "And I'll make sure we get out. Don't try and bring your dad all the way back here. Just get him outside and call me on my cell. We'll figure it out then."

"But—"

"Come on," Krista said, pulling me out the back door.

Each yard had a small blue shed in the back, and we ran from one to the next, but for the most part, we were out in the open. All the disciples and their families were *supposed* to go to Assembly on Saturday, but there was no way of knowing if they really had gone. We just had to run through the backyards, hoping no one had stayed home and would spot us. At least we knew Mira wasn't home. It wasn't safe for Josh to text us, so Liz and Megan had gone to Assembly with him, and they'd sent Krista a message, letting us know she was at the church.

When we got to my dad's shed, we leaned against it, panting. I think I was short on breath more from fright than exertion.

"Can you hear that?" Krista whispered.

"Yeah."

The gate was so close to my dad's trailer that from where we stood the sound of the guards' mumbled voices floated back to us. We couldn't see them, though, and we had a clear line to the rear door.

"Ready?" I asked her.

"I'm gonna text LaVon to let him know we're going in."

When she was done, we hurtled ourselves across the tiny backyard and up to the door. I thrust the key in the lock, and it turned easily. We stepped into the dim kitchen and looked around. Cheap cabinets, mini appliances, and a laminate countertop framed a spotless Formica table. The kitchen literally sparkled, it was so clean. We crept down a narrow hallway, carefully opening each door and peering in. Bathroom. Closet. Master bedroom. And finally, near the front of the trailer, a locked door.

"He's got to be in there," I said. "What if someone's with him, though? Like a guard?"

"I'm guessing they would've heard us whispering by now," she said. "This door is one of those cheap, flimsy kinds."

She was probably right. And then, from inside, we heard a cough.

"That's him!" I said.

"Are you sure?"

"Of course I'm sure. He's my dad! I would know his cough anywhere." That wasn't actually true, but who else could it be?

"Give me a hairpin," Krista said.

I pulled one out of the wig. Five minutes later, the door was still locked and I'd searched all over the trailer for a screwdriver to pry the knob off, but hadn't had any luck.

"It looks so easy in the movies," Krista said, throwing the pin away. "Maybe LaVon knows how to do it."

Another wracking cough came from inside the room, and I thought I heard my dad mumble something, but then it got quiet again.

"We can't ask LaVon," I said.

"Well, we've only got about twenty minutes to get out of here. What else can we do?"

"Fine. Call him and see what he says."

I pressed my ear to the door while she dialed. "LaVon?" Krista whispered. "He's here, but he's locked in the bedroom and we can't get the door open."

I could hear LaVon loud and clear, even though Krista didn't have him on speaker phone. "Did you look for a key?" he asked.

"Ummm . . . no."

"Check over the door."

I ran my hands over the molding, but struck out. I tried all the doors in the hallway too, but there wasn't any key.

"We need help," Krista said.

"Goddammit," LaVon said. "I'm up to my elbows in dishes over here, and you can't even get a fuckin' door open without me, and now I'm gonna go back to jail, and I'll never see my grandbaby till she's grown, all because some fool I don't even know, who can't hold on to his money, gets hisself kidnapped. . . ." He kept going for a while. Finally he told us to chill and he'd be over in a minute. Any other time, we would've laughed at his rant, but we could both feel the clock ticking. My insides were so twisted, I thought I might throw up.

About two minutes later, LaVon barreled in through the kitchen. "Move outta the way," he said. We stepped back, and he bashed into the door with his massive shoulder. The wood splintered; with a second shove, the door gave way and we were inside the room.

The curtains were drawn, and the only light came from the hallway. My dad lay on a pallet on the floor, his eyes large and afraid, but his body unresponsive despite the door being broken open. And then we saw why. Wide nylon straps held him down.

LaVon pulled a huge knife out of his pocket, flipped it open, and reached to cut away the bonds. My dad tried to scream, but all that came out was a raspy gasp.

"Wait!" Krista shouted. She flipped the light on. "I want pictures in case we need proof." LaVon jumped back out of the way as she snapped them with her phone.

"I hear somethin'," LaVon said. We froze, holding our breath, and then we heard it too, footsteps creaking up the trailer's front steps. "You're not here, James," LaVon said. "You got it?"

"But—"

"I said, you're not here!"

I nodded, and he shoved me and Krista into a minuscule closet. He was still wearing his pink rubber gloves, which reminded me that Gyp had told us to wear some too, but we'd totally forgotten. LaVon pressed the knife into my hand and slid the closet door shut, leaving us in the dark. We heard him go out of the room, and then doors banged and men started shouting.

"I SAID DON'T MOVE," ORDERED A MAN'S VOICE IN the hallway. It sounded like the blond guard, but I couldn't be sure.

"Chill, dude," LaVon said. "I thought you trusted me, man."

"That was before God led us to look up from our prayers and see you stealing across the yard," the guard said.

"Oh, yeah, well . . . I was just cleanin'."

"You're not supposed to be cleaning *this* trailer."

"I got mixed up," LaVon said. He sounded so calm. Krista and I held on to each other, barely breathing.

"Where are those girls?" asked a different voice.

"They're in number eight," LaVon said. "Mr. P. left a note there with our money askin' us to do this one too. What's your problem, man?"

"Don't move," the guard said. "Peter, you look around while I stay here with him."

"There ain't nothin' to see," LaVon said. "I didn't do nothin'."

We heard footsteps, and then from the doorway of my dad's room, a voice said, "Samuel, he broke down this door."

"Oh, yeah, that," LaVon said. "I thought I was supposed to clean that room, but there's some dude sleeping in there. Are you sure he's okay? He looks kinda pale."

"Mr. Cross," we heard a voice ask, "are you all right?"

Dad tried to say something, but all that came out was a raspy cough. Krista and I clung together and pressed ourselves into the corner of the closet, holding our breath.

LaVon said from the other room, "Can we take this discussion outside, man? I wanna smoke, and I'm gettin' all claustrophobic and shit in here."

"Is he all right?" we heard Samuel ask.

"Looks about the same as last time I checked on him," Peter answered.

"Okay, brother, let's step outside. I'm sure the Teacher will want to speak to you before we call the authorities."

"You're in charge, man," LaVon said.

"This way."

As soon as they were gone, we sent two text messages. One to Liz, and one to Josh, telling them the guards had LaVon and we were stuck in Dad's trailer.

"Maybe after Assembly finishes they can cause a distraction or something in the parking lot so we can get out," Krista said.

"*If* Josh will even help us. He might not want to now."

We made ourselves wait another two minutes, listening carefully, in case someone was still skulking around.

"Do you think it's safe yet?" I whispered.

"What choice do we have?" Krista asked. "We've got to get your dad out of here before Mira comes back."

When we stepped out of the closet, Dad started wriggling around and tried to scream again.

"Shhh."

"Who are you?" he rasped, his voice barely audible.

I handed Krista the switchblade, and she sliced through the straps.

"It's okay, Dad." I touched his forehead with my hand.

He flinched. "Where's Mira?" he croaked. "What have you done with her?"

"Take your wig off, Jamie," Krista said.

"It's me." I pulled at the long black hair, the pins ripping at my scalp, tears flooding my eyes. "It's me and Krista. We're here to help you."

"James?" he asked. "Is it really you?"

"Yeah, it's really me. You do want to get out of here, don't you?"

"Please," he said.

"Okay, Richard," Krista said. "Time to get up."

She held out her hands to Dad and helped him into a sitting position. He swayed, and I grabbed him by the shoulders to steady him.

"Water . . . ," Dad said.

"We'll get some on the way out," I said. "Where are your clothes?"

"I . . . I don't know."

"Here're some slippers," Krista said.

We shoved Dad's feet into them. His white disciple robe would have to do for now. At least it was a mild day for early March and not raining. We tried to stand him up, and he teetered under our grip, but eventually we got him on his feet.

"Wait," Krista said. "Before we go, I better try to see what's happening outside."

Dad leaned so heavily on me, I thought I might collapse.

"There's a big group of people on the lawn," she reported. "And the gate's wide open, which is good. No cops yet."

"What about guns?"

"I didn't see any."

"No guns," Dad said.

That's what Josh had told us, but it was a relief to know for sure.

"Okay. Let's go," I said.

We took my dad through the back, stopping in the kitchen for a glass of water. I wanted Krista to go ahead and be the lookout, but I wasn't strong enough to hold him up by myself. Once we were outside, we stopped again to let Dad catch his breath. Men's voices carried from the front lawn almost as clearly as if they stood with us behind the trailer. The Teacher asked LaVon if he had taken God into his heart, and he played along with it beautifully.

"I ain't sayin' I never thought of it," LaVon said, laying on his street talk pretty heavy. "There was this dude in the joint who used to talk about the Head Fred, and he made some good points. Know what I mean?"

"God's love is the only point there is," the Teacher agreed.

"I'm hearin' you, man," LaVon said. "But just so you know, I ain't admittin' nothin'. I was just cleanin' that house."

"I believe you," the Teacher said. "Or I believe that's what you intended to do in your heart. Do you know why?"

"Must be 'cause I'm wearin' these pink rubber gloves," LaVon said, laughing.

The Teacher chuckled. "No, because we're all good inside. You just need some guidance."

"Sounds good," LaVon said. "What you got in mind?"

Dad's grip slackened on my arm, and he slowly slid to the ground, too tired to stand anymore. "Krista?" I said. "We need the car."

"You stay here," she told me. "Use the phone to make the video of your dad and send it to Trent."

"Okay."

Krista had only taken about three steps when she stumbled over the brick border around the flower bed and fell onto the grass, writhing in pain, but luckily not making a sound.

"Are you okay?" I whispered.

"I twisted my ankle," she said.

She tried to stand, but couldn't put any weight on it at all and sat down hard on the ground, clenching her teeth.

"Stay here with my dad. I'll get the car." I handed her the phone. "Do the video while I'm gone. Trent's waiting for it."

Crouching low, I made a break for the blue shed and waited behind it to see if anyone had spotted me. After half a minute, I sprinted to the next one. *Everyone's out in the street*, I kept telling myself. *Assembly's probably over, but no one will go home because they all want to know what's going on. You're safe.*

I finally reached Josh's yard and stopped to catch my breath before making a dash for the station wagon. As I was about to start the engine, Josh flung himself at the passenger side and yanked the door open, jumping in and slamming the door.

"Oh, my God," I said. "I think my heart stopped for a second. What're you doing here?"

"There's a whole crowd of people from Assembly in front of your dad's trailer. When no one was looking, I walked around to the back and found your dad and Krista. She told me where you were."

"Did anyone see you?"

"I don't think so," he said. "I want to go with you."

"What about Derrick? Is he coming too?"

"I don't know." Josh's face was the color of watered-down milk, and his eyes had blue shadows under them. "I thought I could only help Derrick from inside, but maybe if I leave, he'll realize he can get out too."

"Yeah, maybe."

"What's your plan?" he asked.

"Not a clue." I eased the car out of the driveway.

"I think you should call their bluff," he said. "They'll never bring the police in unless they absolutely have to. There's way too much going on here that they don't want anyone to know about."

Like how they lock people up and brainwash them.

"Good to know," I said.

Ahead of us, the gate was still open, but about fifty people stood in the road blocking our way. Anger welled up in me, and I wanted to plow right through them, but that would have been really stupid of me because I might actually have hurt someone. Still, I drove as fast as I dared, slamming on the brakes at the last second.

"Jeez, Jamie!" Josh said. "Are you trying to kill us?"

I jumped out of the car without answering. The members of the R&R had scattered because of my crazy driving, but they regrouped and moved toward us.

"LaVon!" I shouted. "Get in the car! We'll be right back."

Josh and I sprinted across the lawn, and behind us, we could hear people running. Liz and Megan were with Krista, and the three of them had helped my dad to his feet, but he stumbled as they tried to move forward.

"They've been starving him," Krista explained. "He's too weak to walk."

Josh picked him up and slung him over his shoulder. He ran toward the car as if going for a touchdown, dodging a couple of disciples who tried to block him.

Krista half ran, half limped along, leaning on Liz and Megan, with me hurrying behind them. "Did you send the video of Dad to Trent?" I asked her.

"Yep. He texted back saying he's already uploaded it to his website."

Everyone's focus was on the Teacher and LaVon, so no one noticed when Megan and Liz climbed into the backseat with Krista. There was no way she could drive with her injured ankle. Josh had already put my dad in the front and was trying to buckle him in when someone shouted the alarm.

"Hey! They've got Richard!" yelled one of the servants.

Josh shut Dad's door, and I scanned the crowd, looking for LaVon. A group of men had circled him on the lawn. I'd parked so they didn't have room to swing the gate shut, and I saw some members sprint out into the church parking lot, probably to get their cars to block our escape. I turned to ask Josh what we should do just as his dad took a swing at him and knocked him against the car.

"You're a traitor and a sinner," Mr. Peterson shouted, "just like your mother!"

Josh put his hands up to protect his face, and his dad slugged him again. The entire group, including the Teacher, stood by without raising a hand to help him. I knew the church's policy was to let a father discipline his son without interference, but I didn't submit to that doctrine.

"Stop it!" I screamed. "Just stop it!" I threw myself between them, and Mr. Peterson's fist rammed solidly into my shoulder, knocking me to the ground. I screamed in pain, and that was all Josh could take. He lunged at his dad, but then Derrick and some of the servants pulled them apart.

LaVon took advantage of the mayhem, and from my spot on the ground, I saw him bang two of the men's heads together and shove the Teacher out of his way. A moment later, he was across the yard, helping me scramble to my feet.

The servants led Mr. Peterson over to the Teacher, who touched his arm and leaned in to speak to him, the wind rustling his long hair and robes. Derrick let go of his brother. Josh leaned against the car, his nose streaming red, and a cut below his left eye oozing blood.

"Josh?" Derrick asked. "You okay, man?"

I shoved him away with my good arm. "This is all your fault," I said. "He only stayed this long because of you. Help him into the car, dammit!"

Josh groaned and tipped his head back, trying to stanch the flow of blood from his nose.

"No," Derrick said. "God will protect him here."

"How can you believe that shit?" I grabbed the front of Derrick's shirt. "I *know* all about you. Josh told me the truth. You can have a *real* life. All you have to do is put him in the car and get in too."

In all the craziness, I had totally forgotten about Mira, and I guess she'd been hanging back with the other women by the fence, but before we could stop her, she darted forward and opened the front passenger door. "Richard, darling," she said. "Come inside. You can trust me, I'm your wife."

I pushed her out of the way, and she stumbled, falling to the ground. I felt kind of bad, but Mira was in too deep to be trusted.

"Dad, she's not your wife. Do you understand? The Teacher can't legally marry you. It was only a secular service. A fake wedding."

The Teacher stepped forward and helped Mira to her feet. A couple of the women led her away, telling her to let Christ handle it. I blocked the Teacher's way to Dad by putting my body between them.

"Richard," he said, leaning over me, "do not let these sinners take you away from the people who love you."

"Don't listen to him, Dad," I said.

"Move her," the Teacher ordered two of the servants, and they lifted me out of the way to get to Dad. In an instant, Josh and LaVon had come to my defense, and I found myself in the middle of a free-for-all. I heard that sickening thud like raw meat being slapped onto a cutting board. My dad curled himself up into a ball and moaned softly, while Megan, Liz, and Krista leaned over the seat, trying to calm him down. The Teacher had retreated to avoid getting caught in the melee, and I took the opportunity to lock and slam Dad's door so they couldn't get to him again.

The fight was ten men to two, but it still took several minutes before they had LaVon and Josh pinned to the ground. The Teacher stepped forward, smiling. "Leave Richard here with us, and we'll let you go without pressing charges."

"I've got the whole thing on video!" Krista shouted from the backseat. She waved her phone in the air. "I'm sending it to the cops right now!"

The Teacher's smile disappeared. "Get the phone!" he ordered his men.

I dove into the backseat, shielding Krista from the men and ignoring my throbbing shoulder. She stuffed the phone down her shirt, and I lay on my back, kicking at the disciples reaching into the car. Megan and Liz scrambled over the seat into the far back to get out of the way and started hitting the men with brooms.

I don't know how LaVon got loose, but suddenly he was there, pulling bodies off of me, hurtling them across the lawn. Then he was in the car, and the engine gunned. From where I lay, I could see the top of Josh's blond head in the driver's seat.

LaVon pulled me up into a sitting position, and I did a double take. Krista had crawled into the far back with Megan and Liz, and Josh sat slumped on the seat next to me. *It was Derrick driving the car.*

In front of us, the congregation made a wall of bodies. Behind them, in the main parking lot, they'd strategically placed about half a dozen cars to keep us from escaping. "Derrick! Don't!" I screamed as the car lurched forward. People dove out of the way, but he swung the station wagon up onto the lawn and around in a U-turn. It scraped bottom from all our weight and made a horrible grating sound as we tore down the road.

"We're going out the back way," he said. "There's an emergency exit in case the compound's ever raided."

"How did you and Josh get away?" I asked LaVon.

He nodded at Derrick. "Some of the church members helped too," he said, shaking his head.

"Wow. Really?"

"Not everyone at the church is bad," Derrick snapped, and I sort of believed him.

He raced the car down the road, gravel spewing behind us. When he got to the Teacher's mansion, he drove right up onto the grass and down a narrow track between some trees. A high gate ran across the end of the path, and he jumped out. We watched him take a key from around his neck, unlock the padlock, and swing it open. He hopped in behind the wheel and eased us over the curb and out onto the street. All around us normal-looking houses lined the streets. Suburbia had never looked so good.

A MINUTE LATER, DERRICK TURNED ONTO THE MAIN road, heading back toward our part of town.

"Uh, James?" LaVon said.

"Yeah?"

"That was all *Charlie's Angels* and shit, but don't you think when we get back to your dad's place the cops are gonna be waiting for us? Breakin' and enterin' and all that?"

"No, we can't go back to the house," Dad said faintly from the front seat.

"Why not?" I asked.

"I . . . I . . . well, I signed it over to them . . . to the church."

"You gave the church our house?" I asked.

"It was Mira's idea," he said. "She told me we didn't need it anymore."

"I'll bet," LaVon said.

I couldn't believe it. I'd have to live in the Regis Deluxe Motel for the rest of my life. Or at least all summer. And now that my dad didn't have a job anymore, I'd definitely have to ask for extra hours at the Coffee Klatch too. I tried to remind myself that at least Dad was free, but it still kind of pissed me off.

"So what about the cops?" LaVon asked again. "Those church people ain't gonna just let me go. Man, my parole officer's gonna kick my ass. And my daughter . . . she's gonna flip."

"Oh, don't worry about that," Krista said. "Right, Jamie?"

I smiled.

"Not only did I get the whole fight scene on video," Krista said, "which I won't show anyone unless I have to because LaVon's in some of it, but while we waited for Jamie to bring the car, Richard told me everything they did to him—starving him, beatings, sleep depriva-tion—" She saw the look of horror on my face and stopped listing them. "Anyway, I sent that video, along with the pictures of him tied down, to Trent. He's already posted them on his website and e-mailed them to every media outlet in the city."

"Plus CNN," Megan said from the back.

"And the Huffington Post," Krista added.

"They're going to be way too busy at the Right & the Real to worry about us," Liz said.

"It still don't mean they won't call the cops," LaVon said.

"They won't," Josh mumbled through the bowling shirt LaVon had given him to hold against his bloody nose. "Believe me. They don't trust the police at all. And their only answer to the media will be *no comment*. If there's one thing the Right & the Real is good at, it's keeping secrets."

We dropped Josh and Derrick off at their aunt's apartment, where their mom was staying. At the motel, LaVon and I helped my dad out of the car.

"Are you sure you don't want to come to my house?" Krista asked.

"I don't want your mom to see him like this," I said. "We'll stay

275

here tonight. If he has any money left, maybe get him some clothes and move to a better motel tomorrow."

"Come on, James," LaVon said. "Let's get him inside."

I leaned into the window. "Thanks for getting the car, Liz."

"Anytime."

"Bye," Megan said.

I gave Krista a quick hug. "Thanks."

"Anything for you, chickie. Call me if you need me."

Dad leaned so heavily on LaVon as we took him through the lobby that Stub looked up from his computer and said, "He better not be dead."

"Just drunk," LaVon said.

"Drunk?" I asked once we were in the stairwell.

"Easier than explainin'."

"Yeah, I guess so."

Half an hour later, LaVon closed the door to my room behind him. He'd brought me a bowl of potato-leek soup, and it sat on the dresser, cooling. My dad lay sleeping on the cot, my Princess Pink comforter tucked up under his bearded chin. I'd wanted to take him to the emergency room, but he'd refused.

"No health insurance," he'd said.

Another thing the Right & the Real had taken from us.

Someone tapped on the door, and I hurried to open it so Dad wouldn't wake up. Trent stood there, holding a shopping bag.

"Hey," he said. "I brought some stuff for your dad."

I stepped out into the hallway and shut the door behind me, leaning against it. "What'd you get?" I asked.

"Electrolytes and baby food."

"Sounds delicious," I said.

"I looked it up on the web," he said. "It's the best thing for someone who's gone without food for a while. He's probably dehydrated."

"Thanks."

It was all I could do not to throw my arms around him, but after kissing Josh in the scene shop on Thursday, I'd been kind of nervous with Trent. Josh and I were definitely over, no matter what happened, but right then, I felt so fragile I was almost afraid I might confess how weak I'd been. And that would be so awful, to hurt Trent when it didn't mean anything.

I didn't know what to say, but I also didn't want him to leave yet, so I said, "You were great."

"Yeah," he agreed, laughing. "I was right there in the middle of it all, saving the day, wasn't I?" He balled up his hands into fists and, scowling, punched the air like he was fighting the men at the church.

"You *did* help," I said. "You got it all up online so fast."

"That's true."

We stood there grinning.

"Never underestimate the need for a computer geek," I told him.

"Which reminds me," he said, "I should probably go because I got so much traffic on my website it crashed. I need to see if I can fix it."

I took a step closer to him, and he set the bag down on the floor.

"All right," I said. "If you really have to."

"I don't *have* to go," he said. "If you need me, I can stay as long as you want. You know, strictly as a friend. Because, I know you said you needed time to get over that Jon guy, and then to figure out everything with your dad, and you just rescued him an hour ago and everything, so that's not actually a lot of time. I get that. And I know

I said I'd wait for you, and I still will, *but* if you needed me *now*, I'm here for you. Seriously. Don't take this as pressure or anything, but I'm totally willing to forgo the thirty-year waiting period and—"

"Trent?" I said. "Just shut up and kiss me."

And then his arms were around my waist, and his mouth was on mine, and I was finally brushing his hair back with my hand. And it was just as silky as I'd always imagined. I guess I'd expected Trent to taste like coffee, but his breath was toothpaste fresh. I traced his tattoo with my finger, even though I couldn't see it, and pressed myself closer to him. As we kissed, his arms tightened around me, and our mouths opened slightly. Very lightly, with the tip of my tongue, I touched his crooked tooth, and a shudder ran all the way through me.

And then a voice growled, "What the hell's going on out here?"

We jumped apart. LaVon stood outside his door, scowling at us.

"Oh, you know," Trent said, putting the width of the hall between us and smoothing his hair, "just the usual. Boy meets girl, boy charms girl, boy kisses girl, et cetera, et cetera. But they don't do anything else because that would be bad. Very bad, and the boy definitely does not want to be killed by either the neighbor or the dad. . . ."

Trent's babbling trailed off into silence, which grew and grew while the three of us stood there not looking at each other. Finally, LaVon's laughter broke the tension, and we all cracked up. "He's as crazy as you, James. You two will make a great couple." He shook his head at us and went back into his room.

"So . . . about that waiting period," Trent said.

"It's over."

"Fastest thirty years of my life." He closed the distance between us.

After a while, I came up for breath thinking we better slow down or I'd need to ask Stub for another room. "I should probably check on my dad," I said.

"Right. Okay." Trent looked a little dazed himself. "And I need to fix my website." He picked up the bag. "Oh, yeah, I got these too." Like a magician pulling a rabbit out of a hat, he produced a bouquet of daffodils.

"Awww . . . you remembered."

"Yep. And your birthday's April twentieth," he said. "Only forty-six more shopping days."

It took us another ten minutes to say good-bye, and the flowers were a little bit crushed by the time he left, but I planned to press them in my complete works of Shakespeare anyway so I could keep them for always.

"James?" Dad mumbled when I came into the room.

"I'm right here," I said. I scooted the folding chair LaVon had lent me up to the bed. "What do you need?"

He opened his eyes a little. "I just want to say . . . I'm sorry."

"It's okay."

"It's not," he said. "It's really not." A tear slid down the side of his face and into his ear. "But I'll make it up to you."

"You'll go back to Dr. Kennedy?"

"As soon as he'll see me," he said. "And I'll talk to the lawyer about the house too."

"Okay. Sounds good." What could I say? He was my dad. So he'd screwed up. We all did. And yeah, this was on a pretty massive scale, but sometimes we mess up big. I knew he'd forgive me if and when I made a disastrous choice or two.

"Know what I missed most?" Dad asked.

"Me?"

"Of course," he said. "But I also missed you reading plays aloud to me."

"I'll do it again," I said. "Don't worry."

"Would you read to me now?" he asked.

"Shouldn't you rest?"

"Please?"

"Yeah, okay." I had recycled all the cartons from my shoes and clothing, but my books, plays, and memorabilia boxes were piled at one end of my bed, still sealed. "What do you want to hear?" I asked, shifting them around.

"I don't care," he said. "Something cheerful."

"No *King Lear*, then?" I asked.

"No . . . definitely not *Lear*."

I dragged the box over by the lamp, used my key to cut the tape. Inside was a large manila envelope with my name on it in Dad's handwriting. I opened it and slid out the contents. There were several pieces of paper, and clipped to the top one were ten one-hundred-dollar bills. A thousand dollars? I examined the first sheet. It was the title for the Beast, signed over to me. The other papers were some sort of bank statement. Next to the account number was my name. In my father's handwriting, it said, *Your grandfather left you this for college, but you can use some of it now.* I looked at the balance: $102,018.86.

"James?" Dad asked. "Did you find something good?"

I swallowed hard. Silent tears ran down my face. "Yeah," I said. "Yeah. I found something really good."

Leave it to Dad to put the envelope in the one carton he'd been sure I would open, and have it turn out to be the box I couldn't face because it contained all my memories and dreams.

"I'm ready when you are," Dad said.

I pulled out my complete volume of Shakespeare, opened to *All's Well That Ends Well,* and began to read aloud to my father.

ACKNOWLEDGMENTS

Michael Bourret—thank you for your insights, encouragement, and for your lightning-quick responses to my never-ending questions. Sometimes you're so fast I think you must be answering my e-mails while I'm still pushing the Send button. *Merci beaucoup!*

Stacey Barney—thank you for your faith in me, and thank you for always asking all the right questions so the story comes out better than I could've hoped. I'm so happy to count myself as one of your writers.

Thanks to the sales and publicity team at Penguin, especially Penny Mason, Vimala Jeevanandam, and Caroline Sun. And thank you to all the wonderful indie bookstores and the staff at Powell's who hand-sold my first book with such enthusiasm. When you grow up in Portland, it's a dream come true to see your book in the window at Powell's Books.

Special thanks to my friends, family, fact checkers, early readers, and cheerleaders. Thank you to Linda Anthony, Frank Anthony, Eileen Cook, Nova Ren Suma, Sarah & Cheryl Tradewell, Kelly & Nicole Berthelot, Alyson Beecher, and Reggie & Mavie Cruz. Also, special thanks to the Brouhahas—Kim Thacker and Alexa Barry—who read so many versions of this manuscript I'm surprised they can see straight anymore. And Joelle Charbonneau, please take a bow for all your assistance with the musical theatre aspect of the story. *I could never really sing!* Plus, it's always better to have two Joelles on the job if you can.

To Ms. Peacock's Grade 6 & 7 classes, I'd like to say thank you for reminding me it only gets done with "less talking, and more writing." Lots of love, and a big thank you, to Ashly Anthony for promoting her auntie's first book to her whole third-grade class (and beyond). Every writer needs someone like you.

Thanks to Mark Cotter for his expertise and for keeping me from making up the law to suit my plot, no matter how inconvenient I thought it was at the time.

I've been waiting for the opportunity to show my gratitude publicly to writer Arthur Slade for introducing me to the idea of the treadmill desk, and now I've got my chance. Thanks, Art! And thanks to Ken Capon for building it for me. Without it, I'd need bigger pants.

As always, thank you to my husband, Victor, for making dinner when I was too tired to think, for growing most of our food, for riding his bike to the store a thousand times for the few items he couldn't grow, but I had to have to keep writing (yeah, I mean doughnuts— thus the need for the treadmill desk), for a wonderful author picture, and for endless cups of tea. You're the best. As before, without you, there would be no book at all. I love you, Pea.